the girl from the moon

the elemental tides

maria beta

Cover design and illustration by Robin Mork

the girl from the moon by Maria Beta. -- 1st ed.

ISBN 978-1987528176

CONTENTS

THE NORTH AMERICAN ALLIANCE - THE NAA

PROLOGUE

....

After failed negotiations and miscalculations, the ozone layer practically faded away. In the process, a wave of horrific earthquakes wracked the planet, showing the Ring of Fire's full-blown rage. Temperatures rose, oceans became larger and indomitable, islands disappeared. The time came to live somewhere else, and that meant to enlarge the small settlements on Saturn's Titan and on Jupiter's Europa.

In the middle of the geological crisis, the Technological War took place and left civilization in the dark for three entire days. Pacts were broken and new alliances were created. The United States, Canada, and the north of Mexico became the North American Alliance—or the NAA, as it was mostly known. States were rearranged in twelve Federations that were to become the New Houses.

The formation of the NAA forced the other nations to join forces as well. Most of Europe and the north of Africa turned into the Baltic-Mediterranean Alliance, or BMA, and Asia transformed into three main entities. The planet later extrapolated its redrawn alliances into space, providing the basis to what became the Aurean Confederation. The Confederation would run every-thing beyond Earth, including Europa and its two human colonies: New Alaska and New Greenland.

New Alaska was originally conceived as an NAA-Russian cooperative, but later it was determined to be better left as an international hub, and both parties were to develop separate cities connected to it—a pro-cess they are still debating how to institute.

A few decades ago, Steban Weelah and a group of scientists, while exploring New Alaska's deep oceans, discovered Zafor, a type of silicate found in Jupiter's Galilean moons. Zafor combined with silicone could maintain itself above Earth's stratosphere, and be-cause of this, it turned into the base of the SZ Sky-Shots. This was the beginning of the Aurean Shield, which is still used today to replicate the almost-van-ished ozone layer. Steban became the most famous scientist in the world.

However, years passed, and Steban decided that it was time to go back to Earth. Both of his stepdaugh-ters, Victoria and Cate, were born in New Alaska, and had never visited what he called home. It was nine years ago when he returned to the NAA's New East with his wife Paula and the girls, and he never went back.

CHAPTER 0

....

W hat was it?" the man leading the group asked. His voice was profound. His steps were solid.

"A she," a man walking to his left answered.

"How was she?" the leading man asked again.

"Silver. Dark silver."

"A quarter of a cycle. How interesting," a woman walking behind them whispered. Her skin was pale as the marble floor; her sight was mellow.

"What else do we know?" the man asked again.

The second man looked behind, to the woman. "Maybe like you, but we don't really know."

"Then we should wait." The man in front had nothing left to ask and left. His secretaries followed him.

"What is it?" a dark-haired boy asked the woman.

"Nothing. Just a girl, in a moon," she said.

maria beta

CHAPTER 1

·····································

ALEX

How *different they look from above*, Victoria pondered. It was a little past 8:00 a.m. when the first morning SZ SkyShot, or ozone replication layer, was released. The shadow inserted itself into the grayish day. She closed her eyes. From the moon, the SkyShots didn't spread over the planet as threateningly as they did from below. From Earth was different. Some days, the coverage became purple, and some others, like those in summer, took on a nasty brick color that felt like blood flowing down to the ground. It all depended on the composition of the Shot according to the time and the season, and how the atmosphere developed that day.

Victoria opened her eyes and went to continue her typical five-mile run. She headed into a track in the middle of an Atlantic white cedar jungle. It was fall, but the foliage still hadn't begun to turn, and the air still smelled fresh. She was visiting her family for a few days. They had recently moved all of their things from FoxStone in Pennsylvania to a new house in Sunally Town now that her father, after a long period of yesses and nos, had completely retired. FoxStone was the headquarters for the University that carried its name, and for the Aurean Confederation's main laboratory, and this was where the family was established when they arrived together on Earth. Sunally was better suited for retirement, situated on a tree-covered mountain facing the Atlantic Ocean; it was soon going to feature the most beautiful one- and two-floor, red-tiled roof, white villas.

The wind was invigorating. Her steps were faster than usual, yet almost at the end she stepped on an unstable stone and sprained her left ankle. She sat on a large irregular rock and took off the running shoe.

It's not that bad; nothing can go wrong tomorrow night, she thought.

On her way back to the house, she walked and tried to slow her thoughts.

Alex Harlow arrived mid-afternoon and parked his black Oceanic-3000 EC in the roundabout, in front of

Steban Weelah's white house. The dark-haired, oval-headed senator for the New East was there to pick up his fiancé, Victoria, and her younger sister to take them to the Aurean Annual Conference in Washington DC the next day. Most importantly, later that evening Alex would give the final speech of the Aurean Gala, the social segment of the event—the same keynote timeslot that Victoria's father had filled a few years before.

Victoria was waiting for her fiancé by the gray steps, wearing her hair loose beneath a bulky gold headband, and still showing a pinkish tone in her cheeks from the earlier run. Long legs and long arms—her shapeless body looked like a long stick. Cate always managed to remind her of that. Her face was flawless, with broad pink lips, a proportionate nose, and deep blue narrow eyes.

Alex came out of the car, impeccably dressed in a dark gray suit with a lilac tie. Tall, he was not seven feet, but he tended to say that he might be. He joined her at the steps.

"Are you nervous?" she asked, detaching herself from his shoulders, looking for something in his sight.

"Of course. Your father always makes me nervous." His Roman nose got trapped between his big grin and semi-closed eyes.

He lifted her into his arms, kissed her lips, put her down, and took her hairband off her head. "I need to practice." He dragged her back inside the house. While he opened the old wooden door, Victoria took back her hairband from his gray back pocket and put it on right away.

They crossed the living room and went straight onto the terrace.

"Dr. Weelah, Paula, nice to see you again," Alex said with his charming smile. He and Victoria sat with them at a gray table, looking onto the ocean.

"Thanks for visiting, Alex. This is the only way that we could see Victoria again," Steban said.

"I was just here some weeks ago," she said.

Victoria had already moved away from home three years before, and was residing in the Aurean Academy Campus in Washington, DC. She was studying political science, while at the same time working for the Senate of the New East. Classes taken at the Academy were co-validated by most of the best schools in the Alliance.

"I'll be back with more tea and those biscuits that you like." Paula, her ultra-skinny, redheaded stepmother, stood up and went inside the house. They didn't see each other very often; no one would think that she was the closest thing to a mother that Victoria had. Victoria barely remembered her mother, and she didn't like to see records of her; in her latest pictures and holos, she looked tired, drowsy and hollow-eyed...she looked miserable. Family was stepparents and Cate—and Alex. A few minutes after, Paula was back with a nice turquoise teapot and a tray full of pastries and cookies.

By then, Alex had already taken off his tie and unbuttoned the two top buttons of his shirt. He kept the jacket on; he always did.

"Alex Harlow! You must help me pick a college. I don't know what to do!" Cate came through the garden waving a midnight-blue-covered book in her hand, wearing a pink pleated dress, and, like her older sister, a similarly bulky silver headband on her dirty-blond wavy hair.

"I promised you I was going to," Victoria said.

"I don't know. The last thing that you promised was to teach me how to drive," Cate said. She'd turned sixteen a year ago.

"I did try."

"We never left the roundabout," the younger sister complained, bringing up giggles from both Steban and Paula. She approached the table and sat between them.

"You refused to use the brakes," Victoria said.

"Plus, you are never here," Cate added.

"You too?" Victoria reacted instantly.

9

Alex raised his hands as if to say, I have nothing to do with this. Both sisters kept arguing about why, a year ago, they could never manage to be together in a car without Victoria being relaxed or Cate being nervous.

Out of nowhere, Steban said: "I'm tired. I'll take a nap." He stumbled a bit to one side and then Paula helped him. He had no problem walking, but his sight dazed him sufficiently that Paula had to guide him using his left elbow.

The three others remained silent for a minute; then Cate finally said: "Okay, at least you offer to, not like my inert boyfriend back then, who didn't even feel acknowledged."

Victoria stood up and moved to where Cate was, and shook her hair fast enough that the silver headband fell down.

"Stop it!" Cate looked at Victoria with narrow eyes.

"That headband is mine, by the way," Victoria claimed.

"You never use it." Cate rearranged her hair.

"Anyway. Time for practice!" Victoria clapped her hands, forcing the others to stand up. Victoria looked down on her sister and put the headband back. "You can keep it."

They went into the library at the end of the living room. The room's walls were decorated by irregular patches of books. Closer to the window, there were two burgundy couches and a rectangular thick wooden coffee table between them.

The two women sat on one of the couches. Alex stood by the window, still wearing his dark gray jacket. "Dear audience," he proceeded, "I was eleven years old when I left Earth for the first time; it was a short family trip to the moon, the classic 'non-gravity' vacation."

"I never had that classic vacation," Victoria said.

"Me neither." Cate laughed.

"Because you two were taken to the moon, as we normal people were taken to the park on the weekends," Alex said. He kept talking and brought up the main points of the speech—isolation and compassion—which the girls agreed with.

Alex, as senator for the New East, had always expressed his full support to the Aurean Confederation and the Aurean Shield—the result of the Quartz tubes and Reflector Panels that spread the SZ Skyshots above in the sky. Yet recently, his appearances had become a little polemic when he showed conflicting views regarding the fact that the NAA was assigning a large portion of its budget for Development and Research to New Alaska and Europa. Instead, he believed some funds should be redirected toward the most affected areas of the New Houses and the Alliance, and as an act of solidarity, eventually to the rest of the badly impacted Earth—as the Baltic-Med Alliance was already doing.

In that environment, the NAA had become isolated, and behaved as it was the only piece of land on the globe. His contradictors tended to mention how difficult and expensive it was to cross the skies and the oceans, and smashed his propositions, but the general opinion was that *something* must be done to turn around the NAA's attitude, and that Alex probably was the right person to do this.

"I know I'm a shield-obsessed Harlow." Alex sat by Victoria.

"They are jealous! You have achieved more than your peers, and they have served at least twice your time in the Upper House," Victoria said.

"I like it, and...well, this speech will also let me keep my front-row seats for the ball." Cate smiled and held her chest proudly.

"They are not front row!" Victoria said.

"What?" Cate threw herself back on the couch.

"You are like second or third in line." Victoria laughed and stood up. She kissed Alex and went to the living room to grab something to nibble and a bottle of wine. She could still hear the others' conversation.

"You will have good seats. No worries. How you've been?" Alex asked.

"I'm okay. Should I not be?" Cate responded. "Is he coming tomorrow?"

"No, I don't think so. His father is, but he is not," Alex said. "It wouldn't surprise me if his father manages to avoid my speech, though."

"Well, you tried to put him in jail." Cate laughed.

"He is not coming! I told you already," Victoria said from afar. Victoria couldn't stand Barrett Mountdragon, Cate's ex, and the fact that he still showed up in her sister's conversation infuriated her even more.

Victoria entered the room and Alex joined her by the door to help her with what she was carrying—some appetizers, wine, and Cate's mint dark chocolate. "And yes, you did try to put Mr. Mountdragon in jail," she added. Both sisters laughed.

Barrett's father was the CEO and main shareholder of Agrippa Corp, and ended up testifying several times in front of the Senate because of his company's involvement with the tubes scandal years ago, Agrippagate. Nothing was ever found to make him go further than that.

"So Paula decorated my room in pastels while I was away. How could this happen?" Victoria immediately changed the subject of their conversation.

They finished the cheese. Within minutes Cate fell asleep in Victoria's lap.

"Alex, are you sure you want to use this occasion to tell these people that they are wrong?" Victoria asked. She couldn't stop tearing her mind apart.

What if it's too much? What if it's not the time?

"I don't even know why they invited me. But if I don't at least say something, everything I have been building so far will be for nothing. Anyway, your father is not coming, right?"

"He is not, and he doesn't want to hear about it. He is becoming day by day more self-involved—more than before."

"What about his sight?"

"Worse, but he doesn't want a bionic iris," Victoria said.

"We should move closer to here. Sunally is too far for me, but definitely something in between."

Victoria extended her arm to grab his, and mouthed a silent thanks.

He did something similar, but whispered sleep.

"Cate, let's go to your room." Victoria tried to wake her up, rubbing her head. "Tomorrow we have a long day."

The next morning, the three of them left in Alex's car at exactly 6:00 am. Fog was beginning to dissipate. They took the New East-100 Aerial Highway, as it had an exclusive lane for politicians.

"I see some blue," Cate said.

"It's cloudy." Victoria didn't even bother to look out-side. She'd seen the weather report when she woke up and that was enough.

"Well, some purple." Cate pursed her lips.

The car was driven by Alex's daytime bodyguard, Marcus, dressed in jade-green—New East's color. His chin would never move, his shoulders always pressed back, even his voice sounded like a robot.

"We'll arrive at Apex Tower at 8:30 a.m.," Marcus said. Apex was the NAA's main building in Washington, DC, and the second-most important building in all of the North American Alliance.

The Aurean Conference was usually sponsored by the NAA, the initials emblazoned on the ubiquitous gold and purple triple-star emblem display, literally everywhere. It was a three-day event full of panels and famous speakers. It reunited the most influential people involved with developments in the outer world and anything related to Jupiter's moons and Europa. Yet, on this occasion, to the discontent of many, the Aurean Conference was taking place in DC. Most of the time was at Atlantic Island in New York.

Alex, in a black suit and green tie, sat on the last row of the large car. He participated in a conference call during the trip. The girls discussed university matters. The car moved non-stop, 40 feet above the ground and at 90 miles per hour, until it reached the

Third Circus, outside DC, where it descended quickly and connected to the main city highway. Safe and simple.

Once they arrived, Victoria took Cate to a few panels. Cate by now should have been used to it; this is what they had been doing all their lives. Later they got ready for the event that night.

The gala took place in the heart of the city; the silicone tent for the party was ready on the Mall, centrally located and connected to both the National Gallery of Art and the Smithsonian. The tent fitted a little more than a thousand people. Transparent walls allowed them to appreciate the surrounding Capital architecture, and randomly exhibited different cosmic scenes from the Haley Telescope on the moon. The pavilion's ceiling was a full-time display from the telescope.

Golden rococo lamps fell from the silicone sky; wild branches ending in ten giant hands held perfectly round twenty-inch light spheres. The branches inconsistently rotated, giving the experience of being absorbed by the ceiling, pretending to be a blue vault. A central hallway separated the area into two blocks and connected both museums. Countless round tables were situated everywhere, white linen with gold triple-star endings, decorated with moon-powder flower centerpieces, some with peachy sans-souci roses and others with scarlet carnations. There was a dance floor alongside one wall, closer to the Hill. By the silicone wall closer to Lincoln, a long-sided table for the most prominent guests rose a few feet taller than the others, with a podium in the middle.

The Weelah sisters had been constant attendants of this celebration. People were accustomed to seeing two blond girls wandering around in beautiful dresses, always matching, every year a different color.

The night went along as planned. A spinning glass of Bouvard, the coveted sparkling wine aged in the moon valley of the same name, was in every person's hand.

Victoria glided in a beautiful pale pink silkgrate dress, long and slightly tight, short and bulky sleeves, a red belt of the same material, and a heart-shaped neckline. Silkgrate was silk photochemically treated several times in diograte, a mineral found on Europa, which made textiles iridescent. If you weren't as popular as a Weelah, it might have taken you several months to get a gown like this. There were only seven more silgrate dresses at the party, two blacks, two blues, a white, a green, and a yellow. Men were in black or blue suits, but women were a combination of feathers, stones, flowers, and flowing dust. Long to the floor, some squared, oval or as a spiral, as some others were tight to women's figures; dresses were competing with comets as the true spectacle of the party.

"I see everyone checking on you," Alex said.

They only care about the ring, she thought.

Alex was in a midnight-blue, glazy three-button suit and a green bow tie, green as the jade-green of the New East, a green pocket handkerchief of the same color on his left side and the NAA gold triple-star pin button on the other.

Victoria and Alex mingled with and greeted everyone, politically relevant or not. Alex gave his signature grin and shook hands with members of every political party.

Dinner started around 8:30 p.m. An hour before, a scientist had taken the podium and talked about Europa, New Alaska, and what was supposed to come 'next.' "Titan is still the second-largest moon in the solar system after Ganymede," he explained. He continued his speech, but centered on the Galilean moons, and despite the small intro, it was like the colony on Titan never happened.

Dessert was an exotic combination of mango and wild berries atop a creamy chocolate soufflé. When coffee was served, Gabe McCully, the extra long-time serving NAA Prime Minister, with his dyed-blond sparkly hair and dressed entirely in purple, moved in front of the stage.

"Here we go again," Victoria whispered to Alex. They were sitting farther on the right side.

Alex grabbed her hand and pretended to be interested in what McCully was saying.

"After the earthquakes, the heat rose in some places, becoming close to claustrophobic. Then the fires. The countries around the Equator suffered the most. Dead cities. Dead. The Amazon was hard to defeat, but it was no longer the rainforest with hidden rivers, inhabited by hippies and the most beautiful animals. Not beautiful, no," McCully said.

"As of today,"—McCully's monologue kept expanding—"there are satellites in the stratosphere connected to the Quartz tubes on Earth. The satellites control the perimeter and width of the tubes' exhalations through Panels. These are the Reflector Panels. All of these, together with the SkyShots, compose the Aurean Shield, the system that creates softer summers and more stable nights. It is the greatest achievement of all eras."

"Every year, his same fifteen minutes of stardom. I can't take this anymore," Victoria added.

"And finally, please let me introduce you," McCully continued.

Alex kissed Victoria on the cheek, straightened his jacket's lapel, and stood up. He proceeded to the podium; his father Arthur was sitting at one of the first-row tables, almost in front of him. A large screen in the back showed a closeup of his face. He smiled deeply, and began:

"Good evening. Mr. Prime Minister, ten Aurors, members of the New Houses, distinguished guests, ladies and gentlemen. It is an honor to be here tonight. I have nothing but gratitude for this invitation." His arms firm on the sides of the podium. "I was eleven years old when I left Earth for the first time; it was a short family trip to the moon, the classic 'non-gravity' vacation. While we were crossing the stratosphere, I awoke to the cloud of dust and to the fact that, unfortunately, this was not the Earth that Galileo and Hawking had talked about. Still, there it was, a perfect blue sphere surrounded by milk and chocolate, as my younger sister had described it."

Sighs dispersed all around. He stretched his neck and appeared more comfortable. He released the podium and lightly supported his forearms on it.

"I joined the Academy at sixteen, and felt privileged for having the chance to learn, and to explore the world beyond the moon"—he raised his right palm and moved it along with his voice—"to what we thought to be completely out of reach. Because we chose to go to the moon, we choose to go beyond."

He paused and beamed to the crowd as applause and ovations boiled in the room. He kept remarking on the Academy and the Confederation's contributions to society, and then added: "But after all, I came to realize that what I wanted was to dedicate myself to the planet itself, and help to move on from the status quo. And not only geologically, I mean."

Some eyebrows rose. Victoria saw two attendants standing at one of the tables in the back. Thus he continued, and then focused on describing the beauty of the planet and the glory of its inhabitants. Soon shoulders in the audience once again looked more relaxed.

The speech went on; with both hands lightly on the podium borders, he spoke confidently, his neck lengthened with his breath, as he went on: "We should be humble and recognize how microscopic we are as an element of the universal plan, and that we can't settle with how we are. We must not stop evolving and looking forward."

He paused for a few seconds and calmed his voice.

"Looking forward to defeat the adversities that came from the destruction caused by climate change, such as drought, fires, hurricanes, and more, and therefore to heal our greatest wound, because after they all happened"—he paused—"they left us divided." He nodded, as everyone else shook their head.

"There are still areas that have never recovered from the time before the Shield was fully functioning," he said, faster and avidly. "We share the Alliance Gulf with many other countries, yet we built a submarine fortress and pay no mind to what is happening south of us. We live in isolation. Friends, what I am talking about is not only expanding the Shield to eventually every inhabitable corner on Earth, but more so, encouraging an Aurean Confederation and an Alliance actively involved with what is beneath the first layer of air." He looked at the audience and continued.

"At the end, we are in this milk with chocolate together." Alex laughed. Victoria laughed too. So did the audience. His sister's analogies had worked well in the focus groups. "The previous generations gave us the Shield, Europa, and more. So before I finish here, I want to leave this question: What are we leaving for the next one? We can certainly do more. Together. Let's work on this. For the future, for the Alliance and this Confederation. Friends, let's stand and raise our glasses." Alex's voice vibrated. He grabbed a sky-blue Bouvard glass from the side table.

The attendants stood up, some with more enthusiasm than others, and raised their bubbly Bouvard glasses.

"It is the compassion for one another that created this Aurean Confederation as a fellowship of people who devote their lives and triumphs to the survival of the species. Compassion is the greatest lesson we've received, and the greatest lesson we can still hand over again." He raised his glass. "Let's toast to this and to the long road ahead. Let's be guides on this journey of history. My fellow Aureans, for what should come, for what should be done—cheers! Thank you!"

Everyone stood up. There wasn't a single person in the rectangular room who wasn't applauding, yelling, cheering, or exaltedly celebrating. Even those who disagreed followed suit. The younger crowd warmly hugged one another; beautiful women wiped tears away. No matter what he said, he was on his way to becoming the NAA's next Prime Minister.

"You will be the youngest ever Prime Minister's wife," an old and heavily bejeweled woman told Victoria while squeezing her hands. Victoria was only twenty-three, but this prediction was not intimidating. Her eyes had only one target. Alex was shaking hands with the first and second tables, and that was when she realized that Cate was gone. Last time she had seen her was before dessert.

maria beta

CHAPTER 2

....

GINEVRA

Catherine Weelah never felt understood when she spoke about New Alaska with others. "It is an igloo, like how the Inuit used to live centuries ago," people tended to tell her. In theory, that was correct: New Alaska was a cluster of large inner-lighted igloos. In practice, however, the grid of lightning bugs, as it looked from above, hosted a network of developments that grew vertically beneath them. She was eight when she left the moon, and arriving on a dying planet didn't make any sense to her. For Cate, the air on Earth was sometimes too heavy to breathe—especially when she would come close to the water, which freaked her out.

The Aurean Gala began and Cate arrived with her best friend, Alice Park. Since Victoria was wearing pink, Cate went for a different color this time, as this was her sister's night. She chose ruby red—a sleeveless dress with spaghetti straps, raw-edge trim throughout, and a ruffled, tiered skirt. Fashion was big that night.

Alice was wearing a halter-neck yellow chiffon dress. She was of Korean descendent and had spent a few years on Jupiter's moon as well, but in the other colony—BMA's New Greenland. Nonetheless, Alice left quite young, and New Greenland didn't drive her conversation that often. The short girl had hazel eyes and gigantic cheeks, and kept her hair loose and falling around her shoulders all year round.

"We are sitting with the Bammies," Cate said to Alice as they were escorted to their table.

They giggled.

The Bammies were a group of sons of the Baltic-Med, or BMA, diplomats who had graduated from the Academy a few years before and were allowed to lengthen their visit in the NAA a little longer—if little could be defined as between five and ten years. Several of them had lived beyond Earth as well.

"Please don't let me sit by Lucca," Alice begged. "He is so egocentric, and I can't handle that twist in his eye. I'm sorry." Alice raised her head, looking for their table.

"I hear you. Let's try to sit by Francis and Pedro."

The Italian Lucca Selv was short and chubby, with a slight twist in his left eye that could easily be perceived from a very short distance. He was smart, and unfortunately, he knew it. And as with every occasion, he managed again to sit by Cate.

"It is not that I'm ignoring your messages," Cate told Lucca. "I just don't come up with anything to say back." She looked to the other side.

"I am single, you are single," he said in his Milanese accent.

That is more than true, she thought.

Her selfish ex-boyfriend did show up to the night's event, and was sitting a few feet distant with his new girlfriend, in a front line table—of course! Barrett was so recognizable by his light-brown short straight hair, combed almost symmetrically to the sides. He was wearing a deep-burgundy jacket that matched his girlfriend's dress. They probably took his parents' seats, since there was no sign of them close by. Cate had never liked Barrett's parents. They hated Alex and Victoria; they wouldn't even mention their names. It was reasonable.

"What are you doing tomorrow?" Lucca asked. His hands and fingers moved like gross tentacles trying to grab Cate's; she moved hers around a few times, but finally put them behind her back to avoid the menace.

Cate exchanged an SOS look with Francis Gaullen-pierre, who was soon moving back to France. He immediately stood and walked around the table to them.

"Cate, Alice said she wanted to discuss something very important with you," Francis said.

She nodded and quickly paced toward the empty seat between Alice and Pedro. She could overhear Lucca greeting Francis, "Il mio ex-roommate, comment ca va?" Francis and Lucca had shared a dorm at the Aurean Academy. Barrett Mountdragon, Cate's ex, lived in the room beside them while dating Cate, and that is how they all met. Francis not only became Cate's very close friend, but he also didn't approve of Lucca's behavior, considering Lucca did have an on-and-off longtime relationship waiting for him back home. A behavior—that Alice later found out—became the source of a couple of encounters on the third floor of the Academy's residences.

The Lucca Show had perfect timing, though. It was when Lucca had sat by her that she saw Barrett escorting his girlfriend, Felicity, to their assigned table.

"Yes, I saw them," Cate said to Alice. Cate hadn't seen Barrett since they broke up around a year ago.

"I can't believe you dated him for a year," Alice said.

"Almost two. My father wouldn't approve because he was five years older than me—oh, and because Barr worked for him too. Crazy," Cate said.

Barrett was one of Steban's senior assistants on his team, but when Steban considered retiring, Barrett decided to leave science for the city and the corporate world—things Cate wasn't considering at the time—so he broke up with her.

"The strange part is how quickly he moved on. He always said she was boring," Alice said. She kept staring at them. "At least he did our homework."

"Stop looking at them!" Cate pinched Alice's forearm. "It is just disappointing. Practically all of our friends forgot I existed—well, they were mostly his. But even my cousin Constance went to his birthday two months ago; she only met Barrett once!" Cate complained. "I'm sure his mother still picks his clothes," she mumbled. She finished her meal, even though she wasn't feeling hungry.

"Well, you know how people are. Who would miss the pompous party co-hosted by Felicity and his parents? I wasn't invited; I had no choice. I don't think Lucca was either. " Alice laughed.

"Francis didn't go," Cate said.

Cate gazed at her French friend. She wondered if all along she had made the wrong choice. He smiled back at her. On the other side, Lucca was blustering about his new Speedshadow 7.0, the latest hydrogen-propelled cycle. Francis looked bored. He raised his eyebrows to Cate.

29

When dessert was about to come, Cate felt the meal too heavy on her.

"I'll be right back," Cate said.

"Are you okay? You look a little pale. I thought it was the makeup," Alice asked.

"I'm fine, I'll just go to the restrooms and I'll be back," Cate said. But she wasn't. On her way to the exit, she felt a weird antibiotic flavor coming up her throat. She managed to leave the tent—felt like forever; immediately she turned right into the women's bathroom, and stopped by a full-size mirror in the small corridor inside. Her hairline was sticky with sweat, and her makeup had slumped into dark-gray smudges under her eyes. It must have been a combination of the food and the teenage drama. A woman dressed in black with the triple-star purple button on her chest approached her, "Have this." She offered Cate water in a Bouvard glass.

"Thanks."

For a moment she felt dizzy, until she visualized a thick gray hair on the top of her hairline. "Oh Lord! I'm old." She finished her water and gave the glass back to the nice woman. *How could I leave at such an important moment for Victoria and Alex?* she thought. She must return, but the stone in her stomach was getting heavier and heavier.

"Some walking would help; the Gallery should be empty now," the nice woman said.

"Good idea, thanks." And so Cate went and sneaked into the National Gallery for a short walk.

"*Everything* on Atlantic Island and in New York is soooo much better," a petulant man in a group at the entry was saying.

"Oh, I can't wait to go back," a woman said.

Cate had never been to New York City. For the Aurean Conference, she and her family had usually taken a nonstop trip directly to Atlantic Island, and stayed in a residential building close to the ivory complex famously known as the Union—NAA's main headquarters and the most important building in the whole Alliance.

While she pretended to check out some art, she very much enjoyed hearing the stories these visitors were telling.

"We still have so many tourists," another woman complained.

"You can recognize them by how they jump with the mini-earthquakes in Central Park," the first one said. "They think the ground will open up and drag them inside."

"Well, that happened once," another man said.

They all chuckled.

"The City was the first that had a satellite and Panel of its own," the same one added.

"Days are clearer, but nights are longer. Rains are thicker, but last shorter—it's perfect," a third woman said.

Cate got bored and left. She finally managed to find her beloved painting, *Ginevra de' Benci*. Cate swung her red dress side to side. The pain in her stomach at least felt a bit better.

"What would Da Vinci say if he could visit Europa today?" a male voice, with a minor French accent, snuck up behind her and whispered in her ear.

"Francis! I am going to miss you!"

"And I am sorry you missed Alex's speech," he said.

"I know! So bad," she explained. "I heard it last night. I like that he mentioned isolation." There was a popular blog running with that name, which Cate was addicted to, written by the famous journalist Marisa Gomez, which covered the topic of the NAA disengaging with the rest of the world and with some of its own houses and states...practically every week.

"My father says Alex is going to change everything in the NAA mess and in the relationship between both Alliances. He just needs to stop the noise about the *Wolf*."

"Oh, God!" Cate laughed.

Francis rolled his eyes. As one of his latest opinions, Alex had openly manifested that it was not the best time for the NAA to help the Meds—what everyone called the BMA—budget their upcoming subterranean bullet-train, the *Midnight Wolf*, which would connect Berlin in the BMA with the Congo.

"And the Meds *do* need a faster train," he said.

"The Eagle is the best," Cate said. The *West Eagle* was the latest hypersonic train that trespassed the mesosphere, connecting the northern and southern hemispheres underground. It went from Dry Valleys in Antarctica to Houston in the New South, where it split either to Washington/New York in the New East, or to San Francisco in the New Sierra.

"Well, in my opinion, the *Tolstoy Dragon* is still by far the most modern and comfortable." He pushed forward his left shoulder. There was a glint in his kind eyes. That train went from Moscow to Beijing.

"That's Victoria! I want to see if I can leave with her now." Cate saw her sister passing by the main corridor with Alex, flanked by two purple-clad NAA guards. She hugged Francis and, while walking backward over to her sister, said: "I don't know if I will see you before you leave. Have an amazing trip!"

"Nonsense! I'll see you before," he said. "If not, we'll meet in Paris. You must visit and see the new Eiffel Tower." His voice rose higher.

"I don't like Paris!" With that, Cate rushed to her sister. Victoria and Alex were chatting nonstop, waiting for an elevator at the end of the hall.

"Can I leave with you?" Cate asked when she reached them.

"Where were you?" Victoria asked. "We are going back to Sunally. I thought you wanted to stay here with Alice."

"I'm not feeling well." Cate shook her head and rubbed her stomach. "Maybe it's because Barr is here," she lied.

"Come," Victoria pushed her into the elevator. Alex was already inside with two NAA guards, waving his hand, beckoning Cate. His head almost touched the mirrored ceiling.

"The Chinese are worried that the tunnel crossing the Pacific could be turned off," Victoria explained to her, but Cate had no interest in the Chinese or their tunnels. Again, she wasn't feeling well.

"The *Wolf*, the *Panda*—what is it with these trains and their names?" Alex grumbled.

"Everyone wants their new toy," Victoria explained.

The two silver elevator doors opened in the lighted subterranean parking lot. The two NAA guards came out first. There they were: three black Oceanic-3000s waiting for them, surrounded by NAA and North East Security, which were distinguished by their purple and jade-green uniforms.

"Senator, Miss Weelah, you are two minutes late." A muscular man approached them dressed in green— New East's color. His name was Anibal, and he was Alex's closest bodyguard, who had been working with him and his father for many years.

They left in the three-car motorcade. They were in Alex's, which was in the middle. Alex and Victoria sat in the third and last row, with Cate facing them in the second. Alex took his tie off.

"What is it with you?" Victoria asked Cate.

"Something in the food wasn't good," Cate said.

"I never got Barrett," Alex alleged. "He is not important. He was your first serious boyfriend, like I am Victoria's. That's all." He winked at Victoria. Victoria giggled.

Alex pulled his Whisper's ring from his left wristband. He seemed to hesitate about attaching the silicone ring communicator behind his neck.

"Don't. Not yet," Victoria said. "Your staff will see you as available."

He pushed the ring back in the silver glass-silicone wristband. "I'll just text Marcus that we are on our way to your parents." He used the holo-arm keytab that came out from his wristband.

"Cate, you should be happy you're not spoiling your youth with him, or with that Lucca. I saw him. I like Francis," Victoria said.

Alex bent his head toward Victoria. "Am I stealing *your* childhood?"

"Don't be silly, Alex." Cate finally joined the conversation. "Victoria was already forty when we came to Earth." Cate coughed. She felt a stitch inside her chest; the pain was spreading.

They entered the eight-lane Columbus tunnel to leave Maryland, and the driver took one of the mid-speed lanes. A few seconds passed and a black Oceanic, like Alex's, landed in the faster lane to their left.

"Senator? We are switching now." Anibal looked back and told the group what would happen next. The Oceanic that they were in instantly changed color from black to silver. Only a few people in the NAA were authorized to have color-shifting cars, and evidently Alex was one. Beyond that, his two cars could switch IP codes for CDD, or Central Driving Department, as well. It was the most secure method of transportation around.

The silver car received CDD authorization and moved to the right, out of the caravan, just before the black "impostor" vehicle took its place. The driver inserted a short blue metal tube below the driver's wheel that would reset the Oceanic's electronic system and re-establish it with the other vehicle's codes.

"Let's take the granny lane," Anibal told the driver. Lanes farther to the right had lower speed limits and manual driving was allowed. The caravan, with the new car in between, moved to the high-speed lane farther left. "We must wait a few minutes until CDD security cameras take them at the exit," Anibal insisted.

"What is it?" Anibal asked the driver, who kept pushing different buttons on the side-screens.

"CDD recognition is not complete. I'm trying," the driver said. "I've tried everything." He looked back to Alex. "Manual driving!" He kept pressing different keys in the main panel. The infrared sensor appeared in front of him to check for reactivity and consciousness, but no light turned on. If a car didn't enter the CDD system, it couldn't be driven by the Driving Department, or by anyone else.

Alex grabbed Victoria's forearm and asked Anibal, "What is happening? Who is driving, you or CDD?"

"It will be fine," Victoria whispered to Cate.

"How fast are we going?" Anibal sounded worried.

"One-twenty miles per hour," the driver said, still dealing with the infrared sensor.

"Can we make it out of the tunnel?" Alex asked with a steady tone.

maria beta

CHAPTER 3

....

AN ANGEL FROM HELL

115°F HEAT INDEX, the sensor at the wall showed.

The city view from the 45th floor of Apex Tower—NAA's complex in DC—was sheathed in purple haze; it hadn't stopped raining in the last twelve hours. The only element in sight through the thick glass window was the Obelisk's red eyes, two burgundy oval dots floating on smoke by themselves. The room was luminous, the lights reflected on the glossy floor, and a fifty-person-long table was perfectly set up with note tablets and glasses ready to be served.

Victoria, camouflaged in the white of the surroundings, saw through the glass curtain-wall the reflection of Patrick's flawless sand suit as he entered the room.

He came closer: Dark ash-blond hair and a slender, humpy nose. She turned to him. In another situation she might have given him a hug.

"Why is it taking so long? And why can't I see her?" Victoria interrogated the man.

"It's complicated. They don't know how to address the situation," he replied with his plummy tone, his hands in his pants pockets. Patrick Jameson was one of Alex's closest advisors, and one of Victoria's best friends.

"Address what? For how long? It's been two days. I should have never left her with them." Victoria pressed her forehead to the glass.

"Don't blame yourself. She was brought here to be safe, and you went with Alex to the hospital. He was unconscious. You had to go with him," Patrick justified for her.

"Where in this building? They legally can't do this."

"There is a video going viral in every medium. I am afraid they are trying to link her to the accident. There hasn't been anything like this...ever," he said. "They are calling it..."

"Stop," Victoria firmly interrupted him, showing him the palm of her right hand. "I still can't believe that cheap gossip satellite found us before CDD or the police department." She went back to the smoky sight. Victoria paused her breath and tried to calm her thoughts.

He cleared his throat.

"What else do you know?" she asked.

"That she is fine, they are just asking questions, and for better or worse, nobody is willing to touch her."

Good, Victoria said to herself.

"Victoria, I think they want to know about her. I think they are making it about the accident to keep her in for longer. What is it? Is it a suit? Did you know?"

"Patrick, don't, please." She darted from him but stopped a few feet away when her right hip began bothering her again—a souvenir from the accident. "Help me get to her," she said.

He nodded. He truly seemed to care. The media was calling her sister an "Angel from Hell." The video that Patrick was referring to showed Cate staggering around on the upside-down car, pulling the doors away. Two Hercules robots showed up from behind and tried to stop her, but she easily took off the arm of one of them and pushed the second one twenty feet away.

"Give me another day. The entire team is behind this."

She looked outside; her shoulders felt heavy.

"I'm so sorry, again. You must be gutted. Is your leg better?" He sounded conciliatory.

"I don't know. It's my hip; it's just bruised," she said.

"Alex should be out of the hospital soon," Patrick added. Alex had a couple of broken ribs, a dislocated shoulder, and a concussion.

Victoria closed her eyes. Despite the pain, she strode fast across the room. A gross tear managed to escape anyway. She didn't want to bring up that she hadn't been able to see or talk to Alex after the accident, two nights ago on Saturday—today was Monday. A moment of silence passed and Patrick rubbed Victoria's right shoulder.

"I'll call you in the evening," he said.

Victoria slightly bent back her head to him. "Thanks for everything."

He left.

*****

"Good afternoon, Miss Weelah. I apologize for the delay," the New East Chief Deputy Attorney General greeted as he finally appeared in the room on the 45th floor, around an hour after Patrick left. A heavy man dressed in a jade-green suit and a dark purple tie with golden symbols embroidered on it.

Victoria was sitting at the center of the table. She stood up and met him on his way in. They shook hands. The golden symbols embroidered on his tie were NAA triple stars.

"No, please, I appreciate your time very much," Victoria said—*though if it was Alex who asked for you, you would have come crawling yesterday...even if it was Sunday*, she thought.

"Catherine has to stay. No parole. And no, you cannot see her. We need to define what caused the accident. We are still gathering evidence; it's a special situation," he explained.

"You don't even have charges. I will go to the Alliance Truthful Court if I have to," Victoria interrupted.

He left without saying anything else.

A few minutes later, downstairs, Marcus, in his jade-green uniform, picked her up; he was driving her blue Tolsa. "Nothing. Let's go to Alex's," she said. Her thoughts wandered. She had always thought herself capable of handling anything. Unfortunately, in this strange and unusual situation, she was finding out how much weight she could really carry, and it wasn't as much as she'd thought. She put the Whisper's ring behind her neck and the Whisper's semi-transparent device around her ear, and listened to her messages.

"Call Indersol, ask to clear an elevator for me. I should be there in..." She sent a request to Alex's building concierge.

"Fifteen minutes," Marcus said.

"Fifteen," she completed the request.

Coming out from the city's underground tunnels, she arrived at Indersol Towers. The four 54-floor dinosaurs had entrances on the ground and top floors, since the latter were heliports set up to receive even the large new Aero-Cobra 7-14 that politicians liked to have these days. A couple of them were hovering, probably waiting for permission to land. The thickness of the purple fog had cleared in the last hour.

Victoria entered the building through the subterranean parking. The elevator was waiting and took them directly up to the 32nd floor. She hobbled across the hall to the apartment door. Marcus accompanied her.

"Thanks again. Paula is coming. Can you please make sure she makes it here easily?" Downstairs had been a jungle of journalists over the past two days.

"No problem," he said.

Victoria got in and hung her black bag on the large wooden coat rack that stretched along the entry hall; it was full of Alex's jackets and one long white one that belonged to her. She took two small yellow transparent tubes from her bag.

"Good afternoon. It's 3:24 p.m.; 73 degrees Fahrenheit indoors, 102 outdoors. All shields and curtains are closed," the residential core system saluted her in a mellow voice.

"Core: Open them."

She headed to a studio, which looked like an extension of Alex's office at the Senate. Some pictures on the walls, mostly of Victoria. Two big ones of them at

Walker Lake in Alaska, with matching yellow shirts and navy jackets. They were in a boat, Alex holding a 19.9-pound Arctic char that he had just caught and Victoria beside him holding the fish's mustache. She looked as if she might be ill. The only reason she was touching the animal was because she lost a bet with Alex that he wasn't going to catch anything bigger than two pounds. In the other photo, she was squeezing his cheeks, while he was trying to pull away. In this one she was smiling. *It made things even*, she thought back then.

To her left, a big interactive blue screen took up an entire wall. The screen was connected to the one he had in the Senate, and covered in plans and strategies—lots of 1, 2, 3 and a, b, c. She opened one of the yellow tubes she had taken from her purse and took a pill for her hip pain, then she took another from the second tube—these were to keep her from producing tears. She didn't want to be seen as weak. One every twelve hours for the first month, then once every day—that was what the doctor had said.

She lay on her side on a full-grain leather chaise longue, looking nowhere near the balcony on the other side. The sky was light violet; it was not raining anymore. No more than five minutes passed and the building core system spoke out again: "Mrs. Paula Weelah is coming up in the elevator."

"Yes, open the door for her."

Paula came into the studio with her long red hair in a ponytail and wearing a plain beige knee-length dress. She sat on the bench and bent to kiss Victoria's hair.

"My father hasn't done anything...nothing," Victoria said, rising to her feet and re-arranging the bun in her hair. She looked at the floor and could tell her mother-in-law was wearing different colors of flat shoes—one black, one brown.

"He won't talk. I explained to him in detail and he locked himself in the library. I know he has made some calls, but I don't know to whom," Paula slowly explained.

"Paula, I don't know what else to do." Victoria deposited her head in her palms. Her elbows dug into her knees.

"I am so sorry we never talked about this before," Paula mumbled and gave Victoria a weak smile. "Perhaps. I don't know."

"What do you mean? *Before* what?" Victoria asked.

"Victoria." Paula paused for a bit, "Your father said that if this time ever came, that he would handle it. Time passed; we never thought we would have to deal with it again. I think that is why he is still figuring out how to react." Paula couldn't focus her sight on one place.

"What do you mean by *again*?" Victoria stood up, with both hands on her waist. She looked above to the ceiling and deeply exhaled. "I am going nuts," she added. Victoria knew that whatever Cate had turned into, she herself had also turned into some version of it. It was dumb luck that no one had caught Victoria on camera. It was so fast, sharp, and painless; her thoughts commanded her body. She had no idea this kind of transformation was possible, but how could she know? *It is not important now,* she thought.

"Paula, Cate is different. She had a sort of shield around herself—I don't know exactly how to describe it. Is that what you are talking about?" Victoria's voice was dry and firm. Patience was gone. Paula seemed intimidated by Victoria's fierceness, but she had no condolence for her stepmother this time.

"I know. I've seen her." Paula's voice was shaken. "Shining, lustrous. Not rigid but solid. It's an anomaly, your father said."

"He *said*? He *knew*? Ugh, how long have *you* known?" Victoria interrupted the older woman's attempts at explanation and advanced closer to her.

"We never mentioned it because she probably would have been taken away. And we thought it wouldn't happen again if she didn't know," she explained.

"Who would have taken her?"

"Others like her," Paula said, her eyebrows creased with worry.

Others like me, Victoria thought.

"I'll tell you everything I know. It's not much." Paula kept talking. "After the day of the pool, your father never spoke a word about it again. He wouldn't even react the few times I asked later. What I know is what I saw," Paula said. Her eyes were bright and rounded.

Paula is an honest person. She is definitely telling the truth, Victoria thought, as her heart beat faster.

"What pool? When Cate fell in that pool in Europa?" Victoria asked.

Paula nodded.

The residential areas in New Alaska were crossed by a railway system and by thin two-way streets, wide enough for a moon-car on each side. Houses were dynamic cubes. Areas were divided according to the different cubes' dimensions. Larger cubes came with more amenities; like Paula's friend's, her family lived in a cube Type XI—two floors and a backyard, with a pergola and a pool.

On a quiet afternoon, Paula and her friend were chatting in the kitchen, and Paula's friend looked through the window, disturbed: "Something..." Then she immediately yelled outside: "Where is Cate? Kids!"

There were two children, a boy of 10 and a girl of 6. They were staring at the bottom of the small rectangular blue pool. The girl came running to the kitchen after hearing her mother. Paula was already running to where the kids were. She jumped into the water, pulled Cate out, and sent the boy to tell his mother to call for Steban, and that everything was fine.

Cate was wearing a red dress with a wide white silk band on her waist. When Paula saw her, she was a pale brightness beneath the red waves of her dress. When she took her out of the water, the little one put her arms tightly around her stepmother's neck, and then Paula could tell she was well.

"Honey, it's fine. You have to calm down. Shhh," Paula said. Immediately, Cate recovered the pinkish-peach color of her skin. Their eyes met. Then Paula said, "Honey, close your eyes. Keep them closed until we get home." They were swollen, semitransparent, and silver, extremely reflective, like fluorescent glass bulbs filled with water.

Paula related how later, after hours of questioning, Steban revealed to her that Cate had always been different. But he didn't go into detail.

"We—well, mainly Steban—decided that you two shouldn't hear about this, and to keep it from happening again, it would be better to be far, far away, on Earth," Paula continued as she remained seated with both of her palms on her knees.

"Far from these *others*?" Victoria asked.

"Yes," Paula responded plainly.

"Who are they?"

"I don't know."

"So how did he know Cate was always different?" Victoria asked. She pierced Paula with her sight. She breathed steadily. *Always* was too long.

"He said he knew when she was born," Paula said. "*How* she was born. I thought it had something to do with Jupiter and its moons; people were developing reactions and allergies to different components, or whatever your mother was doing back then."

"How was she born? What is it that my mother was doing? Why have I never heard this before?" Victoria's mouth was stiff. She was holding her temper. She stepped back.

"Your mother...well. I knew your father for ages, from working together, but we got together as a couple years later, after she passed away."

Victoria released air through an O-shaped mouth. Tons of answers, but still no solution to her main dilemma—what was Cate, and how could she get to her?

Paula walked over to the other side of the room. "When we met Sarah, your mother, she already had a beautiful golden blond girl—you. She was a geologist, she was helpful, but there was no real reason to retain her. But Steban liked her; thus, she was kept around. A year after joining us, she became pregnant, and she was devastated. It was very unusual to have more than one child on the moon colonies in those days, so she was going to have to come back to Earth. He asked her to marry him and she said yes. Easier to approve her stay if she was married to Steban Weelah."

For Victoria and Cate, the subject of their mother had always been complicated. Sarah seemed like a vague and unhappy character, with no real explanation of her life. Steban never talked about her, and if the girls asked, he always avoided it with a smile. Everything the girls heard about their mother growing up had come from Paula: what Sarah did for the lab, how obsessed she was with generating energy from liquid hydrogen, or how sometimes she would disappear for an entire week. When Victoria asked her father how her mother had died, the answer was "Talk to Paula," and then he flashed that same smile again.

"What does this have to do with Cate?"

"Sarah died shortly after having Cate."

"I knew that already."

"It wasn't Cate's fault that she had grown inside a gray scar instead of a normal placenta, and we believe that is how Sarah contracted the blood infection," Paula said.

Dry eyes, no tears; the drops were taking their effect. Victoria couldn't cry.

Paula sat on a chair in the corner. "Cate came out covered in something that looked like lead, but it wasn't. She wouldn't stop crying. No one knew what to do. Her skin was arid, she had no hair, and her eyes remained sealed until the fourth day—or fifth; I don't remember well. But that was the day her gray paper covering began to crack."

"Are there any videos?" Victoria managed to ask. She couldn't swallow properly. "Holos?"

"Nothing. Only four of us saw her like that. By the end of the week, her little body was like wrinkled frozen lava. And a few days later, the gray veil tore slightly apart. By the end of the month she was smiling and pink, like you met her. We all thought she had no chance at survival, but she made it. I thought that was it, until that day in the pool," Paula added.

"And two years later we were on Earth," Victoria finally spoke properly. "Damn, Paula. She should have known. I should have known. How could you? Both of you!" She walked back, holding her forehead, toward the chestnut leather sofa.

"He thought it was better to come to Earth and leave it all behind. He could have stayed on Europa and sent only the three of us, but he decided to return to work on the Panels—there was still more to do; there was no sign of ozone recovery. The perfect excuse was there," Paula finished the story, staring at

Victoria, who was stretching her temples with her two hands.

"Could my mother turn like Cate?" Victoria asked, trying to assimilate the new scenario.

"No," Paula said.

"How do you know?"

"It's true. I couldn't know." Paula looked down.

"Who is my father?"

I want to know. It can't be just anyone.

"I don't know. Sarah just said that it was some-one with a life somewhere far. Somewhere on Earth, she said once; on Titan, she said one other time. We thought it was easier to tell you that he was someone we never met who then died," Paula said.

A few seconds passed and Victoria's stepmother broke the silence: "But I came to tell you something else. You must find Mr. Rogers," she said with thunder.

"Mr. what?"

Victoria wondered if Paula had a vague idea of what she was talking about, but then Paula stood up and said, "During that time in transition before we moved back to Earth, I heard Steban talking to a Mr. Rogers several times. When we got to FoxStone, your father said that if something happened to either of you, and he was not around, I must look for Mr. Rogers in the NAA Department of Space Affairs." Paula stopped, pressed her palms firmly together in front of her chest, and said, "I'm sorry I didn't bring it up yesterday. When you told me this morning that people were trying to link her to the crash, I asked your father what would he do. He said nothing, but I left the house right away."

CHAPTER 4

....

SAKI

I n Apex, deep underground, Cate opened her eyes. She instinctively swung her arm and pushed a dark-gray-suited person a few feet away. Three men wearing what looked like stiff moon-suits surrounded her bed. She stood up and they immediately moved out of her compartment to another area on the other side of the glass. Inexplicably, she felt taller than she had a few hours before; she could tell that now her sight aligned lower than before. Still wearing a torn-up version of the red dress from the party, one of the straps hanging on the back.

A week? Too long. Perhaps a day, but it definitely feels longer, she thought.

She hadn't seen a familiar face since she'd become conscious the day before. She was not feeling sick anymore; yet her thoughts had moved so fast that she'd barely slept. Time was burnt by looking at her arms and hands, and trying to connect the dots of that night of the party. She remembered talking to Victoria and being asked by officials dressed in purple—probably from the NAA—to get into a black car. And then she turned up inside this glass cage. It was all blurry.

She lunged forward and pressed strongly the glass of her cell, a big crack appearing in it.

"Where is my sister?" she said, slowly, pretending to be in control.

The three moon-men left the room. Then a horrible thought came to her mind: *What if something happened to Victoria and Alex*? There was no possibility that they would leave her alone like this, not this long. She lay down on the bed and rolled over to the wall; a couple of tears streamed from her eyes. Her face covered by her hands, she cried.

***

With no further explanation, Victoria put her white high heels on and took off.

"I'll wait for you here," Paula said.

It was late in the afternoon, but there was no time to spare. She headed downtown to a separate building of the NAA. Marcus was driving her in a batter car from the public car-sharing system, PCSS. On her way, Victoria made at least ten calls; suddenly everybody knew the existence of the important Mr. Rogers, whom she had never heard of, yet no one knew where he was.

"Marcus, our friends in New York will help you. Let me know if you find him first. Good luck!" She got out of the two-person batter or disposable car that Marcus would drop at the Eagle Station before taking the train, heading to the Union Building in New York, both of them chasing this mystery man.

The street was almost empty—parking was not allowed at this time; only pickup or drop-off. A row of Virginia pines divided the ample two-way avenue in front of the granite building. The few people walking around were wearing the characteristic purple NAA uniforms, a stiff set of pants and a square jacket with rounded shoulders that looked like a set of dark gold cupolas. Golden embroidery continued down through the sleeves, ending and merging in slim golden cuffs. She knew the street perfectly. For Christmas time, the Department put lights in every single tree—she had driven around it several times. The building hosted the second-tiered offices that didn't fit in Apex Tower.

It had no more than twenty floors, but took up almost three blocks of space.

She walked up the broad stairs, dodging puddles.

Victoria's credentials—her ID card and fingerprint as part of the staff of the Senate for the New East—got her into the Space Affairs Department on the eighth floor easily, yet she was told not to cross beyond the waiting room, where two women at their own desks sat with the mighty faculty to let people pass to the other side.

"Hi! I apologize in advance for the late hour. I would like to see Mr. Rogers, please. I tried to call..."

"He is busy," a dark-haired woman said.

"This is a matter of extreme urgency for New East. I'm Victoria Weelah and I work directly for Alexander Harlow..."

"Impossible," the woman interrupted her again—an annoying character who wouldn't even raise her head to answer Victoria. She merely moved her sight from her black bangs to the monitor in front of her, ignoring Victoria's presence. "That office is halted," she said to the other secretary, a cute chubby old woman with silver hair and lavender cat's-eye glasses, who looked up at Victoria.

"New East is not halted; who told you that?" Victoria assured this demon incarnated. If only she could crush her monitor with her fist—but this one was not a matter of strength.

On the other side, the woman with snow-colored hair gave her a smile tinged with pity. "Come here," she said to Victoria.

Victoria approached the old woman, who said, "I met your fiancé at a charity event a few years ago. So good-looking. He was talking and talking. I couldn't stop staring at him. No one could." She was crisp and sweet.

Victoria's nose was burning. *I miss him*, she thought.

"Mr. Rogers is in New York. Come back tomorrow; there is nothing more for you here today. I'll talk to him directly." She whispered these last words.

"Can you put me in contact with him by phone? You have to tell him it is Steban Weelah's daughter."

"Just go..."

Victoria gave up and left. She insanely wanted to believe this old woman; so far she had been the only one who had come up with a positive answer.

Back at Alex's place, Paula had dinner ready for Victoria. Victoria explained what had happened in the middle of several yawns and sighs of frustration. *Am I always be going to be like this?* she thought, *frustrated and angry?* Then Victoria went to the studio and took a second pill from the yellow tubes.

"I could barely feel my feet anymore." She took her shoes off. "And my hip is starting to really bother me."

"Try to sleep. I'll wake you up if anything happens," Paula said from the living room.

"I can't," Victoria responded.

Victoria opened her hands and extended her arms in front of her. Her right arm suddenly seemed to be covered in golden dust. Right away, she brought both her arms close to her chest. She rested on the chestnut chaise longue. There on the floor, she saw *The Frontier of Tomorrow*, one of Alex's favorite books. She had never gone so long without hearing from him.

I'm not an idiot. She knew there was something wrong.

Victoria had no books; hers were passed to Cate when Cate was learning to read, and Cate tore their pages out as soon as she read them, just as she'd cut the dolls' hair when Victoria turned her sight away. "Different season styles," Cate had said to justify herself. The two of them didn't have much of a relationship until one time, around two years after they had moved to Earth, when Victoria had gone into her sister's room in FoxStone and caught her melancholically looking out of the window.

"What's wrong?" Victoria had asked.

Little Cate began crying so hard she couldn't breathe. "A girl in school, she makes fun because I'm afraid of the water in swimming classes," she said while sobbing. "She is bad. The other girls laugh too."

"I promise it will get better," Victoria said, and she meant it. From that next day she began making short visits to Cate's building in school, and spent time with her and another girl named Alice who had recently moved back to Earth as well. But still, the two sisters felt distant. At those ages—ten and sixteen—a year's difference is a whole stage in life.

It wasn't until later that Cate was desperate to see Saki, the new pulserock sensation, who happened to be Victoria's favorite singer as well. Cate begged her and promised to do anything that Victoria asked for a year if Victoria would take her to her concert. They went together, and from that night until Victoria left for college, they were inseparable. They used to say that Saki's record *The Lonewolf Project* was the soundtrack of their life.

Victoria fell asleep on the chaise longue, still wearing her white suit.

*****

Cate was rocking herself in a chair. In front of her were three people on the other side of a long table. This was in a room adjacent to the synthetic glass cell where she was usually kept. The glass was made from a composite of carbon and iron, she was told.

"I was in the accident as well. I don't understand what you mean by me causing it," she said. "This is nonsense. Argghh!"

"Why don't you want to change your clothes? There is a suit by your bed."

"The orange suit?" Cate was still wearing the ripped red dress from the party. She was going through another session with "Debika, the shrink." That was how she had introduced herself. An eagle-looking woman, she wore a white robe so puffy it was easy to tell that she had three chain-metal layers underneath. Her dark and short sleek hair fell by the ear line. Her chin was always defiantly held upward. She was probably fifty, but looked twenty years older.

"Why am I here?" Cate was getting tired. However, it was not a game; this woman wanted her to say phrases in front of a camera and sign documents, not only about what happened on that night, but also about "future guidance for her safe life," as Debika put it. Cate could see how these enforcers of the law were tense and nervous around her, even though they had been trained to act as masters of the universe. *How would normal people react?* she couldn't stop thinking.

"We want to protect you so we can protect other people. It is our duty. We don't know what you are capable of," Debika said. She was the only one who acted cold and confrontational. "The murder of two noble servicemen of the New East House; there hasn't been a murder in the New East in decades. You are aware of what you did," Debika said. "You saw the videos; I showed you the accident report. The car security system shut down because of a major electromagnetic force. By you. I am not making this up. I know this is tough. What do you need? Is the food okay? More water? You drink a lot, but we see you don't go to the bathroom. How can I help you? Your sister sent a bag for you; unfortunately I can only give you the mint chocolate." Debika picked a green plastic-wrapped bar out of her pocket and handled it to her, but when Cate's silver arm approached, Debika instantly dropped it on the table.

"Don't be afraid of me," Cate said. "I'm the same person. I just want my family present. Or a lawyer. Someone." Cate quietly broke down. Her elbows resting on the table, she rubbed her eyes and nose with her thumbs.

"Darling." Debika was trying to be tender. "No lawyer needed. That can make things worse. Public, no. Just do what we ask you, and save yourself from this pain."

Cate looked at the woman, and then looked at the bar.

"Pain doesn't last forever." Cate set her sight on this small woman. She stood up, sassy, and twisted her head slightly backward so she could see the reflection of her flawless dark silver metallic body in the synthetic glass wall of her room. She looked down and saw her shoulders and arm muscles slightly defined. She was solid but flexible, and something like a thick liquid metal covered her all over. It was no longer her human flesh. Her silver hair was wavy, loose by her shoulders, like a tough single thread. The first time she saw her reflection she went into a panic, but after being alone and afraid, she relaxed. The metal coat protected her.

She dropped the chocolate bar on the table and strutted back to the carbon cell. It was not dark chocolate, as her sister would send. Debika should never had used such a cheap lie.

My sister makes no mistakes.

CHAPTER 5

··

MR. ROGERS

The next day, Victoria woke early and prepared for the non-scheduled meeting with Mr. Rogers, assuming the snowy woman was going to stick to her word. She had picked a short-sleeve, bulky dress in navy blue, and put on some makeup; Paula said that she wouldn't get anywhere with that unhealthy look.

"Mr. Harlow is coming upstairs," the mellow voice from core system said. She ran to the door and saw him coming out of the elevator. Khaki pants and a blue blazer. He looked tired, with a bruise on his temple, and a bandage on his swollen nose—the hump looked bigger than before—but he was still handsome. She went to him, hugged him, and kissed him.

"I missed you so much," she said.

He smiled, staring at the ground, and replied back: "Me too."

"I've been so worried." She pulled him into the apartment by his left arm. "I knew I had to be with you, but this whole Cate thing... They say it's a general questioning, but I don't believe it; they don't let me see her—it's been terrible. Do you want some coffee?"

"I was told she is fine. I will go myself later. I had some coffee already," he said.

"Paula was here. I got answers, and I found someone who will help me. Come with me." She pressed his hands with hers. I need you more now than ever," she said, using a soft and sweet voice, in contrast to her tough tone of the past two days.

"I can't go with you." He detached from her and went into his studio.

"Do you mean, like, today, or like..." She followed him.

"Victoria, the polls, they just..." Alex said, looking out the window into nowhere. His hands were in his pants pockets.

"The *polls*?" Victoria interrupted him.

"Victoria, you will understand eventually. This is what we both have worked for all of this time. Together," he said.

"*What?*" Her tongue felt heavy and numb. "I understand that I love you, and that my sister is in some sort of secret room. Don't ask me for more than that," she yelled at him.

"I saw you. I saw your arms." Alex finally looked at her; he was still in shock from what had happened that night.

"What?"

She realized it was not about Cate and the polls. It was about her.

"We were in the car," he said, moving his sight away. "Cate started coughing and suddenly she was silver; you were holding her arms. I saw them; your arms were golden from below your shoulders. We crashed, the smell; it is still in my head." He walked slowly to the window. "I won't ever tell anyone about you; don't ever worry about that." He wouldn't even look at her; he sounded convinced that he was doing the right thing.

Her throat was burning. Even if she had words to say, she wouldn't be able to pronounce them. It wasn't longer than a minute, but the moment felt like eternity—yet she finally opened her mouth and said: "Alex. Alex, you have no idea what compassion is." She took the ring off, left it on his desk, and abruptly left the room. She grabbed her stuff from the wooden bar at the entry. "Core: Door open!" The door moved to the left, inside the wall; she stepped outside and she was gone.

Forty minutes later, Victoria was parking her Tolsa in the granite NAA building's underground parking. She released the wheel and punched it with her right fist. All her life, all her plans had burst into nothing. *What is this?* she thought. *What is this that even Alex is afraid of?*

Once again she made an entrance on the 8th floor. The annoying woman—again— didn't even raise her head to look at her; the snowy one received her warmly and told her to take a seat on one of the couches in the waiting room. Nothing. Time passed and Victoria received a text from Marcus; he assured her that Mr. Rogers was not in New York, but he couldn't guarantee that he was in Washington. After two hours, still smiling, she approached the women. "I'll be right back," Victoria said. The sweet old woman responded with the same smile that made her eyes squint shut. Victoria went downstairs to stretch her legs by the pines, which wasn't a good idea with her high heels, since the trees were still dripping rainwater from their branches. She crossed to the other side of the avenue, where all of the water had been vacuumed out earlier.

She put the Whisper on and called Patrick Jameson. He had asked for another day; that day was gone, yet he still had nothing relevant on Cate.

"The only reasonable explanation is that CDD's system overlapped for a few seconds, precisely when the cars switched—and that happens in tunnels all the time," Patrick said.

"But has never ended in a crash," Victoria concluded.

"Precisely. That is what they say. Well, and also we still can't find anything to reject Homeland Security's version that an electromagnetic wave, emanating from the middle of the vehicle, burnt its electric system," he continued.

"And the cause was Cate? Nonsense! The system stopped working *before*," Victoria, irritated, said back.

"Before?"

"Before the crash," she said. *Before she transformed; we don't need more confusion.*

"About Mr. Rogers—I've never met him. It seems like he only relates to the Aureans," he said. "I spoke to Alex earlier when he left the hospital; he is recovering well. How did you find him?"

"Never better. I have to go." She took the Whisper from her ear right away.

Victoria returned upstairs. She was not a fan of this snowy woman anymore.

"Just tell me where he is and I'll go," she said.

"Go eat something filling and come back," the snowy woman said.

Victoria gave her a forced goodbye beam and took the elevator to the parking floor underground, not because she was going to get something to eat, but because she'd decided to go to the Senate. There were two things that she must do right away. First, get a lawyer for Cate—a real lawyer; no longer using Patrick or the New East. Second, offer her résumé to the Senate of Texas in the New South; they hated Alex. Probably the South could help her better for her future purposes.

Disturbed by her thoughts in the dark parking lot, her hands became stupefied, forcing her to shake them strongly. "Aw, not now," she said. She was afraid it was a side effect of the pills she was taking, plus all of the stress of the last two days.

"Victoria!"

She turned around.

"I am Mr. Rogers. You have been looking for me."

A man dressed in a light brown suit that matched his hat advanced. He came closer and took the hat off; his cornea, iris, and eyelids changed to a metallic copper color. He blinked and smiled. They changed back to flesh and human-like eyes, and he graciously put the hat back on. Light hair, olive skin. He had an approachable presence, an old baby-like face with an elegant tie.

"I've been looking for you everywhere." Her voice trembled.

"I'm unreachable, sort of; that is the idea." He elegantly moved his right-hand fingers. "But your father Steban found me, and I've been busy dealing with your sister's situation since then. I should had contacted you last night but I still didn't have my final authorization," he said calmly. "Cate is fine. And you can pick her up now," he said.

"Pick her up? How?"

"Call it an executive order from beyond. There was no reason to keep her for more than five minutes." He sounded mysterious. "You should go soon; I don't trust humans." He shook his head.

"Humans?" she mumbled.

"The Tolsa? Yours?" He indicated her car with his sight.

She nodded. He began walking toward the car and she followed.

"Put your thumb here." He pulled her right hand and pressed her finger on a gray card's black window. He kept talking at a steady and fast speed.

"Go to NAA's Apex. You will be clear to move around anywhere for two hours starting at 7:00 p.m. tonight. She will be waiting for you on the 5th floor. Don't lose any time. Dr. Debika Sanders is obsessed with your sister, and she managed to build a case, but that case is over."

"What is this? You, copper; me, gold."

Instantly she became golden; her golden hands grabbed his jacket. Her arms, what she could observe of her legs, they were golden.

He stopped. "Gold? We are Alliafied."

"Alliafy?"

"Alliafied"—he put emphasis on the *d*—"that is what we are. I might have felt you, barely... Nobody's explained it to you?" he asked.

She moved her head saying *no*, and recalled Paula's useless attempt to clarify.

"We can feel each other when we are converted," he kept walking.

My shaking hands, Victoria thought.

"I think your sister may have felt me the night of the party. I was sitting close to her with two other Alliafied, and that may have altered her system. I had no idea about you," he continued. "We always knew about her, but we respected Steban's decision. This is all new for your people." They arrived at the blue-sonic.

"Give me your hand," he said.

Victoria showed him her golden right palm. Her long thin fingers looked splendid.

"Don't be nervous. It's only your skin. Think of it as like foil wrapping paper. The blue suits you." He grabbed her hand and examined it. "Gold. Carbon. Some diorite. Some quartz. You will be fine."

"I am not like Cate. I tried to hold her and I couldn't. It was like she was burning at the end," Victoria said.

"She *is* different. She is in the high end of the range. People call her a monster; we think she is perfect. I saw the video. Her state was probably reaching gas."

"Gas? How? She was a rock." Victoria felt clueless.

"I mean above that. Being Alliafied is about the components that our shell can absorb, and it is also what we can do with them. You are familiar with the states of matter, are you? Can you go beyond solid?" the mystery man asked. "Think if you want to make it larger, stronger." This suddenly became an intensive chemistry class.

She looked at her hand. Sticky liquid gold glided on her skin. "This is it."

"Leeve 2," he said.

"Leeve? Levi?" she asked, while staring at her hand.

"Leeve. Level or category. There are four."

"Is 2 okay?"

"Yes, more than okay," he added.

"And Cate?"

"Three, maybe 4."

Victoria returned her hand to normal and pressed her fingers on the handle tab; the driver door moved up and open. "What about after? I mean, after we leave that building?" She was pulling her best nerves, interiorizing this avalanche of information.

"This was a big mistake; I assure you nobody will take Cate back in," Mr. Rogers said, confident. "Then we will figure out a way to get her back on track with human life. The NAA will have to conform with her having a quiet life."

Before getting in the car, she asked, "You *do* know Steban is not our biological father?"

"I know," he said.

"Do you know my father—that is, not Steban?" Victoria was eager for an answer.

"Get in the car," he said in the same tone that he had been using for the last three minutes, as if the subject hadn't changed.

She did, but when he was about to pull the door down, she asked, "Okay, but one more thing. Was Cate's transformation really that strong that it messed up everything in that car?" she asked.

"Maybe, but that doesn't make her a murderer. If anything happens, alliafy; don't let them forget who we are, and that we will be here for a while. Come visit my office next week and we will talk more. Good luck!" Mr. Rogers pushed down the door.

*****

Traffic was absurd. Victoria had been in an underground city tunnel for an hour, and not a single vehicle was moving. There was an accident at an exit, and the Highway Connected Mode or HCM lane was so dense that it was impossible to connect. Rows and rows of vehicles; the ones moving slowly in HCM were completely shuttered. Passengers were probably sleeping or watching TV.

"Entering HCM in three minutes," a female voice from CDD unexpectedly said. It was like a boost in her chest.

"Finally. Take me straight to Apex." Victoria opened her right palm and turned it to gold metal. She closed it and it went to her pink flesh again. *This is it*, she thought.

"500 Liberty Boulevard."

"Yes," Victoria said.

"On route. Arrival is calculated at 6:43 p.m."

Victoria arrived at 6:42 p.m. at the glass tower. "This vehicle is not authorized to enter the tower's parking premises after 6 p.m.," CDD indicated. "Underground public parking lot located 550 feet away."

"Leave me here. Head over to the parking lot. Accepted," Victoria confirmed.

Everything went as Mr. Rogers said. She entered the building and three lines were still open. Two security guards and two dark gray robots at each of them.

The new-model robots resembled a classic Greek sculpture, but they only feigned it; the Hercules was the deadliest machine on Earth. She went in with her credentials, thumb and iris recognition—just as she did on the morning the day before. Two violet luminescent strings ceased to interfere and she passed between the robots. The hip-height strings could give an electrical discharge, enough to numb both legs.

She took Elevator Alpha to her left, heading toward the 5th floor. Once there, she noticed a small foyer and two black doors in front of her. She looked around. It was quiet. The black doors opened and her silver sister came out.

"Victoria!" Cate's eyes and mouth opened wide; her voice was faded.

A shiny and familiar face loomed out from the dark with her.

"I told you to come back," the snowy woman said.

Victoria grabbed her silver sister by the sides of her face, making sure she was okay. "Let's go," she said.

The elevator behind her opened, and a string of a voice came out, "Victoria Weelah!" An eagle-like woman dressed in white came out from Elevator Delta, putting herself in the way of their destination.

"Who is this?" Victoria asked Cate, and stepped forward; immediately she was golden and moved Cate behind her golden arm.

The short woman's eyes became wide and bright.

"Debika, my recently assigned shrink," Cate answered.

"I'll leave you here." Snowy woman went back inside. The black doors closed.

"I see. Let's go." Victoria walked toward the doctor, indifferently, and pushed her sister forward.

Debika began moving her arms in different shapes.

"No one is safe with you out there," Debika howled.

She can't be right.

Debika grabbed Cate's arm, but Cate pushed her, and Debika fell to the floor.

"You shouldn't leave this facility, either of you," the doctor said.

Victoria pressed for the Lobby by the reader and Elevator Alpha opened again.

"You are a threat to our perfect community," Debika cried out loud, still on the floor.

"You spend too much time down there," Victoria said. She crossed the silver doors.

Cate released a quiet snort, and walked into the elevator.

"Security will stop you," Debika said. She rose back to her feet and went after them again.

The doors closed.

"Tolsa, pick me up," Victoria said to her Whisper, but there was no connection. She unalliafied and went back to her human skin. "Tolsa, pick me up; send my coordinates," Victoria commanded. "Are you okay?" Victoria asked Cate, rubbing her sister's head.

Cate hugged her. "Yes, I am. But she told me," Cate stopped.

"She is wrong."

"You can turn back to you," Victoria said.

"How?" Cate shook her head.

"Just think about it."

"Not yet."

The doors opened.

The area was clear, as Mr. Rogers had said. The guards looked away; the Hercules didn't move. The violet strings disappeared as before for Victoria. The strings reappeared, but Cate crossed them as if they were air. Crossing the white lustrous floor lobby, Victoria and Cate moved toward the exit.

"Hold on." Victoria stopped before crossing the tower's main exit. She checked her Whisper band.

"What is going on? How did you get me out?" Cate bent forward, looking for her sister's eyes.

"You should have never been there in the first place." The Whisperband beamed; she saw the blue car approaching. "Let's go."

Coming down the gross white steps, they passed NAA staff; the purple-dressed men and women stared at them and remained motionless. A few regular citi-

zens saw them; some took pictures, others videos, holos, anything. Their Whisper rings turned immediately to red while they walked away.

"Unlock," Victoria instructed her Whisper. The vehicle stopped in front of them; both blue pearl doors
moved up like wings, making a cross-air sound. They
jumped in and headed north.

maria beta

CHAPTER 6

....

COPERNICO

I don't understand anything." Cate was sitting with her feet on the seat, squeezing her knees. She was looking to her right at the full moon's reflection on the ocean, not paying much attention to her own reflection on the glass window of the car. The rain had stopped and cleared the stratosphere. The moon could only be seen on certain occasions, like that night, after days of heavy rain.

Traffic was decent. Victoria was driving; she probably wanted to avoid CDD.

"On the first day, there was a doctor. I swear I've seen him in FoxStone before; I am sure he is in one of Dad's pictures in his library." Cate stared at her arms, twisting her wrists.

"I am so sorry. There were people I would never have doubted, and they didn't return any of my calls. Did this doctor hurt you?" Victoria asked.

"No." Cate's voice was dry and apathetic. "What is this? You too?"

"Yes, but not like you. Happened the same night, but just my arms that time; it's weird."

"What is it? What are we?" Cate asked again. She pushed a button by her side, looking for a holo-mirror on the window on her right. Her features were perfect; her face bones shone indescribably, like having a silver fluid attached to her. Her eyes were dark silver too, with a tiny darker iris. Every fiber of her hair had a metal shine of its own.

"I am not sure yet. It is called Alliafied. Apparently, that is what we are. It has to do with the elements. And you are a very special kind." Victoria simplified the chemistry lesson from Mr. Rogers. "I'm heavy in gold. I don't know about you yet, but we'll find out." She grabbed her sister's left palm.

"Did we get this on Europa? Are we the only ones?" Cate asked.

"There is someone else; the one who helped me get to you, this Mr. Rogers. I'll meet him soon. We'll find out." Victoria said, and by pushing with her index finger on two bright yellow lines on the panel to her right; an image of a band came up. She swiped and a teenage boy dressed in yellow plastic appeared; swiped fast again, and a sleek, dark long-haired woman emerged. Victoria pushed the image, and Saki's latest hit started playing:

The depth of your soul will determine
How dark can you go?
The silence of your spirit will lift you
There is no limit for wings made of dust

"How do I come back? Is it safe?" Cate moved her hands.

"Yes, just think about it. Think about being normal again." Victoria grabbed her left hand.

Cate closed her eyes and so she did. She was a little anxious about seeing her own self again, and went back to the mirror. All the same, not even a bruise. A sting in her chest—she lowered her legs.

"Where is Alex?"

"We won't see him anymore," Victoria said.

"What? Is he okay?"

Victoria didn't look well. Her nose was red and her lips frowned.

Victoria remained quiet for a moment and stopped at the wayside. She grabbed the wheel.

"Victoria, what is going on?"

"We broke up, and there is no way back."

"Was it because of me?"

"No. Because of me." Victoria got out of the car, slammed the door, and dashed forward. Cate got out, but stayed behind. The moon and the ocean on one side, the darkness of the mountains on the other. She could hear the waves crashing nearby.

"What exactly happened that night?" Cate asked.

"I sat by you; you were coughing blood. I didn't know what to do. I tried to calm you. Everything happened so quickly." Victoria pressed her forehead with her right palm. "I saw you turning silver and passing out, and everything went dark. It was like the Oceanic turned off, and we crashed. I was holding you; I felt you slipping away, and that is when that horrible smell showed up. I guess our arms engaging released a horrendous smell of burned metal. I still can't get it out of my head," Victoria explained.

"So that's what the smell was." Cate bent her head backward.

Victoria looked at her and nodded. "You slipped away anyway. Your safety belt broke, and you were shot to the back of the car with the impact," Victoria added.

"I don't remember much." Cate was worried.

"I tried to open the door. I punched the window and I saw my arms like that, golden. That is when I saw you crawling outside of the car, still coughing; you saw me and came to me. You tore the door like paper and helped me push Alex outside the car," Victoria continued.

"And Anibal and the driver?" Cate asked.

"We may have been driving at more than 120 miles per hour. That is the last record. We were out from CDD's reach and the protective screen didn't work. They instantly died with the hit." Victoria seemed hopeless.

"Oh no, it was true," Cate said. Her shoulders felt heavy.

"It had nothing to do with you," Victoria said.

"They explained to me how transforming into this shut down the car," Cate said.

"No. The Oceanic crashed; that's it. We were swapping cars, and in a tunnel. You must believe me. Maybe it was because both of us were there," Victoria said.

No, no, this can't be happening. Cate crushed her thoughts.

"How did they find us?" Cate asked.

"Once Alex was out, I put his ring behind his neck and Marcus got the signal. In between, a helicopter from that gossip show appeared. The light was terrible. There was a fire in the car and you were trying to get the people from the front, and that is when the Hercules appeared and began shooting at you. You turned around, and your body was—I can't describe it well." She wobbled her hands. "Not like today. It was like a gas layer, shiny, dust, like sparkles. You went to them..."

"I wasn't thinking," Cate said.

"You thought right," Victoria said, and moved closer to her sister. "I came to you and somehow my arms were back to this, flesh again." Victoria was not crying but her eyes were small and her face was neutral. "The NAA security guards said they would take care of us. And I believed them." Victoria supported herself on the car and released a dreadful gasp. "I'm sorry, I should had never left you alone."

"And Alex?" Cate asked, looking for her sister's eyes.

"He saw my arms punching the door, and he was worried he might not get reelected, having a metal girlfriend like me by his side." Victoria's voice was soulless, flat. "Interesting—he did promise not to mention to anyone who I really am."

Cate's anxiety began to build as she gasped intensely.

"Alex is a coward. That Debika would have kept me down there forever." Cate stopped for a bit. "I don't understand anything about what this is or what is this for, but I don't care. I hate them all." She realized her words didn't make much sense. She barely knew who she was anymore. "This is not fair."

"I know. It is not." Victoria went to her and hugged her. "Let's go home for now," Victoria walked in front of the car and got back in. Cate followed her.

A few minutes later Cate saw the medieval gate of her parents' house in Sunally.

Victoria drove in and left the car by the roundabout where Steban and Paula were waiting. They welcomed Cate warmly while Victoria went straight inside the house without a word.

"I think you have lost some weight," their father stupidly remarked, which a few days earlier Cate would have considered funny; however, tonight she pretended as if she didn't hear it. Paula took her in, while Steban remained outside, probably watching the stars.

"As soon as you feel okay, we can talk and maybe call a doctor. Anything you need, when you feel right." Paula sat her in the library room. A bunch of mint dark chocolates were set up in a dish. She went upstairs to her room; she saw the pink curtains and tore them out. She took a pillow from her bed and walked to Victoria's room. Her sister was lying on her side; she saw her and moved farther right. Cate lay down beside her sister, looking to the other side.

"What is going to happen now?" Cate asked.

"Nothing. Everything will be the same," Victoria said.

Cate woke up the next day, looked at her hands and arms, and she was dark silver as the day before.

Things are not the same.

*****

It was a Wednesday.

"Paula, I want to get rid of all the pink in my room."

"No problem. I will do it for you," Paula said. She was cleaning her magenta gardening gloves in the sink. They kind of resembled a porcupine, and the supposed quills moved along with the level of moisture in the plant's leaves. Her duties were limited to spraying the bushes and their few flowers with a treatment that helped them with the photosynthesis process.

Cate was sitting at the round table in the kitchen when she received in her tablet the fourth rejected college application in a week. She sank her chin to her chest and then tried to recover.

"What is it?" Paula asked.

"Am I supposed to stay here forever?"

No one, besides a few TV shows, would talk about having Cate around. The only person who energetically tried to reach her was Debika the shrink, with constant threats about how she was going to take the Alliafied back in and next time it would be forever, but the threats weren't even close to materializing. Only once she did manage to appear at her door, but Sunally security took care of her right away.

"Victoria is doing her best." Paula stopped the running water and looked at her.

"It's that video! Maybe I should have stayed in that basement forever." She left for upstairs.

Cate wasn't oblivious; even though she wasn't charged with anything and no one else knew about her short stay in Apex, with that video out, people were aware of how massively strong or dangerous she was. In mere seconds, she destroyed two Hercules, considered by some to be humans' major protectors. She thought about the situation over and over, never reaching an agreement with herself. She got tired of strolling around Sunally and, afterward, seeing how distressed people became when she was close by. No one visited her house anymore. She and her father would sit and read for hours, not talking to each other; soon, she would pick a book and take it upstairs to her room, to avoid the silence.

A couple of months after, on a Sunday, the four of them were having lunch on the terrace on a nice lime-green sky winter's day.

"Patrick Jameson will join my team next week," Victoria said. Public opinion started liking her as result of the pity and empathy generated by her situation:

metal sister and gone fiancé. And she took advantage of it to position her name quickly in the New South.

"Would anyone mind if I moved back to the apartment in FoxStone? Where we used to live?" Cate said seriously.

"Are you sure?" Victoria asked.

Steban nodded.

Cate moved to FoxStone practically the day after, but when it was six months from the day they left the NAA building, Cate sunk into a depression. Her life was built around the two-floor apartment, which she almost never left. Sometimes she showed up at some conferences in the University close by; some of the professors had seen her grow up, so they gladly extended invitations. But that wasn't enough.

One day soon after, Cate was on the terrace, alliafied. As usual, she was dressed entirely in black. She was wearing a Letiqa long-sleeved tight jumpsuit. Letiqa was a waterproof synthetic material that resembled leather but was as warm as two insulated layers. But it wasn't like she needed it. Weather was not an issue while being silver. She was sitting legs crossed on a metal chair with wide and heavy rococo arms, in front of a holo-screen set on a rounded table of the same heavy style. On her right palm, a silver-translucent sphere made of dust and matter was slowly spinning. A tiny silver ray of light was fighting to get out.

The screen was showing some recent studies on palladium, which she believed was her main component. An announcement appeared. She clicked on it and saw Victoria through the camera at the apartment entrance. Victoria was with Alice, Cate's best friend from high school, who visited Cate every two weeks, and this time was carrying an orange plastic box by its hanger. Cate closed her palm, the sphere disappeared, and she kept reading.

Victoria came in and Cate swiped her index finger on the screen, leaving it on pause.

"You couldn't find a bigger coat," Cate said.

"It's freezing."

"I guess," Cate continued.

They discussed nothing important until Victoria said, "Cate, I want you to come with me, to the moon. To Apollo. I'm going there for a short trip, but you will stay there for a year."

"What for?" Cate stood up, a bit worried.

"You will be working for Alice's mother's team. You will run into some friends as well; Francis Gaullenpierre is there."

"I don't want to see him."

"Take this as fresh air. And then come back to Earth, here. FoxStone University will take you in then; it is almost set in stone."

Cate's heart began to beat in a way she hadn't felt in some time. She had thought it had already turned into cold metal.

"Take me in as what?"

"As a student. Do you still want to study physics? They told me they will use your previous scores for it, or you could take new tests if you want something else. You will be joining two years later than scheduled; it's nothing—they would even take some of your work with Alice's mother as credits," Victoria said.

"You shouldn't have gotten involved. I don't know if I want to go."

"Cate, I promise you that time will fix everything," Victoria came close to her sister. "It's just that time takes time," Victoria whispered.

"Does it?" Cate said bitterly. She had already lost her faith in time.

"I am counting on that," Victoria responded sharply.

Alice, smiling, entered the terrace wearing a purple hat with many fuchsia mini-pumps. A tiny golden-brown furry creature escaped her hands and ran to Victoria, who picked it up and gave it to Cate.

"What is this?" Cate was dumbfounded.

"This is your new roommate. He just got all the certificates and is allowed to join you on this trip."

Cate grabbed him and lifted him through the air. He kept twisting his four legs. She always wanted a dog, but her parents had denied her since she'd kept saying it was hard for her to breathe. They thought she might have developed an allergy in New Alaska, a condition that was resolved as soon as she became an Alliafied.

"What will you name him?" Victoria asked.

Cate left him on the floor, unalliafied, and said: "Copernico."

maria beta

CHAPTER 7

....

LOST-TOWN

When Catherine came back from her one-year moon exchange program, as she liked to call it, she was 19, and started undergraduate school at FoxStone University, where she ended up studying physics. She fully redecorated her parents' apartment, thanks to a generous welcome present from her older sister. Colors and wood practically disappeared.

Alice was wearing a white dress stamped with strawberries. "Wow, this looks so much nicer than last time. That is my favorite part." Alice indicated an island with a steel base in the open kitchen, and four tall silver stools.

They sat by a round and simple white table with four short white chairs, before a long window that enabled them to see the terrace. Cate had kept the rococo table and its chairs. A mustard-yellow hammock was on the rococo table, waiting to be installed in an unknown future—a welcome present from Paula.

"Did you plant roses?" Alice asked.

Cate nodded.

"This is great! And you look great! I can tell you change your outfit pretty much as your mood tells you to," Alice said.

Cate felt nervous—her friend was right; she changed to her silver skin whenever she felt uncomfortable.

"It's not an outfit, Alice; the metal cover is me," Cate explained.

"And I heard that you are not changing that much anymore, not at all for chemistry."

One of the agreements between the University and Cate was that she wouldn't transform when she was attending classes or wandering around the campus. However, especially in the first two weeks, people tended to stare at her disproportionately, and Cate's instant reaction was to alliafy, or just to show a subtle silver gleam, and to leave the place right away. Teachers had asked her to stop, and she'd promised she would. She had tried. Nevertheless, she soon received a letter from the Department threatening to expel her. When she tried to imagine Victoria's reaction, she reconsidered her actions. At the same time, as classes advanced, her confidence kept moving forward. Not even her hands would shine in chemistry or two other courses, which happened to be the classes in which she excelled.

"Where do you hear all these things?" Cate was curious.

"I have people everywhere." Alice raised her eyebrows, and they laughed.

The new life in the two-floor apartment worked well. It exceeded Cate's expectations. And college life had seemed to be working out well too—until she realized she wasn't really participating in it. She had been invited to the show, but she was a mere spectator. She became close to a pair of genius twins, Sabrina and Martina—math prodigies who had approached her after she showed up with the only A+ on the first Physics 101 test. And that was all.

*****

The week before summer vacation was over, Alice called her. "Cate! I'm being transferred to New York City, at least for six months. You must come visit me."

"I'll try," she said.

"Come on! I am sure you can miss a day or two. You advanced in two courses this summer. You deserve it!" Alice insisted. "Do it as a reward for staying in college during the entire summer."

It's not like she'd had many options of where to go. Two months in Sunally with her parents was a round no.

"You even assisted in one of the summer labs!"

I may deserve it, Cate agreed.

Cate didn't think about it too much, and three days later it was Friday and she jumped on a bullet train heading to Manhattan. She arrived at Penn Station and the wave of human beings swamped her own innerspace. Their clothes, their hair. Everyone had their Whisper's ring in red, languages that she had never heard before. They pushed her more than twice. It was energizing.

Later in the evening, they went out for dinner—hot pot in Koreatown, followed by French dessert at the New York location of Paris's most famous patisserie, La Magieclair. Then they walked to Alice's dorm in Greenwich Village. They crossed Washington Square Park and sat on the fountain edge. The two of them talked about Paris, and whether travelling across the globe would ever be the same.

"Well, it's hard to fly with the Panels moving up there—at least that's what they say. And the hypersonic trains are too expensive," Alice said.

"Do you think we will ever have an ozone layer again?" Cate asked. She took a last bite from a pistachio éclair and passed it to Alice.

"Don't know. I wonder if these Aureans will keep trying. I mean, we have had the Panels for, what? Sixty years? No one has an allergy to Zafor anymore. So, I guess we stick to this," Alice said. She finished the green pastry.

"At least we get these multicolored days, almost like your winter hats." Cate moved her right hand circularly, looking up at the sky.

"They are the best part of my winter."

"Coper loves your hats, in any case," Cate teased Alice and pushed her shoulder.

"I am glad you came." Alice seemed happy.

"I am too. I know some people at FoxStone. But I don't have friends."

"Why do you think it's hard for them to understand that you are different?"

"I don't know, but it's not like I try much either." Cate paused. "It is just that I always have the impression that they are expecting me to do something, like grab the tables in the class and throw them through the windows, just like that Hercules in the video."

Alice chortled. "That would be fun."

Cate for a second had a reproduction of the idea in her mind. "Yes, it would."

The next day, on Saturday, Alice had to set up her new apartment in the school dorm, so Cate went to see some of the museums Uptown on Fifth Avenue. On her way back, she took the subway to head back to Alice's, but she forgot to change trains and by the time she realized it, she was already deep downtown. Everyone could go south, but after 5:00 p.m. special permission was required to go up north; so she would have to go back by foot and get Alice to authorize her ticket back.

Before then, though, she decided to get lost for a while under the dark burgundy sky. People were disconnected. No one turned around—not to see her; not to see anybody. She glanced through the dark streets lit by long-armed, vintage-type lamps. New bricks merged into different types of glass. She entered a bar; the place was simple—dark and loud. She touched her wristband, sent her location to Alice, pulled up the keyboard, and texted "Come, I'll be here."

An hour later, Alice entered the bar wearing a black hat stamped with silver hearts. "Cate, you are crazy. This is where everybody comes to disappear," Alice said.

A guy came up from behind and pulled Alice onto the dark dance floor behind them. His friend came and took Alice's seat.

"I am Martin," he said.

"I am Catherine."

"Do you dance?"

"No."

"Me neither. What do you like to do then?" he asked, searching for her sight. His dark skin emphasized his clear green eyes.

She stayed quiet and then said: "I like Mexican food."

"So you *do* like stuff. Two spicy margaritas, please!" he asked the Gothic bartender.

"I guess," she said, laughing, a little nervous.

They talked for hours about her life on the moon and Europa. She lied and said her last name was Walker, not because she was afraid of what he would find about her, but because she didn't want to be identified by her famous father. Martin seemed so far from the world she'd grown up in. He was in advertising, and he described his work with enthusiasm, but Cate interpreted it as pressing the right buttons to push people to do what was required of them.

The night was a success. The two gentlemen escorted the girls to the border, where Alice passed her ID through the gate, proving that she lived farther north.

Before they said goodbye, Cate asked Martin, "Do you ever come to this side?"

"I can, but why would I?"

The next day she went back to college and felt that the gap between her and the rest of humanity was not as wide as she'd believed. A week later, Cate and Sabrina were sitting in the University Amphitheater, eating apples and talking about math. "Have you ever been in Lost-Town, in New York?" Cate asked.

"Oh no! I'm not allowed!" the ginger-haired Sabrina responded.

"Does your mother know we study together?

"No." Sabrina lowered her tone. "She might say something."

"I see," Cate said.

"I prefer to avoid the conversation. I really don't care."

"Do you want to go to Lost-Town sometime?"

Sabrina nodded.

Cate visited Alice another couple of weekends during the fall and winter, once with Sabrina, but stayed in a hotel, always south of the border.

*****

Before winter was over, Cate went to her parents' house in Sunally for a Sunday brunch, mostly because Victoria would be attending as well. Victoria was wearing a shimmery wide-leg blue jumpsuit, and Cate was in black as usual. When the two of them were bringing dishes and food back to the kitchen, they were finally alone.

"Have you ever considered having an apartment in New York City?" Cate asked.

"What for?" Victoria responded.

"Investment, maybe? You can rent it."

"Where in New York City?" Victoria inquired. "I wouldn't even know how to pick a place. I always stay on the Island."

This might be the end, Cate thought. She hesitated but gave the answer: "Downtown."

"Do you mean...Lost-Town?" Victoria said scornfully with her eyes semi-closed.

"I would rent it. I need an apartment in New York. I am running out of money staying at hotels. I don't have the rating to get a loan, and I don't have the money for it either. I'll pay you back. We can figure out something."

"Oh, Cate!" Victoria left a teapot on the table and turned to her sister with both hands on her waist. "Get a random job and then think about it more patiently. Build your credit rating. I am sure you will start high. I will call the bank and make sure you are in my category," Victoria said, and continued to put some cylindrical teacups in a robo-box.

Cate felt powerless. The conversation was going nowhere.

"I don't need a platinum category to get into the fanciest places only allowed for the ones that match your financial behavior," Cate said. "I don't want to be segregated. Not anymore."

Victoria turned to her. "And you think Lost-Town is not segregation? Don't kid yourself," Victoria said. "Some streets are more expensive than DC, full of eccentric people who want to live out of order, and who put value on the fact that police never go there. They even have systems to block satellites and CDD." Victoria moved her hands in denial and walked to the storage closet.

Cate followed her.

"Well, I call that luxury," Cate said back, laughing. She remained by the storage door. "If you want to and you can afford it, I am fine with it. In any case, we don't need law enforcement anymore. But the fact that you need a special résumé to be allowed above a certain street? That I find another despicable chapter of this NAA dictatorship. And these people you talk about, could not care less if I shine silver or blue. I would never be allowed to live Uptown, even if you bought an entire block." Cate fought to make her point, even if it was not worth it anymore.

Victoria came back and passed her. She was shaking her head.

"I'll lend you half of the money to buy it," Victoria said. "You will have to manage how to get the other half. That's my final answer."

Victoria left and headed over to the living room.

This is happening! Cate followed her.

"Thank you so much. Thank you. Thank you!"

Steban was standing by the window. "I'll give you the other half," he said.

The childish reaction faded, and she felt some pressure on her chest.

"I promise I'll pay you back," Cate said.

"No need," her father calmly said and went out to the terrace.

The next day, Monday, she decided to pay a long-delayed visit to the Dean of the Faculty of Physics. She arrived early in the morning. She entered the elegant brick building and requested an appointment. She was told to wait for a few minutes. The place looked like a doctor's waiting room, all white with no decoration. A thick glass door opened sideways and half the Dean's body showed through.

"Catherine, hi, come," he said. He waved his pale and venous hand. He was dressed casually, in beige, which matched the color of the day outside. What was left of his hair was pushed back in three lines, and an inch-sized mole took the right side of his forehead—*A little creepy*, she thought.

The room was plain with diplomas and awards on the walls. He sat behind his desk, a thick copper sheet with two screens on it. Behind him, a holographic screen showed a constantly changing matrix—names, places, projects, highlighted in different colors.

"First of all, congratulations on your outstanding grades. I'm glad you finally came to visit. I've sent you several lunch invitations since you arrived," he said in his squeaky voice.

"I am sorry I haven't come before. I was hoping to have an idea of the college experience before I said hi and thanks, and then time just passed by. I'll be forever grateful to the institution, and I wish there was some way I could repay the Department," Cate politely said, knowing the Dean had been key to her college acceptance.

He seemed very happy to hear her words.

Then she went straight to the core. "I was hoping you could give me a job. I have free time and I think I'll be useful to the University."

"You have advanced faster in your classes than anyone of your generation. I am very proud of you. But I am not sure; maybe an internship. Let me see," he said.

I need to get a job, a real job, she pressured herself.

"Well, the thing is, I happen to have an unusual characteristic," she said solidly, her eyes fixed on him.

"I am aware of it." The Dean bent the chair back. "Is it safe for you to turn silver like you do?"

He seems interested, she thought.

"It is mostly palladium, and some platinum. It's fine. It is just my skin. And my body adapts perfectly to it; no side effects." Cate smiled.

"Interesting." It was hard for the Dean to hide his enthusiasm; he was rocking his chair.

"I'm stronger than anyone in one of your special suits. I don't need a suit, in fact." Cate had no intention to prove this, but Victoria had said that according to Mr. Rogers, a multiple series of lightning bolts would be like regular rain for her.

"Palladium has the lowest melting point of all in the platinum group," he brought up.

"Well, it's a mix of things. I can support any temperature, cold or hot, while I'm transformed; I don't need to eat or go to the bathroom either, at least not for a good amount of time." She laughed, and so did he. "Send me to Venus. I know you have been struggling with the base over there. Sulfuric acid rain is delaying the missions."

He nodded, and so he did.

Three months later she went on her first mission beyond the moon, and Cate finally built a life schedule for herself, one that she was really fond of. She studied and worked hard at FoxStone from Monday to

Friday, then took the 6:15 p.m. train toward New York, where she spent every weekend. A year later she led an expedition to Mars. Her goal was to eventually be sent back to Europa, which she did when she locked herself a spot for the new Renewables Station to be set up there. She stayed in New Greenland for almost a year, and it was fantastic.

"These projects really fulfill me. They give me purpose," Cate said to Victoria when she was about to come back.

"I'm so glad."

"And you, how you've been?"

"Busy, busy as ever."

CHAPTER 8

....

THE ECLIPSE

In HCM, the car was under the Central Driving Department's full control. The direction was northeast. Cate grabbed her coffee from the cup holder and watched the major news headlines displayed on a holo-screen before the windshield: "...and that is why general elections may be postponed once again," the youthful female news anchor said.

"Screen off," and the screen immediately vanished backward into the transparent crystal sheet behind. The gray-lighted intelligent tube that crossed the northeast underground appeared in front of her. The vehicle was going 145 miles per hour. Emerging from the underpass, the car slid to the right, toward the exit, taking the glass-covered 1A1B Interstate. The landscape was radiant; waves hit the long miles of breakwater that protected the highway, brightened from the east by a misshapen yellow spark coming from what was definitely somehow the sun.

Soon after, she circled the roundabout and parked in front of their parents' house. She got out of the bright green Triton S16, her new three-wheeled car— two in front and one behind.

The door of the white house opened.

"I've been here since 6 a.m.," Victoria complained in her silvery tone. She came down the gray marble steps. Fast but elegant, dressed in a long, square-shouldered navy blue dress. "I was dying to do some gardening with Paula," she added.

"I'm sorry," Cate said.

Cate was wearing a white polka-dotted diagonal-sleeved shirt and the same black tight pants she had worn for the past three days. *I may need new pants*, she thought.

"Welcome back," Victoria said, and gave Cate a big kiss on her left cheek. She pushed Cate back and rearranged her younger sister's hair.

"I missed you too," Cate replied.

"Where is Coper?"

"I left him at the house; Steban doesn't like him." Cate trapped her laugh in her smile.

Once inside the house, a dark Brazilian cherry-hardwood hallway led the way to a large arched window at the end. Medieval paintings hung on the left side, and family pictures on the right. *This is new*, Cate realized. She stopped at one of a pregnant woman with a long honey-blond braid; a whitish-blond toddler in a navy-and-white décor dress sat on her lap.

I never got to meet her.

They turned right at the end of the hall, where Paula greeted them from the living room: "Come! Come! Say hello to your father; he is in the library. You haven't been here in a while." Paula welcomed Cate with chortles and hugs.

"A year. You can say so," Cate said.

I hope this doesn't turn into a whole day...

Cate ignored the ocean view and kept walking to the other end, where two red wooden doors embellished the room. She pushed one aside and walked in, and she saw Steban sitting in repose on a long burgundy couch in front of the window, with a direct view of the ocean.

"The testing was a failure from the start." Latima, his three-foot-tall silver reading robot, was giving him project reviews from the latest issue of *Science Wisdom*. "A waste of taxpayers' money." She sounded like an algebra teacher.

The walls were covered with books of different types and colors, and rocks—some shelves were only decorated with rocks. A Roman desk that hadn't been used in centuries sat to the right, at the end, in the dark. The glass of the window in front of Steban was covered in a thin veil that automatically adjusted so that the light in the room was maintained at a constant level all day. Victoria had updated Cate that Steban had become completely blind in one eye in the last year.

"I wonder if they say the same of my Refinery." Cate carefully sat at his side and pushed the silly rounded robot's head with her left foot. "Move!"

She took Steban's old hand.

"Dad. Hello," she said softly. She could tell a year was more than a decade when old age was unrolling.

"Catherine! You look so grown up." He was probably lying; if she hadn't spoken, he would have confused her with Victoria, as he had done before. "Anything on Europa? Cold, still, I assume," he asked.

"All the same mess," she said.

He smiled.

After a brief summary of the current situation in New Alaska and its diplomatic issues, her father's eyes closed for a long moment and he yawned a couple of times.

"Maybe I can go back there in two years or so," she said.

Steban looked to the other side and then back to the window. Shortly after, he fell sleep.

"Watch him," she whispered to Latima. The stupid robot nodded.

Paula was gardening outside, as always. She wore her funny-looking magenta gloves.

Cate headed to the kitchen, where Victoria was walking in circles. She saw Cate, and pressed the lower button on the Whisper around her right ear. She took the semi-transparent device out of her ear and off her neck, and left them on top of the dining table.

"What is fresh here?" Cate went to the pantry to see what she could find.

"So, how does it feel to be back? Have you spoken to someone besides Alice? Francis? The twins?" Victoria asked.

Cate came back with a red apple and took a bite.

"Not really." Cate bit the apple again. "What's new with you? I saw elections were postponed... again." She didn't want to get into a conversation based on her social skills.

"You are unique. People will want to be around you," Victoria said. She smiled at Cate.

Cate looked to the other side and sighed. She supported herself on the table.

"The elections, yes. Actually, they weren't even proposed," Victoria said bitterly. "But things will change. Let's take a walk. Leave your Whisper here."

"Marisa Gomez yesterday called this government 'the survival of the unfittest,'" Cate said.

"It's true, but it doesn't matter anymore, soon it will change."

"I don't know what you can really do. All these laws that protect McCully were enacted decades ago." She left all of the Whisper's toys on the table as well.

"They had a purpose; times were different, unstable." Victoria grabbed a mug with tea. "This Democracy 2.0 works for no one." She opened the terrace door and it swung automatically outwards. They stepped outside.

"Well, Steban says that was how the NAA overcame bankruptcy, and is now stronger than ever," Cate said.

"That is just a slogan. We, in the New South, have less clean water than the Meds in the North of Africa." Victoria paced toward the white cedars. "But we have a plan. All the New Houses and us are getting some help. And you can be a part of it. You picked the best time to come back."

Why would I? Cate mulled over the thought. She took another bite.

Victoria looked up to the sky.

"I agree with you that something must change," Cate said. "But you and I are completely aware that your friends would want me not because of my civil rights interpretation." Cate couldn't care less about civilians, much less about their rights.

"Cate, I know that. But you are equivalent to a whole division of Hercules. I know what you are capable of."

"Yes, but I am the one who *doesn't* know what I'm really capable of."

"We need to use all our bullets. The time has come."

"No, no. Even if I can, it doesn't mean that I should." Cate stressed her tone. "What do you want me for? I can't unleash myself if I truly can't assimilate the implications of my acts. And much less for the NAA."

"I know it's not simple. I just wanted to let you know that something will happen, and soon."

The day had turned gray and it was only past noon. The ocean's color was black and the green surroundings looked opaque. A warm breeze approached.

"This is supposed to be the best time to watch the solar eclipse today," Victoria complained.

Crossed arms. They both lifted their heads.

"You still have hope," Cate said. She turned her sight back to the ocean. It was impossible to watch anything through the gray clouds, yet her sister kept staring at the sky.

"Have you re-engaged in your meetings with that Mr. Rogers of yours?" Cate asked.

"Sometimes." Victoria looked to the other side.

Of course she has, Cate thought.

"Just please don't depend on Alex Harlow." Cate had to bring him up in the conversation; she didn't trust him, and Victoria shouldn't either.

Victoria nodded.

"If something happens, I promise I'll go and find you." Cate grabbed Victoria's elbow.

"I know you will." Victoria smiled.

A moment passed. "When was the last time you became gold?" Cate asked Victoria.

"Six months ago; don't know. When was the last time you turned into silver?" Victoria looked down on her, to her left.

Cate released Victoria and stood up properly. She looked up to the sky, and among the gray clouds, a weak blue dot showed up. Three seconds later it disappeared.

"This morning."

CHAPTER 9

....

THE UNION

Cate was in her apartment at FoxStone and woke up to the constant vibration of her Whisper band; she'd forgotten to take it off the night before. Cate had fallen asleep on the living room's big silver couch, her favorite nap place; its material looked plastic, but it was as soft as silk. She had been watching Marisa Gomez's show on the big screen in front of her; the screen was still on but the sound was muted, and the classic headline *Breaking News* ran across it.

She rolled over and pulled herself together, found the ring on the table in front of her, and put it on behind her neck.

"What?" She jumped off the couch. "Volume up." Slowly, her gut twisted. The image was NAA's Union Building, the multiple-square white building, NAA's largest and most important center. The image switched to her sister, standing in front of a podium, at what seemed to be a press conference, and she was golden—an Alliafied.

Cate had only seen Victoria once since that day of the eclipse. They'd had lunch at FoxStone a few weeks ago. She claimed she had never been so busy before.

What is this? Cate started changing channels.

"This Wednesday, during the weekly North American Alliance meeting at the Union Building, Victoria Weelah from the New South joined the members of the New Houses to discuss..." one AAB journalist said.

"A group of rebels with a golden Hercules entered the main conference room at the Union and kidnapped all of the members that were gathered there—including Gabe McCully, who has remained Prime Minister of the NAA for the last twenty years. It took them less than thirty minutes to seize the building," another channel said, euphorically describing the situation.

"Patrick Jameson from the New South, after a two-hour meeting, forced Prime Minister Gabe McCully to resign and to convene an special election. They guaranteed later that they have the support of the Senate, and that the only thing they demand is the return to real democracy. They are probably speaking the truth, since the chairman of the Senate, Alex Harlow, has only said that he needs time to see how facts evolve," the South Channel announced.

"Another one! Are there any more among us?" the Soupy Show schemy host warned. Cate stopped switching channels until she recognized the "Angel from Hell" video from the night of the crash. That famous image of herself: silver, surrounded by a thin layer of silver dust, her wavy silver hair floating, like with a life of its own.

"TV off," and the Whisper turned it off immediately.

Coper came into the room, rushing his yellow legs. Cate rambled around the couch, and tried to decide what to do first: whom to call, what to eat, where to go. Coper, on the other hand, sat on the silver couch and barked.

"Not now, terrace." She scratched his head and went to the kitchen for one of his treats. On her way, she slipped the Whisper on her right ear.

"Call Victoria, sister." The response in her ear was: "Unavailable."

"Leave message: Saw you on TV. Call me. Do call."

She listened to the messages; most of them were from Paula. "Text Paula: I'll call you later; she will be fine." Cate saw Victoria that night when she took her out from Apex and from that devil shrink. Plus, Victoria wouldn't dare do anything without Mr. Rogers' blessing. Cate had only seen him once, but she knew he and her sister talked often. She didn't feel the man was friendly with her.

Out on the terrace, she sat by the old rococo table while her puppy damaged what was left of the last summer's roses. A few rays of sun managed to penetrate the overhead viridian fog. She suddenly looked at her shoulder, and a strand of platinum hair was moving like a single wave. What if this Victoria show meant that she would end up losing the freedom she had gained?

People will remember how different I am.

"Text Alice P: What does your mother say? End. Text Francis G: I will call you in an hour. Thanks for your thoughts. End. Call Paula."

"Cate! This is unbelievable," Paula said.

"She is doing the right thing." Cate defended her sister, of course.

"Cate, she is gold like you," Paula added.

"I'm silver."

"Well, yes," Paula said.

"What does my father say?"

"Nothing. Cate, do you know Mr. Rogers?"

"I only met him once, briefly." Cate responded. *The strangest character*, she thought.

"Do you think he is part of this as well?"

"Probably, but I'm not sure." Cate was speaking the truth; she had no idea what was going on.

"I believe the military is with her, because they haven't gone onto the island," Paula said.

Yes, but for how long? Cate wondered.

"She is using New East troops right now." Her stepmother seemed more informed than her. Cate had always underestimated her.

Alex, New East means Alex, Cate thought.

"I'll call you later." Cate took the Whisper off her ear.

The day passed just like that, Cate watching the news unfold. She tried to reach to Victoria a few more times, but again to the same response. Alice visited and reiterated how her mother had no clue about what was going on. Before she knew it, it was 6:00 p.m. She saw the band showing 'Francis G—Caller' and immediately took the call.

"It's crazy, I know!" Cate exclaimed.

"Cate, straight to the point. I spoke with my father. He is worried about this, and he is worried for you. He wanted you to know that if anything happens, you can move to the BMA if you need to," Francis said.

"I don't think it's necessary," Cate disagreed.

"He said there will be serious repercussions for Victoria's acts; those were his words."

Aldrick Gaullenpierre, Francis' father, was very high in the ranks of the Baltic-Mediterranean Alliance. He was even one of the ten Aurors two periods ago. Cate had met Monsieur Gaullenpierre ages ago, when she and Francis were both in their teens. Her ex, Barrett, had always looked for an occasion to talk privately with him, but Mssr. Gaullenpierre always managed to be unavailable for him. Cate knew that Francis's father was also one of the people who'd helped Victoria get Cate off Earth for the year she was away in Apollo, in the moon. He had even offered to receive her in Europe if necessary. "Europeans do not care about eccentricities," he had said. That's what he called Cate's abilities—eccentricities.

"I'd appreciate it, do tell him," Cate said.

"I just wanted you to know. Good night!" Francis said.

The next morning, she tried to reach Victoria again; worthless. It was Thursday, but it was like the world had been put on hold. She took a quick shower and put on her usual uniform set of dark clothes and a black, unpolished letiqa jacket.

Repercussions of what, from whom? The Bammies? Cate snorted.

Cate finally received a text from Victoria: "Everything is fine. Right now it is kind of chaotic. Give me a week, and feel free to show up any time. Love, V."

"I'm on my way there; we need to talk ASAP," Cate texted back. She was concerned about what Francis's father had said.

Coper was sitting on the couch in the living room, pretending to watch the news.

"Who do you think you are teasing, eh?" She scratched his belly and he rolled on his back, extending his furry legs. "Come on!" They both left the apartment.

"Triton, doors open." The dog jumped inside the green car through the pilot door before her. She dropped him at PetVida in FoxStone, for the whole combo—haircut and pet intermingling. Coper had never interacted with other dogs while on the moon, and not with many after, so he had serious social issues.

Back in the car, she took the highway heading east. Cate had barely been in Manhattan since she'd left for Europa more than a year before. Work in FoxStone had been exhausting, and every time she was about to take the train for a long weekend, she'd had to take a jet to Apollo somehow.

"Can I take the Lincoln Tunnel?" she asked CDD. The tunnel was the best choice; it crossed Manhattan and had an exit straight onto Atlantic Island, where the Union Building, the NAA's Headquarters, was.

"Closed. Entry only for authorized members."

"Call my sister, or Patrick Jameson."

"No response. Traffic is reaching Level 8," the system said. At Level 10 vehicles didn't move.

After more than an hour, she reached East Harlem and soon she saw the 100-foot-wide bridge in front of Atlantic Island. Between Coper's spa, the closed tunnel, and a stop at the car's battery station, it had taken her around five hours to reach her destination. *This day really can't turn worse*, she thought. It was the end of September.

She got out of her Triton and approached a sentry box on the right side, realizing that guards were taking aim at her from two watchtowers bordering the entrance.

"No one is allowed in," a young cadet in jade-green told her.

Green, Alex's New East.

"I'm Catherine Weelah. Golden Victoria's sister."

"No one is allowed to go inside," he reiterated.

She went into the box, and a Hercules robot behind him stepped closer and turned its arms inside-out—attack mode.

Cate thought twice about whether she should alliafy completely; the outcome was never good.

"You are clear," the cadet said. "Take one of the cars; leave yours there."

The gate opened and a batter car with no driver and enough space to fit two passengers picked her up.

When was the last time I was here? Eight years ago? Maybe more. She couldn't recall. Despite the fact that she had her second house in New York City, she never went back to the Union again after the Apex episode. In New York, she was Miss Walker, a resident of Lost-Town, as Victoria would say—and had zero involvement in political affairs. Cate had the pass to move up and down in Manhattan, but she always remained down from the borderline.

The droid car crossed the bridge, and there it was: a beautiful pure green meadow of perfectly maintained grass that could reflect whatever version of sun rays managed to cross the shield. Following a path at the left of the magnificent green square, Cate remembered when she, Victoria, and Paula had once crossed the big yard through the avenue in the middle. It had taken them around an hour to reach the multi-cube building coming from the gate.

Cate's right hand turned intermittently silver; she closed her fist and turned it back to normal flesh. She trusted Victoria, but she couldn't stop wondering how long her sister would be able to keep this up. People were weak, and their intentions tended to fade. And if a better bidder to solve this situation came along, she may lose support. Victoria had to move fast.

The building hadn't changed at all. Ivory. A main structure with two smaller cubes on each side, decreasing in height, combined with gray glass towers between the cubes' edges. It's said that the Union could be separated in blocks and transported to any other place in the NAA, just in case.

As the droid car got closer, the size of the building looked more imposing than it did on TV or holos. It could resemble the bottom half of a pyramid of blocks. Broad steps opened their way at the bottom of the middle tower; ivory in the center, opening sideways in opaque gray marble on each side. The car turned around the building toward the main entrance, located on the other side, instead of facing the green meadow. The car left her where a long burgundy carpet began.

"Good afternoon. Miss Weelah is fixing to expect you in the Celestial Room now." A woman with a southern accent received her.

"Who else is here?" Cate asked.

The woman smiled.

The entrance was packed with soldiers dressed in yellow—worn by troops from the New South. She was escorted inside, and ten minutes later Cate was on the top floor—also filled with yellow-clad troops—standing in front of two colossal black doors made of a matrix of metal and rubber. These slid to the sides, revealing an impressive view of the emerald lawn below. Cate made her way into the Celestial Conference Room, where the day before the main body of the ex-government was gathered for its weekly meeting before it was taken down by her sister, Jameson, and others. Between Cate and the panoramic view sat a long transparent table—decorated with a glass piece filled with bluebonnets—and square white chairs.

To her right, standing beyond the table, her golden sister was giving instructions to two New South personnel. Patrick was with them. They laughed and the two people in yellow left.

Insolit, Cate pondered.

"Welcome!" Victoria said. She shone in her golden skin, her hair loose, combed to one side like a single wave of rich metal. Her navy suit fit her well. A main screen filled with data was behind her.

Patrick left a tablet on the table and walked toward the exit; he opened his eyes wider when he came closer to Cate. Cate responded with a funny face. She did like him.

"So, what do you think?" Victoria said, beckoning her sister to come closer to her. She unalliafied from her golden shade and pulled back a chair from the table, making room for Cate to sit.

"Well...I see you are here, and McCully is not, so I think it's okay, right?" Cate hugged Victoria and sat.

Victoria sat at the head chair of the table.

"They call it a mini-coup. Ridiculous. We were here; there were a lot of arguments." Victoria extended her right arm. "We demanded he announce elections. And he wouldn't, so then we threw at him all the articles that he was infringing, we built a good case, and then Patrick told him he was under arrest," Victoria said. "It also helped that we have control of Homeland Security, which conveniently controls the Hercules and CDD."

"Gone Hercules; that is all you need," Cate laughed.

"But McCully had his own security robots, not controlled by CDD. So that is when I transformed and everyone shut up. It was easier than I'd thought. They saw me and went into a panic. But we are asking the media to keep it low-key," Victoria explained.

Low-key? Really? Cate wondered.

"But now every state is hiding information; they don't want to show their real messes," Victoria complained.

"Where is McCully?" Cate asked.

"In the Presidential Suite, in the hotel here on the Island. He can't complain. Either he takes the deal or he will go to trial next month."

"I am sorry I have to ask this: Do you have a Plan B? Are you willing to stay golden forever if this doesn't work?" Cate asked.

"Why?"

"This is kind of a coup. What if it doesn't work?" Cate added.

"I'm not considering that chance." Victoria pushed herself deeper in the tall-backed chair. "If things were easy, anyone would do it. I don't know how much of the plan will work, but if we can achieve something, it will make all of this worth it."

"You think you are untouchable, and you are," Cate said. "But what about the others? They could all end..."

"That is why it has to work." Victoria stood up and walked around the table. "I'm of the idea that in life you must take a position, and how you stick to it will define the weight of your words. Soon Arthur Harlow will run for election, and he will win. He will then extend pardons to all of us, if anything. Come join us. You still can be a part of this." Victoria sounded pretty sure of her strategy.

"You don't need me. I don't think people like me really." Cate rotated in her chair.

"Cate, you are overestimating people's memory; most of them barely remember what happened that night of the crash."

"Evidently you haven't had time to check the news these last two days. That Angel video is probably in the top-10 most-seen already. Anyway," Cate continued, "my point is that things could end badly for Patrick and for all the rest who cannot alliafy—and that is why I'm here. The Meds." Cate stopped rotating her chair. "They know something. They think this won't work."

Victoria turned around.

"I was offered some sort of asylum. *Me?*" Cate continued.

"Who told you that? Francis? The sleazy Italian? Lucca?" Victoria asked.

"Francis. He spoke to his father. I feel bad telling you, but listen: he said that repercussions were coming."

"Repercussions? We have so much to do here, I cannot be concerned with everyone else in the world right now."

"It's the Meds. I wouldn't take it lightly," Cate suggested.

"I will do something." Victoria released a big breath from her chest.

"Also, you should call Steban and Paula."

"Oh, yes... Take this." Victoria went back to the table, opened a drawer, and gave her a new Whisper. "This is not tapped; just put your code in it."

"Oh thanks!" She picked up the new band and inputted her keywords. "I honestly thought you weren't really going to do something, when we talked back then; I mean, you just said things will change. I guess you will be stuck on this island for a while," Cate said.

"Likely." Victoria sighed. "Come on, let's take a walk and I'll introduce you to the transition team." Victoria paced toward the door.

"Is Alex here? I saw his green people around; so annoying," Cate asked. When Alex needed someone for the dirty work, he suddenly didn't mind that Victoria was golden, or that the whole world would find out about it.

"No. But it's complica..." Victoria was interrupted.

Out of nowhere, the earth rumbled, like those noisy earthquakes that people said happened when the ozone layer faded away. The panoramic window trembled and the chairs moved out of place. The flower arrangement in the middle of the table fell to the floor. Victoria supported herself on the table. It lasted close to 20 seconds.

maria beta

CHAPTER 10

....

THEM

"What just happened?" Victoria exclaimed.

"I don't know!" Cate approached the window. "It's all smoke. But it's all above. A SkyShot. Has a Panel ever broken apart?"

The sky turned into a thick sheet of dark purple clouds and smoke. The sound rose again and became a dreadful noise, despite the fact that there was no ground movement this time. It stopped. Silence. And then the sheet of clouds and smoke in a single harsh move moved down.

"What?" Cate couldn't believe what she'd just seen.

And then the layer of smoke melted; it lowered and became wider, until it took any sight away.

"I'll find out." Victoria went back to the screens on the wall. The main one, crooked to the left, showed the scenario on different floors; people were in distress, and the words at the bottom: "An incoming call from P. Jameson."

"Victoria, do stay there until we know what it is. Is Cate still with you?" Patrick said on the speaker.

"Yes, she is with me," she said to Patrick. "Cate, come back here," Victoria said, but Cate remained by the crystal window.

The smoke slightly dissipated and turned into some patches of dark and light gray; something started showing from behind. Cate's saliva got stuck in her throat. Two iridescent dark purple turbines advanced through, crossing the gray cloud. A spaceship nearly the size of the Union Building showed up. The environment was silent. The purple vessel hovered in front of them. Between the purple circles, there was an asymmetrical rounded façade with a rhombus in between.

Not only had this gigantic object interrupted, unnoticed, guarded NAA space, but the entirety of the Union was now covered by a violet force field expanding from the ship, pushing the thick gray and purple clouds back to the river. Hundreds of yellow and green guards came out and covered the building; Special Forces soldiers in white uniforms began to fill the strategic places of the field.

The purple ship remained over the green field for a while, until the first line of white soldiers shot two batches of uranium torpedoes. These turned out to be harmless. A few NAA Shadow-Jets flew close by, but they couldn't cross the violet force field and were forced to turn around.

"What is that?" Cate said to herself. *This can't be the Meds*, she thought.

The ship came closer to the grass; a bottom compartment opened, and a bridge lowered until it touched the peeled green ground. A group of beings jumped from it. The purple machine rose again and turned backward, close to the river, and landed on the water.

Victoria approached the glass where Cate was standing.

"This is not the Meds; what is that?" Cate said.

"I've never seen anything like...never." Victoria remained open-mouthed. In the middle of the field, there was a black square of what could be giant ants. They weren't many—more than 50, but less than 100—but it was the speed with which they moved that made their intrusion panic-inducing. At a certain distance, about 10 feet, one of them stayed in the back, circulated backward and forward, looking around 360 degrees with its two heads, covering the perimeter, moving closer to the ivory building.

"I think we must leave," Cate said.

"Message Patrick J: I'll meet you downstairs, send the rest to the basement," Victoria said to the Whisper. "Go to the basement," she said to Cate. Victoria alliafied; she stretched her golden neck from side to side. For someone who was currently profusely active with her golden aptitudes, it was obvious from the outside that she didn't feel comfortable in her alliafied skin.

Cate watched how these perfectly aligned spider-people advanced across the island. Effortlessly, some rolled and some sprinted, leaving the NAA soldiers motionless on the ground. And then she saw them. It could have been a visual effect from the smoke. Cate's throat closed. Approaching the gray and ivory steps, two shiny blue creatures emerged, stumping from within these spider-people. She went into the form she felt safer in—her solid and non-breachable dark-silver form. And then, as soon as she alliafied, she realized that one of these creatures raised its head—or what seemed like it—and pointed at her. The other one followed and pointed as well.

A twist in her gut, the same from that night at the party before the crash, but with a strong burning in her chest.

"I think they might be like me." Cate looked back, but Victoria was already gone.

What now?

Two spider-people kneeled approximately 20 feet from the building and launched two bazooka-type rockets toward it. She jolted back. All of the electricity shut down; the lights recovered, but the screens remained black, and the black door opened sideways. She peeked outside and saw that the floor was empty; she went back into the Conference Room and locked the matrix-like door from inside. *Too late for the basement.* She grabbed the Whisper band—the ring didn't work while she was metal—and brought it close to her mouth: "Text Victoria: Where are you? We need to leave." A third rocket crashed through the panoramic window and she fell to the ground. Sparkling dust. Pressure dropped. It was like oxygen was being sucked out of the air. Cate crawled to the end of the meeting table, where she'd been talking to her sister a few minutes before. She was about to faint. It was like that night she alliafied after the party—no blood, but, incredibly, worse. There was fire in her chest. *Let's breathe. Breathe more,* she said to herself. A fourth rocket struck the building. The lights were gone; the room was only illuminated by the gray daylight from the window. She managed to stand up, but she couldn't distinguish anything in front of her; there was a veil of dust everywhere. She heard another sound, closer this time, and saw a black block flying away and breaking the panoramic glass. She realized that all this time, all these years, she hadn't been afraid—rather, she'd been sad and frustrated over being rejected. She saw a blur of two blue figures. This was what it felt like to be scared.

They were like two columns, one blue and the other darker—could be purple. They paced toward her. The purple tower stepped closer. It looked like a he. When he was about ten feet from her range, she tripped on a chair and fell on her knees, but immediately extended her right arm, twisting her right hand down and then up; she released a magnetic field. She tried to keep it steady, although her fingers couldn't stop shaking. His head moved down in a slow and threatening way, he took another step closer, and with a swipe in the air with his right purple hand, he dismissed Cate's shield.

"Did you really think you were the only one?" he said, his voice ringing with a slight echo.

The other one came closer. The scene was clearer but still dusty. They were men, as metallic as her, one dark blue and the other dark purple, dressed in suits and knee boots made of the same metallic material, and they were wearing capes that flew like thin liquid metal behind them. Everything matched their alliafied colors. Cate's heart was beating too fast. The blue one turned to his purple counterpart, the cape waving as his right arm twisted, and said something to him in a different language—nothing similar to what she had ever heard before. She only recognized the last word: *Victoria*. The purple one turned around, and with no rush left the room.

"I'm not going to hurt you," the blue one said, looking straight down at her, his hands on his hips. "I'm Kanio from Turnfeld"

She came up on her feet.

He unalliafied from his blue shield, and, amid the dust, revealed his pale skin and dark hair, and a square human face alike with long ears. He came closer.

She looked to the window behind her. She looked at him and then looked back again. She ran and jumped through the glass.

*****

"Send one of you to her," Kanio said, still hands on hips, moving his head slightly side to side.

"For now, or permanently?" an elderly voice asked from behind.

"Permanently," Kanio said, "for now."

*****

Cate fell on her back, making her landing on a terrace on one of the gray towers adjacent to the core building, usually used for summer cocktail receptions.

She looked down to the field and saw that it was conquered by the spider-people.

Now what? she thought.

"Where are you? Respond!" Cate tried to reach Victoria a few times, but nothing; the Whisper wouldn't even say *"unavailable"* back.

A few hours before, her task had been to convince her sister to reach out to the Meds, which seemed difficult but not impossible. Now, the equation has gotten more complicated. Nevertheless, the only feasible choice seemed to be to go back to the building and try to find a way out from there. She broke the terrace's carbon-glass door and went in. She quickly crossed over the dark and shaken salon.

"Catherine, stop," someone called in, something between a whisper and old man's voice.

She turned around, and that was precisely what she saw: a white-haired sheer creature covered by a flowing white robe.

"I'm here to help you. Now, think you are light as air." His voice was steady and concrete.

"What is this? Who are you?"

I'm losing my mind, she thought.

"I know you better than anyone. I am your Ereo. You will be able to come back for Victoria, but right now..." he said.

"How?" she interrupted him. "Are you with them?"

"No, with *you*. And you will be able to come back, but if you stay, you may end up doing something you regret later. You need to think you are as light as air, count to five, and then open your eyes and feel your weight again," he said.

"What? Stop!"

"I know what happened that day in the pool. I know how you felt in the spaceship, when you came to Earth, when you couldn't see your mother. You will never be alone again. And you are like air. Fast. Count to five and open your eyes," he said in his old voice.

Cate felt light-headed. "How do you know?" she asked.

"There is no time; do it," he commanded.

"This is crazy. I'll do it and then you stop talking." And so she did. She closed her eyes and counted: 1, 2, 3, 4, 5...opened her eyes, and she appeared to be on her back. She realized she was in the parking lot, with the same creature by her side.

"What?" She couldn't close her mouth. Above was a dark gray concrete ceiling. She turned around and sat on her knees, still wrapped in her liquid metal skin, which made the idea of trespassing through objects even harder to believe. The thought that she was much more capable than she had ever imagined was firing up her heart. She came to her feet.

"Iterization," he said. "It is because of your hydrogen composition; when you allow yourself, you can become the lightest element on Earth."

"Hydrogen?" Cate recomposed herself. "That is what it was!"

"Cate, you must take the Thunderbolt-cycle in parking A301 to your left, by the corner. You will be able to cross the bridge and you should go east to your father's. Wait there." The Ereo kept talking as he floated slightly above the ground. The Ereo, she realized, had no feet.

"Aren't they going to stop me?"

He moved his old face slightly sideways. "Kanio had already instructed the Letaneos to let you pass. He wants you to trust him."

She ran to the spot and took the red cycle. She came flying up the ramp, out of the underground, and took the same lateral path where she'd come in earlier during the day. As the Ereo predicted, she crossed through two guards and took the bridge to the other side—no questions asked. However, she had other plans. Lost-Town.

CDD indicated that FDR was closed, as well as some other main avenues. Cate drove straight to Times Square, still the most crowded place on Earth, trying to reach West End Highway. A theater show was about to begin or was just finishing; she could see a group of people in line fixing their sight on her. Victoria might have been right that few remembered the incident in Washington years ago, but that had changed in the last forty-eight hours. She unalliafied and squeezed in between the ocean of vehicles in the next avenue—illegal but necessary. She saw the crowd on the main stage of the square. The big screen on the back was showing a commercial of the latest Iliada System, a set of family profiled robots designed for each family's own features and needs. The advertisement showed the Iliada Nanny robot coming out from the screen with two children dressed in sailor suits through an emerald green park—the kind of hue and freshness that was hard to imagine in those SZ-shielded days. *The elms give hope,* marketing research had said. *People still believe that Earth will become one day as it was before.* Right when the trees went back to the screen, the screen to the side showed the latest cola design; guaranteed to make you thirsty in less than 30 seconds, Lost-Town Martin once explained. The four main screens were coordinated so that only one of them could extrapolate 3D outside of the screen at a time.

Miraculously, she saw it in one of the midsized screens: 'The Atlantic Island receiving visits from beyond,' the headline showed: 'Nothing to be feared; more news to follow.' Once again, she was disappointed by the obliviousness of humankind. She managed to reach the highway, direction downtown. She only had one image in her mind: her sister.

"Text Francis G: Repercussions, right? We need to talk," she said to her Whisper band.

Soon after, she was in front of a seven-floor blue glass building. The Mexican taco place on the corner with its OPEN 24 HOURS sign, like nothing had changed. *People should be panicking; people will be asking one another for ages: Who were they? Blue? Purple? Where were you that day? I was right there. Why does no one care?* She was in shock. She left the Thunderbolt carelessly by the entry. Home. She rushed in and took the elevator.

"Good evening, Cate. Going up. Seventh floor. Can we order some food for you?"

"No food," Cate said. "No calls. I am not here."

Cate entered her apartment; the lights turned on, and she saw some clothes hanging on the right, including her favorite red letiqa jacket. She'd thought she had lost it. A deep sound of air escaped her mouth.

"Core, ask CDD to bring my Triton back."

"Done," a mature male voice responded.

"And I have somebody's Bolt parked downstairs; tell them to take it back too. To fine me or see how we can amend it; whatever they prefer," she continued.

"According to the legislation, that will involve 3 years of jail."

She strode inside and, grabbing her head with her two hands, a second and third apprehensive sound followed.

"Just ask them for a fine," Cate insisted.

"The system does not have authorization to ask for that."

"Then I'll go to jail," she said.

She crossed the living room without paying attention to the Brooklyn skyline to her right. *I am not alone; we never were.* Still the pain in her stomach continued; it was tight and compressed. Soon after, she was in the bathroom, head between her legs, throwing up even the scrambled eggs she'd had for breakfast. The smell was of rotten fish—disgusting.

She sat on the floor and alliafied her arms and hands. She saw them become slender and lineless; they were liquid metal gloves, and little tides defined her muscles. Hydrogen. She covered her eyes and cried.

maria beta

CHAPTER 11

....

KANIO, THE AEKIOU

Early morning, on the top floor of the building, Kanio was watching through the broken window how his arthropod-looking Letaenos, his most trusted fighters, were taking control of the entire island. The residue of two hundred Hercules was being finally taken away.

"It is done," Nnox, in his purple cover, said as he entered the room.

Kanio was alliafied, and his color was dark blue, as sapphire and carbon were his main elements. "Is Victoria well-kept in your Ryder?" He meant the purple ship floating by the river.

"Seu. This building is not set up to have a captive alliafied. I despise these people more every second," Nnox said.

"You will end up liking them; you always say the same thing," Kanio said. "Is she gold as described?"

"Yes. And she is not like the one here." Nnox added, "She is plain, mostly gold."

Kanio wasn't sure if this small detour had been worth it for him, the Aekiou, and his pair, Nnox. But when he was told that Onerio was experiencing a breakup in its pillars, he and his father had decided that a visit would remind humans that they belonged to a system more vast than they could imagine. A situation created by a recently hidden Alliafied was not going to be allowed—that was the bottom line. He did know about Cate's existence—a human Alliafied flooded in hydrogen as no other Alliafied was—but he'd never contemplated that she might be in the building as well.

"She is different than I'd thought. Seems she has no idea of how she bends the air," Kanio said.

Nnox was already sitting at the middle of the table. "So much nitrogen..." he complained.

"We need to increase Zafor in those Panels above," Kanio said. "But let's fix the air situation in this cube first. Today. But not drastically; it may be tough when we are unalliafied," Kanio said.

"You know I don't do that. I'm not the Aekiou." Nnox laughed.

Kanio picked a blue tablet up from the floor and threw it at him. He hated it when Nnox brought up the fact that he had fewer responsibilities than him.

"I want humans to move around freely. I don't want them asphyxiating in that staircase below," Kanio said seriously.

"By humans, you mean Catherine Weelah?" Nnox laughed again.

*****

"It is between amusing and miserable," Kanio said. He looked through the fixed panoramic window, drumming his knuckles on the meaningless long table. "They are more than condescending."

"More on the side of amusing," his Ereo said. The flowing creature wore a white, slightly silver robe, and a long and wide white beard covered all his neck and touched his flowing chest. Only a few Alliafied had had the privilege of having Ereos: the Khun, the Aekiou, and whomever they decided.

"Everyone is childlike to you," Kanio responded.

"You are mad about how things turned out; I cannot help you with that," the Ereo said in his deep hoarse voice.

Kanio was still confounded by the instant he had felt Cate for the first time. *I may have frightened her*, he thought.

"I was walking into the building, and my chest started burning. I looked up and there she was. I felt faster. Stronger. I was told about the existence of an Alliafied, on a world that wasn't ready for her. Why is she here, then?" Kanio asked.

"She wasn't ready for yours, either. Not contacting her was part of the pact sealed between Phelaries and humans cycles ago, since, Alliafied or not, she is human after all."

"When I knew she was here, I had no other choice but to go straight to her. She is different, and not in a bad way," Kanio said. "Is this like magnets?"

"It always is, and she is not a threat to you," the old creature added.

"I have to make sure of that." Kanio paused. "How is she going to change things?"

"Radically," the old flowing Ereo responded.

Sometimes it was hard to interpret Ereos. They had a different understanding of the future than what time represented for Phelaries and Onerians—when the relevant change he was referring to took place, it may no longer be relevant.

Kanio walked around in what was known as the Celestial Room until the prior day, but was now the

Aekiou private department, or Aekiou Kof. The Union Building was now recognized as the Phelaris headquarters, but only for formal matters. He still ran everything from Nnox's Cross-Ryder—the purple ship that crossed the stratosphere the day before and currently was floating in the East River by Atlantic Island.

Kanio pressed the sides of his left wrist.

"I want to see Victoria Weelah. I am leaving the Kof now," he said.

He stopped at the new, refactored room's exit. It opened to the side and cleared his way. Every floor and room in the building was being recycled by the Phelaries, citizens of Phelio, one of the purest systems in the Universe.

Phelaries were easily recognized by their pale peach metal skin coat and their dark shimmery hair. They could also toughen their skin, but never like an Alliafied. Their clothes were made of a thick carbon-black material, like paneled neoprene; pants and high-collar shirts for men, long stretch skirts with boat-neck shirts for women. Kanio and Nnox were Phelaries who also had the privilege of being Alliafied.

He went into the first elevator. A Letaneo joined him.

"Three," Kanio said.

"The force field from the Ryder has been successful; nothing can get in or leave without being authorized," the Letaneo said.

"It was not necessary to have mine here as well. Good work," he added. The Letaneo nodded. Kanio's Ryder was left in space, behind the moon.

The elevator's full window showed the large green meadow. He touched the crystal. *Everything here is like paper,* he thought. The doors opened, introducing the third floor, which was the official lobby; its ceiling was high enough that two other floors could fit in it, he had been told. He proceeded through the left side to a magnificent plain ivory staircase, guarded by gray neo-classical granite columns, which connected the third floor to the ground level.

"Juveo." Kanio greeted the copper Alliafied man waiting for him at the bottom of the steps. Juveo wore a spotless human suit and a hat. Kanio had been trying to avoid the encounter with the Alliafied in charge of Onerio—what Phelaries called planet Earth—the whole morning. Juveo never seemed to pay much attention to the Aekiou, and Kanio did not pay much attention to him either.

"Aekiou," the man greeted back.

"I would like humans to feel comfortable with us. I have realized they halt doing whatever they are into to stare at Nnox or myself," the blue Phelarie said.

"It takes them time to get used to different things," Juveo said.

"Everyone in Pirthee is pleased with what you have done here," Kanio said. Pirthee was the capital of Phelio, and Phelio was the most important system in a far-off area in the universe known as K4. "I wanted you to know that our coming had nothing to do with your work here on Onerio-13, Earth." They walked outside the building.

"I understand. I wish I had known," Juveo said.

"We didn't want to pass on any message that could alert the moon base... Apollo?"

Juveo nodded. "Just thought I could have collaborated in the plans you had in mind," Juveo added.

Kanio didn't have much in mind, really. He knew taking the building peacefully would take a matter of minutes, and there was no need to deploy any forces in cities or other buildings. He just needed to reestablish control in the Americas; the BMA told him that they would maintain themselves apart and keep an open dialogue with the Asian communities.

"This ceiling; gray, green, purple clouds? Nothing is as blue as Phelio," Kanio said, he looked above and shook his head as they walked down long marble steps that led into the green large terrain.

"Tomorrow, when the rainy clouds dissipate, you will be able to see some violet."

"We will see. You do know the golden Alliafied, right?"

"Yes," Juveo responded.

"Have you ever met her sister?"

"I saw her once but we didn't talk much, just as I was instructed," Juveo continued.

"What Leeve do you think she is?" Kanio pretended he was not interested, and kept looking straight while stepping on the green ground.

"Two, probably. I don't think she can trespass liquid," Juveo answered.

"I mean the dark silver one." Kanio's voice was firm.

"Maybe like you." Juveo sounded a little vague.

"Are you sure?"

"Yes, but from a different Genyi. They are both Larios. Air," Juveo responded. Kanio was a Thendor, and his symbol was solid earth. Juveo was a Balio, water.

"How did two humans turn out to be Alliafied?"

"Their mother was human, that is for sure. The missing link is their father, who is not Steban Weelah, the human who worked with us for the Shield. Perhaps he is one of us, probably a Lario as well," Juveo said.

"Are you coming?" The blue Phelarie pointed out the ship with his head.

"No, I prefer to stay in the building helping in the setup." Juveo had never seemed comfortable in Nnox's presence. The purple Phelarie was approaching them, inside a purple capsuled Helo-Ryder, a small capsuled vehicle that worked well on Onerian terrain.

"We need to talk later about Colt and Brogio; he may need a new pair. A Balio should be here, but now that we are visiting, you may want a recess," Kanio said. Balios related to Water and it was easy for them to change shape in a minimal way, facilitating their interaction with new systems. Colt from Behar was one of Kanio's closest Alliafied, and he lived on the green planet Brogio. Colt was a Balio as well.

"How long do you plan to stay here?" Juveo asked.

"Juveo Rogers, Seu Kalema." Nnox jumped out from the vehicle.

"Seu Kalema. Seu Kalema Aekiou," Juveo greeted him back and walked back into the building. The environment was quiet—only the faraway sound from the river and far-off construction noise from the building structure. Nnox raised his eyebrows.

Kanio looked the other way and jumped into another blue Helo-Ryder standing by the end of the stairs.

The Helos moved toward the purple Cross-Ryder through a path that was built to easily move cars and elements from the ship to the Union Building and vice versa. They glided approximately one foot above the path.

Once in front of the ship, a purple corridor came out and connected it to the green ground, where two Letaneos in their convex shape, four extremities on the floor, were expecting them. Immediately, the two moved their arms up, stood, and walked behind them into the Ryder.

"How much is nitrogen affecting your breathing system?" Kanio asked them.

"Some," the black Letaneo to his right said. They all had the same voice, so Kanio recognized who talked from where the sound originated. When one spoke, it did so for all the others. And any of them would do anything for the Aekiou.

"It will be fixed soon," Kanio said.

*****

The two Phelaries entered a large bright purple room; the two black Letaneos waited outside. The ceiling was a wrinkled dome. In the corner to the right was a large transparent cube with a purplish shade. The cube had a bed, a table, and two chairs, and a door behind the table, which was probably the bathroom that the Phelaries had built especially for her Onerian requirements. They tried to build a confinement space as comfortable as possible. When they approached, he could see Victoria on her bed, lying on her back, alliafied, reading a tablet. Kanio came closer to the security veil.

"Victoria. I am Kanio, the Aekiou."

She went closer to the cube's transparent wall, dressed in navy blue; one of her sleeves was torn between the elbow and the wrist.

"I wanted to come here earlier and introduce myself, but I have been busy coordinating...stuff; the mess that you left, in fact," Kanio explained. "Perhaps Juveo Rogers mentioned me before." He looked around; she was using the rubber gray shoes she had been offered, but had left the suit on the table.

"Kanio Turnfeld, maybe, but not much," she said, while observing him up and down.

Kanio could tell, even in her golden shape, that there was a physical resemblance between the two sisters.

"Is the headache better?" he asked.

"Gone," she said.

"Now, the air inside this room has the same conditions as outside. Perhaps better."

"You can't tolerate nitrogen, right?" she interrupted him.

"And you already met Nnox." Kanio pointed to his pair. Nnox came closer and stood right by him. "You should have come to us. Why didn't you go to Rogers?" Kanio went straight to the point; no more air quality chit-chat.

"What for? You knew what was going on already; what could I have said to make you intercede? Probably the inertia in the system made everything simpler for you," Victoria said. She didn't look at Nnox.

"The only thing that we have been aiming for is that your people don't consume the planet. It belongs to all of us. It is called Universal Equilibrium." He stepped back, arms crossed, and observed the big purple room. "The loss of the ozone layer was predictable, considering how all of your governments kept lying to one another. And when it happened, as you know, we intervened and helped to create the Shield. Before yesterday, we retained the final decision on planetary issues, while humans dealt with the micromanagement. Not anymore," Kanio said. He turned to Nnox, who looked like he was swallowing his own smile.

"History repeats itself, Kanio. You won't achieve anything," Victoria said sassily.

This gold Onerian—empty arrogance, he pondered.

"You were not going to achieve anything either. In your history, you always fought so hard for what was supposed to be right; yet once you were about to have it, you betrayed it," Kanio said.

"You humans reject anything that would involve giving away a little something, and instead go straight for the cheap, short-term deal. You see, this is not a negotiation," Nnox said. The two Phelaries went on talking, almost ignoring her presence.

"We are here for the long run," Kanio said to her. The Khun agreed to show Onerians what Phelaries were, and to clarify whatever they may have been thinking being an Alliafied meant, given Catherine's track record and Victoria's recent spectacle. Yet her father never mentioned anything about the long term.

"You seem rational, Victoria. We have been watching you for a while. At least it seemed like you don't pretend to hide behind an empty promise," Kanio continued.

"Empty promises are our expertise." She gave him a full sealed-lips smile. "And perfect solutions that never take place. But nothing really changes, and it turns worse for the ones who needed it the most." She paused.

"Why do you think that was?" he asked.

Useless promises. Useless conversation.

She shook her head. A moment passed. "In the Alliance, we have taken what we have for granted, and have blindly chosen to leave things as they were, for decades, and blackmailed the rest of the world with the Shields that you helped us build. The Shields that my father designed are better than the others, you know," Victoria said. She sounded uncomfortable, but looked confident. "Whatever your plan is, you should look outside, Aekiou. The Alliance is not the North East. And the rest of the planet is not the Alliance."

"Things will be different. You see, we are not like you," Nnox said, jumping into the conversation. He stepped closer to the glass.

"Don't look at us as a complete failure. We kept our word that a collective calamity won't happen again. Those three days—banks, electricity, communications—everything was gone. Chaos," Victoria kept going.

"We know the end of the story. The Alliance. And that nobody trusts anyone," Kanio said. "We will help bring balance."

"And what is your plan, then?" she asked.

"An independent Controller. It is simple. And a real one," Kanio said.

"How will it match our democracy?" Victoria asked.

"It is not relevant," he said.

She pursed her lips and took a step back.

"It is funny how what you call democracy has evolved over time," he added, both hands on his hips, "considering that nobody actually votes anymore, but behaves like they do. What you have is a modern version of a feudal system. We are going to trigger a tiny reset." Kanio felt that the conversation was going nowhere, and he hated wasting his time. "But that is not relevant; you are here because of something else." His voice rose higher but remained neutral. "How could you take advantage of the fact that you are an Alliafied? Who is helping you? You would not dare go ahead with this alone." Kanio saw blue vapor coming slightly from his body, but he rested his breath to control it.

Victoria remained quiet.

"I hope you start enjoying this place," Kanio said.

"I don't mind being here forever." Victoria went to her bed.

"That is because you don't know what forever is." Kanio said in a croaky voice.

Victoria stopped and looked back to them. Kanio dashed out; he was not used to being lied to or left without an answer.

"If you need something, call me," Nnox said to her.

"What?" she said to him.

"Just call me. I'll find out," Nnox said. "I am this— this place." He followed Kanio.

The sliding door closed behind them. "You have to find out if someone close to the Khun is willing to betray him, or has already," Kanio said to Nnox.

"Easy. I'll have the information by tomorrow." Nnox left him without saying more. The lustrous purple mirrored-looking walls of the hall emanated a hint of purple gleam where he passed. He must have also been very annoyed.

maria beta

CHAPTER 12

....

THE UGLY DUCK

Cate woke abruptly. She was having a nightmare. She was still in her dirty clothes. She opened her eyes, and her first words were, "What did I do?"

I should have stayed at the Union with Victoria. She couldn't get the thought out of her mind. She had barely slept five hours. Before she went to bed, she spoke with Francis; he'd mentioned that his father said her sister was fine, and as the fluffy creature said, she would be able to go back for her. The blue one said that he wasn't going to hurt her—would he, eventually, if she went back? *I will definitely go back.*

Dressed in black, she drifted around the living room, drinking coffee and swallowing green cookies. For Catherine Weelah some things were becoming clear. She was made of hydrogen, and that explained why she could break and melt palladium when she played with it. And there was what was missing in the equation—metallic hydrogen. She called Paula.

"It's cameras all around the entrance. I don't want to leave the house," Paula exclaimed. "There was even a helicopter around the whole of Sunally all night. You can come—once you are inside, you will be fine."

"I can't. I have stuff to do here. Can I send Coper to you? He is at this Pet-Vida Spa," Cate said.

"No, no, Cate, you know your father doesn't like him," Paula responded instantly. She truly lived in a separate dimension sometimes.

"Okay. I'll ask them to send him here then," Cate said.

"Are you going to see Victoria again today?" Paula asked.

"Well, hmm. Victoria is not exactly hosting these visitors, as the TV says. I probably will." Cate realized that may not have been the best choice of words. Paula remained silent. "Paula, what more do you know about them?" Cate asked.

"Nothing," Paula said.

"Kanio, Ereo, nothing?" Cate kept inquiring, trying to get an answer. But nothing came back.

"Nothing."

"Why did you tell me that I dreamed of being silver that day in the pool? And that I was never in that pool for more than five seconds?" Cate could imagine her stepmother's face turning white, but at this stage she didn't care anymore. She sat on a red couch in the living room.

"Steban said..." Paula tried to answer.

"Why did he never tell me that there were more? How could he let me believe that I was a rare result of my mother's experiments in the moons?" Cate alliafied as she spoke, stretching her metallic arms.

"He said that, well, we just don't know them." Paula's voice was a bit shaken.

Her father was right. She didn't know them either.

"Don't tell Steban about Victoria. Not yet."

"Is she going to be all right?" Paula sounded worried.

"I think so," she lied. She had no clue. "Who is this Mr. Rogers?"

"Isn't he like you and Victoria?" Paula responded.

Paula didn't understand that Cate and Victoria were different, and that Cate had seen Mr. Rogers once before—*he definitely wasn't like these two.*

"I see. I'll call you later." Cate hung up.

"Flowing old man? Are you there?" she said out loud.

I might have lost my mind, she thought.

But the semi-transparent creature appeared in front of her, in the middle of her living room. She laughed. '

"It's Ereo. It's man. We are many, but I am the one assigned to you. Only you can see me, and I can only show up if you are alone," he explained.

She stood up. "How did you know about the pool?" she asked. She needed to know if he was true to his word—if she could trust him. "I sometimes dream about it. I can't forget."

"That was the first time you ever alliafied. You were scared, this child was upsetting you, and there was another Alliafied close to you—similar to the night of the party. When you have others around, it is like when particles try to escape. You will get used to it with time."

"Others? Those two from yesterday?"

"No, no, those were like your sister," he said. "These two are like you."

"Were you there?" Cate asked.

"We have always been there. And I'll be with you from now on, whenever you need me. Or while Kanio thinks it is appropriate," he said.

"He said he won't hurt me; will he?" Cate finally asked.

"Maybe, but not in the way you think. And not today," he said, and chuckled.

"Who are they? Where are they from?"

"You should ask them yourself." He smiled.

"Should I go back today, then?" she asked.

"Kanio, the Aekiou of Phelio, would like to see you again. There is an open invitation for you, any day, any time. You can come onto the Island and leave the same way you did yesterday."

*****

And that is why two hours later Cate was once again in front of the tremendous gate before the bridge that connected Manhattan to Atlantic Island. She was riding the same red cycle that she had taken the day before. Her dark-silver skin shimmered under her black clothes, her silver hair bent back in a single wave.

The gate bar opened. None of the black aliens that she'd seen the day before, at the gate or the parking entry, either on their two feet or four, had tried to stop her. They'd just looked away. She made it to the parking floor beneath the building, and left the Thunderbolt in space A301, right from where she'd taken it from. She walked toward the elevator, but she needed to pass through a crystal wall—but she was not her sister; she had no useful credentials. Breaking it? Two peachy metallic men were standing inside the crystal wall; one of them looked at her and pressed a control panel by the wall. The crystal doors opened sideways. She passed. She said nothing; they said nothing back. In front of her, the six main elevators, ten feet high, dark opaque gray, each with a different engraving, all full of the NAA's golden triple-star emblem. She knew the two in the middle were the only ones that reached the top floor. One of them opened. She looked back at the metallic peachy creatures, but they remained staring outside. She went in. The doors closed. The letter K highlighted in blue on a silver panel by her left—*K? A new floor?* Outside, that purple thing floating at the end of the meadow. The doors opened and she walked through a hall to her left. That heartburn appeared again. She stopped in front of where it used to be a complex door made of carbon and rubber. Now there was a dark gray polished rock, with no way to open it. She looked around. *Worst case, I just clash against this rock, and it's not like I'm going to get hurt,* she thought. She closed her eyes, and with only the thought that she was as light as air, she crossed it. She opened her eyes and there was the panoramic display in front of her: gray vapor, a purple sky, no sun, bordered by that emerald grass underneath and the purple ship at the end.

"Someone was going to open that access for you," a male voice said.

She felt the lack of air from the day before, but she managed to stand tall. To her right, there he was: in dark sapphire blue, crossed arms, his flowing cape behind him, in that same spot where her sister and Patrick Jameson had unfolded their failed future of the world the day before.

"Only a few can iterize. You are extremely privileged," Kanio said.

"Hello," she said, remaining close to the door.

"Come inside; you are here to talk to me right," he said.

He was guarded by two of the spider-people, who actually from a close distance didn't look like spiders at all. They were short and bulky, entirely black, polished as if made from obsidian, with no hair and very similar features—fissures as eyes and mouth; surprisingly, they didn't show anything that could resemble a nose. Both were raising their front legs and turning them into arms. Kanio bordered the table toward her. Cate walked to the other side, around the long table. He stopped and went back to where he was, shook his head, and unalliafied. She kept circling the table the other way around, by the panoramic window, but she had no intention of letting go of her dark platinum tone. She got a few feet away from him. He stared at her in a way that made her slightly uncomfortable. His skin was pale nude, and he had a square face and straight black hair that fell a little longer to one side. His eyes were almond-shaped, almost giving him a vaguely Eastern appearance. His deep sight hooked on her. She tried to avoid it and hid her shaking hands behind her back.

"I'm the same one who jumped last night from that window behind you." She pointed behind him.

He looked back to the spotless glass and tilted his head a little to one side. He remained quiet. Maybe that wasn't a good intro.

"The Ereo thing said I could come see you any time," she added. He stayed quiet. Again, another mistake, she presumed. But then he smiled. She did too.

"You can," he said.

"It's just..." She hesitated; vulnerability must be kept behind the curtains, but she couldn't hold it, and looked at the ground, looked at her sides. She was finally there, and despite practicing hundreds of sentences for hours, she didn't know where to start. She should have written something down.

"Are you hungry?" he asked.

Suddenly he was by her side and grabbing her left arm. He bent his head down. She looked at him and could distinguish his clear blue-sky eyes. He alliafied. She blinked; his shine was like a deep blue pearl that felt like it would blind you if you stared at it too long. She blinked again. The shine came down one level.

"Is my sister okay? Where is she?" Cate asked. This was the reason she was there. If she wanted to eat, she would have just ordered Mexican from downstairs.

"Of course; we'll see her after," he said. He dropped her arm and walked away. "Come; I don't trust your people yet. I heard leaders get stabbed in their backs here," he whispered.

"I don't think they are aware that you are their leader. You can still feel safe," she said, without being able to take her sight off him.

"Like you have felt all these years."

And then the free and easy feeling vanished in less than a second.

"Are you okay?" he asked.

"When I began sleeping unalliafied, it was because I didn't care if I was taken away by that crazy shrink," she explained.

"That was my father's command: to instruct your sister to get you out of there, no questions asked, and that no one would ever take you back there, or anywhere. It was a mistake," he explained, while standing again by his alien creatures and putting together some documents on the table, without raising his head.

"Who is your father?"

"My father is the Khun, Protector of the Law on this side of the Universe."

"Who are you? All of these people in this building."

"We are Phelaries, people from Phelio, that until now you haven't heard of."

He walked toward the new black door, followed by the two black things—animals or men, it was not exactly clear to her what they were; they had a bulky button-shaped tail.

"Where is Victoria?" Cate suspiciously raised her voice and followed him.

"There." He looked to the window and kept walking.

She realized he might mean the metallic purple vessel.

"Why?" she asked.

"She is visiting. We will go there after; come on," Kanio said, without even looking back. She increased her pace. They left the room and stood outside the same elevator that she'd come up in just a few minutes before. The doors opened and he went in. She followed. The two black creatures remained on the upper floor.

"What are they?" she asked.

"Letaneos," he said.

"Eh?"

"Letaneos. They have a few tricks. Their arms can shoot their own generated electro-shock; they can knock out anyone, no matter the shape or size, instantly. But that is not relevant. For you, they are harmless. The Phelaries, for you, are harmless too."

Cate's thoughts wandered. He had the same seriousness as Barrett, and the same vibe as Martin, that Lost-Town guy she'd kind of dated for a while.

"It's funny that we are not heavy," Cate said.

"I know." He looked down at her. He was probably one foot taller than her.

The doors opened on the fifth floor to the other side. The crowd. The sound. The fifth floor could fit two other regular floors in height. The third and fifth floors shared this attribute; there, on the fifth, was where the most important receptions were regularly held.

"I'll meet you there. We will talk more after. Do not unalliafy." He showed her to the right—west—and he went to the other side.

"What?" Cate unconsciously said. A little consternated, trying to avoid some journalists and their video and holo-cameras, she headed into the West Hall where official dinners were held. *How could he leave me?* she thought.

"We will review all the pictures, in any case," two peachy metal men were telling the journalists.

Most of the damage in the building had been repaired; if it wasn't because she'd evidenced it with her own eyes, she would not have believed an invasion had occurred just a day before. She stopped in front of a large, light-colored double wooden door with gold arrangements. A peachy man opened them for her. She could hear the flashes left behind. She was no longer the main attraction.

Not heavy? He must think I am dumb. She struggled with her thoughts. *Probably that is why he left.*

"Catherine. Come with me." A pretty peachy metal girl dressed in black and with a funky, overexcited voice approached her. Her face looked like a doll's. The hall looked like a big gallery; an extremely long dining table crossed it as if it was set for an important diplomatic event: crystal glasses, silver cutlery, and flowers—white and lilac orchids. The room was full of people whom somehow she had seen before, either on the news, in FoxStone, or in Sunally. Some looked like the apocalypse had begun. Others were pretending to be chill, kissing cheeks and hands of whomever they could. Nobody seemed normal.

The room was set up for approximately a hundred guests, maybe fewer. To the left was a wall-size grayish window; to the right, a wall covered by a complex stucco mix of pastels, gold, and silver colors and small mirror-like star shapes. Three humungous teardrop lamps hung over the table. The ceiling was also decorated with some drawings mixed with white stucco, and many golden triple stars—the NAA emblem.

"What is new?" Cate asked the peachy girl, while the latter was escorting her inside.

"In general, the other centers are calm, as we'd expected. They have told the North Americans to deal with their own noise," she responded. Her voice was a little annoying.

"As they have always done," Cate said to her. As they got farther into the room, almost everyone had turned around. She wished Victoria could be here as well.

"Apex in DC, in particular, was relieved that these rebels were overcome with such a high level of efficiency. Should be a fast transition," the peachy girl said proudly. Victoria wouldn't have liked the rebel quote.

In the group, Cate distinguished Eugenia Santos, a Portuguese scientist whom Cate could drown in the Arctic happily any time. Marisa Gomez, Cate's favorite blogger and talk show hostess, was there too; always wearing her metallic-framed sunglasses, even indoors. That was exciting. However, at almost the other end of the table, was her ex, Barrett Mountdragon, still with his Franciscan monk haircut, whom she hadn't seen since that night at the party almost seven years before. He saw her and looked immediately away.

"This is really annoying," Cate said.

"What?" the Phelarie asked.

"Nothing; the color of the day," she said. Barrett had never even sent her a text to ask how was she dealing with her new Alliafied situation. Supposedly, he was her most important relationship so far, yet the emptiest. And farther, standing and chatting with two other people, was Alex Harlow—spotless in a blue suit, purple tie, and probably wearing all the NAA praised symbols. It was true that his nose had become bigger after the accident. He glanced at her. *Now he wishes he was made of metal.* Cate ignored him.

"Where is Gabe McCully, the previous NAA Prime Minister?" Cate asked.

"He is not invited." The peachy girl stopped by two empty seats right in the middle, on the window side facing the stucco wall. "You will sit here." She touched the one to the left. There was another empty seat in front of these two. The peachy girl left.

Cate was still disconcerted. *How will being here help me get to my sister?* Luckily, a familiar voice called from behind her.

"Catherine! Catherine Weelah!" Cate turned around; Marisa Gomez was trying to clear a way to her.

"Oh my God! Hi! I'm such a big fan," Cate said happily. She felt like hugging Marisa; she resisted and pushed her arms back.

"Hi! I am a fan of yours, as well! I mean, I've sent you tons of invitations," the famous reporter said, drawing out the O in "tons" and moving her hands in circles, just like she did on the show. It was funny how familiar it felt. They'd just met, but Cate listened to her voice and read her thoughts every week.

"I know. It is just that I am not... I wanted to leave the accident episode behind."

"Well, the first time I wrote you"—again the effect on the O—"was about the show, but then I only wanted to have some lunch or coffee. Get to meet you. Then you left. Then you came back. In and out since then. Your life seems fascinating. You are like, what? Twenty-one?" Marisa was sharp, just like in one of her regular appearances.

"Twenty-four," Cate said back.

"Are you like them?" Another question. She was good.

"I don't know," Cate responded.

"But I'm sure, I guess, this feels right." Marisa was totally right. Cate remembered the story of the Ugly Duckling. What if this was her pack? This was so strange. But then, these characters also had her sister, probably against her will. Not exactly the same story. And then the room's atmosphere changed; the air became dry again. Peachy girls asked everyone to go to their seats.

"I'll see you soon!" Marisa gave Cate her card.

She saw the blue and purple heads entering the room. Their capes flowed behind them in the same way. She felt a little light-headed; it seemed that was their effect. Kanio came closer, and everybody stared silently. Shiny. Solid. They looked imposing. Kanio stopped at the empty seat in front of her.

"I'm glad you are here. Do sit," Kanio said to everyone, making a welcoming gesture with his hands.

The purple Alliafied took the empty seat next to Cate, looked at her, and raised his eyebrows. These two would look a little similar if it wasn't for this one's bigger, humpy, purple nose.

Cate tried to avoid looking at Kanio; nonetheless, he was not paying attention to her at all. She recognized the two people sitting to her left; they were the ambassadors of England and Japan. They looked astonished. This was probably the first time they had seen an Alliafied in real life—actually, three Alliafied, an alien spaceship, and pink shiny people. It was understandable. But it was different; she was not as embarrassed by her unusual characteristic as she had been before.

"Hi, I'm Catherine Weelah, Steban Weelah's younger daughter." She tried to exchange a few words with them; they had to know her father.

"We know, and Victoria's sister," the Englishman said, and returned to his conversation with the Japanese.

"I am Nnox." The purple Alliafied bent his head down to her. "Nnox from Levantone." His voice was bold. Kanio was much more familiar.

"I'm Cate," she said.

"We wasted too much time in the picture show. But you see, we need to keep the press happy," Nnox added. His tone grew a bit softer. "We are trying to be approachable."

"Is it working?" she asked.

"We will see," he said. "I may have scared you last night, and that was my intention. But let's start again." His purple teeth were perfect.

"Is this you saying you are sorry?"

"What?" He looked surprised.

"Don't you regret how you made me feel?" And she hadn't gotten to the main topic yet—Victoria.

"I want to take off. This doesn't look good." He stared at his full plate. Neither of the two Alliafied had touched their meals. "This is getting complicated. I was trying to be polite. Kanio tells me you may stay with us," he said.

"What? Why? I'm here for..." She wanted to talk about Victoria, but she was interrupted by another female voice from the right. Nnox turned his head to the right as well.

"Cate," with a nasal long a, "did you know about them before?" Eugenia Santos asked. Of course, it had to be her; dressed in gray, looking like a disconcerted scientist from the movies.

I don't want to admit it; I don't want say no, she pondered, although that was the truth.

"Of course, we knew about her," Kanio said. Nnox nodded.

"That is fantastic," Eugenia said. "How?"

"We just know things," Nnox said. He nudged Cate.

"We want to visit the stations," Kanio said, completely ignoring Eugenia's further comments. "The tubes and the Zafor combination." The main tubes were located in the four driest areas on the planet. "We are very impressed with everything related to the Shield, but we think there is room for improvement," he added.

"Huge space," Nnox murmured to Cate.

Cate giggled.

"I can assure you that there is not much space, really. I would be happy to take you and show you. The tubes are being constantly upgraded." Barrett Mountdragon's silly voice came from the other side of the table to Cate's left.

Kanio shifted to Barrett.

"You can come, but you are not in charge anymore," he said.

"Then who?" Barrett sounded bitter.

"One of us, clearly."

Kanio looked finally at Cate and she felt aroused.

Is this for me? Or for planet Earth? She didn't care—this was the slap in Barrett's face that she had been waiting for...for seven years?

"You do know he means me," Nnox quietly said to her.

"Eh?" She looked at his purple eyes—so annoying.

Kanio stood up: "We have to go, but stay and enjoy the event." He headed outside.

Nnox, standing by Cate's right side, looked down. "Come on."

Am I part of "we" now? She stood up as well. The three of them took off.

Crossing the wooden doors, Kanio said to her, "Follow me. Don't walk behind me."

"I'll walk by you," she said.

"I meant that. We will always have translation issues," he said.

They took the elevator. She felt so small between them.

"Your English is very good," she said. She wanted to be nice as well. The time to visit her sister needed to come soon.

"Who do you think taught Anglo-Saxon to you?" Nnox said.

Kanio raised his eyebrows.

"Ha. I am hungry," Nnox added.

"I know. You told me practically twenty times; we could not leave the place after five minutes," Kanio told his friend.

"Of course we can," Nnox said back.

The elevator's doors opened and they proceeded into the Celestial Room or whatever new name it now had. Cate watched them from behind, both of them pushing each other. It was like she wasn't there. They got into the room and walked to the left. The table had plates with some creamy green leaves and brown elements that smelled like chicken. A big bowl in the middle contained what could be dirty bones.

"Wait, can you read each other's minds?" Cate asked, bedazzled.

"Of course," Nnox exclaimed, looking back at her, knocking his head with his index finger.

"No," Kanio rectified Nnox, while the purple one was already seated and eating. "We have a device like your Whisper, but inside our heads—behind our ears—so we can communicate while being alliafied," Kanio explained.

"I can't tolerate your food. It is too savory." Nnox kept swallowing.

"We only need to eat once a day," Kanio said. He grabbed one of the bones and bit it. "Do you want to try it?" He sat at the head of the table, farther left.

"No," she responded. It looked disgusting.

"It is healthy," Kanio insisted.

She shook her head no.

"Why blue and purple?" she asked.

"Sapphire," Kanio said.

"Corundum," Nnox responded as well. "It is not like we picked it. I wanted to be black," he added.

"Of course you did. I wanted my father's dark blue," Kanio said.

"This was good. But I have to leave now for Death Valley, before your ex-boyfriend starts changing the system codes." Surprisingly, Nnox's voice became serious and steady when it was about work.

"Barrett. How do you know?" Cate exclaimed.

"We know everything, Cate Weelah, because we read minds," Nnox gave her a wicked smile and left.

Kanio couldn't stop laughing. Whatever.

Cate sat close to Kanio. "What are you? Am I like you?" She bit her lip by accident. Somehow her interests slid away from her sister's safety. *I need to find out.*

He kept eating and checking a board full of lights. She could only recognize shapeless blues and reds.

"You might be," Kanio said. It was not what Cate had been expecting to hear.

"Might?"

He pushed the board away; it remained hovering at his side. He stood up and went close to the panoramic window with his hands behind his back. "Our compositions are clearly different; you are strongly based on hydrogen, and most importantly, your composition doesn't get brittle with it. I am sapphire, platinum and carbon, among others. Your sister has gold; Nnox has carbon too. Also, our crio-time was different; I believe yours was a quarter of a cycle, nine months, and that is probably why you absorb hydrogen so well, which is very unusual. But beyond that, we are similar not in composition but in form."

"We are *and* we are not?" she asked. She stood up and followed him to the other side of the table.

"We are Alliafied." He took a step closer to her; he opened his right palm and a small blueish sphere floated on it. He flicked it with his fingers and pushed it in her direction. "We are all unique in different ways, but we are all the same."

The sphere came to her and became silver. She tried to touch the gaseous globe with her index finger but it vanished.

"I'm so confused. I still can't figure out what this metal thing is." She sat at the table, the weight of her shoulders pushing her down.

"You will. Do not overwhelm yourself; not yet," he said. He sat by her.

"I had an accident. Well, not precisely an accident, according to whom you ask," she said.

"I know. The crash. You have nothing to explain. It was a misfortune that it happened in front of a younger civilization; it had nothing to do with you."

He makes things seem simple, she thought.

"Are you always like this—metal? Cape, arm covers?"

"It's a suit. I'll get you one," he said.

"Aekiou? Kanio? What's your name?"

She felt so small. So insignificant.

"Aekiou is like a title, because I fulfill the prerequisites to eventually take the place of the Khun. It is not related to my being his son, though some think it is." He sighed, "But Kanio is my name, as yours is Catherine. Nnox uses it because he is close to me, as Victoria is to you."

"Victoria is my sister," she said reluctantly.

"It's the same. We grew up together. I gave him his first hit; he gave me mine." Kanio laughed. "That was cycles ago," he explained.

"I am sorry to disappoint you at this stage, but it's totally different. We share something called DNA."

"It is not relevant. We are both Thendor. My father brought him to live with us when I was in my second cycle, and that is enough for me. You can call me Kanio as well."

"Kanio, I want to see my sister."

"Seu. It's time. Let's go."

185

maria beta

CHAPTER 13

....

THE STATES OF MATTER

The spacecraft's inside had a pale violet shade and dark gray appliances. The walls were window-like, with some transparent concave curves at the edges. After walking through a long hall, they turned right.

"Purple? How convenient." Cate looked at Kanio. Her voice had an echo.

"It is his; it has his sequence—what you call DNA," Kanio said. His voice had an echo too.

"You guys are a little too robotic," Cate said, kind of bothered by the echo. "Ugh." She covered her nose. There was a strange smell.

"We are, by your standards. By ours, believe me, we are not. I have tried to break every permissible convention. I was told to have Seemo from Fendple by my side, but I chose Nnox from Levantone," he said.

"Seemo Fendple?" she asked. "Another purple character?"

"He is kind of yellow."

"And why not him?"

"It was not a no. It was an alternative. I am strong enough already. I don't want a partner that would further enhance my alliafied state, like my father chose. I wanted someone I trust, and whom I can build ventures with. And I do like Seemo, and we would be ruling the universe by now; yet I prefer to wander around with the purple joker."

"Partner?" she asked.

He walked faster. They took a few more steps and he stopped in front of two purple doors.

"This is it. She has been well taken care of, and this soon will be over. She needs to understand that we are the side she should appeal to. When you leave, someone will guide you outside," Kanio said.

"Why won't you come?" Cate asked him.

"Or ask your Ereo to do so." Kanio vanished behind one of the curvy walls; his liquid blue cape followed, crisping in the air.

The purple doors turned to suspended violet dust and then vanished. She crossed.

"Hey!" Cate howled when she saw golden Victoria reading on her bed on the other side. She walked to her and touched the glass, slightly punched it, and realized that it was quite stiff—different from the stupid cage where she had once been kept.

"Hi! Yes, I know, it's not breakable," Victoria said. They both smiled. She was wearing a gray uniform.

"You will be out soon," Cate said impatiently.

"I don't know. But at least something did happen. Where are Patrick and the others?"

Cate didn't want to say that everyone had been sent home with a transitional domiciliary arrest and a red card blocking them from ever going back into politics. Victoria was the only one behind a crystal cage. *Even Gabe McCully is back in his home in Virginia,* Cate moaned in her head; he did have a future trial to attend to, though.

"Somewhere, but they have nothing to do with the government anymore," she tried to lie; she didn't want to upset Victoria—a gray uniform and a purple room was enough.

"Somewhere? Have you seen Mr. Rogers?" Victoria asked.

"Is he like us? Like them?"

Victoria nodded. "Copper," she said.

"No, I haven't seen him, and I think your Mr. Rogers has no authority over the Thendor Alliafied command," Cate continued.

"They are Phelaries," Victoria said. She walked in circles.

"God, I'm still confused. Too much info for one day," Cate said.

"They are Phelaries, as we are humans. In their alliafied state, they are Thendors. Their sign is Earth as we are Larios. Our sign is Air. Our alliafied processes behave differently. And we can reach different levels, similar to the states of matter. I cannot get into the state of gas, but you can. When it is about the third state of matter, they can't match you. I don't know how that translates, though." Victoria shook her head; she looked tired.

"And the fourth state?"

"I think you can turn into plasma. That video is a little confusing. You probably were in the third or fourth state that night. But if you happen to find a Phima, and you are both on the fourth state, it doesn't mean you have no chance. It's all about the compositions," Victoria responded.

"Phima?" Cate asked.

"Fire. That is all I know," Victoria said.

"We are all unique in different ways, but we are all the same," Cate said. Kanio was right. She supported her left side on the glass.

"Yes." Victoria nodded.

"What happened that you haven't told me? Kanio said..."

"Cate, be careful. Those two are like you, and they are two," Victoria interrupted her younger sister. "They are not our friends."

"Then what are they? They have given me more answers in the last 24 hours than you and your Mr. Rogers have in the last five years. What is this Lario thing? Did you just happen to find out?" Cate was tired of realizing that she knew nothing about herself and everyone else did. She knocked on the glass again.

"It wasn't simple, Cate. Mr. Rogers began explaining with time. But after I took you out of Apex Tower, I agreed to not tell you anything more than was necessary. People here were afraid that you'd join these Phelaries, and we don't know them well. It was better if we remained as an independent planet." The golden Weelah looked upset.

She is right, Cate thought.

"It's okay, I trust you; you are the one with the good decisions."

The two of them kept talking for an hour. Cate left, promising she would be back with a better update on her release.

*****

Cate drove her Triton back home. She was unalliafied. It was completely dark—and it was only 7:00 p.m. When she arrived at her building, she distinguished a man with golden hair, dressed in a navy suit, standing at the door below the pale neon-yellow light.

"Francis!" she exclaimed. "Triton, parking lot," she instructed her Whisper, and the car took off.

"Aren't you afraid of me? Were you ever?" She moved closer to him, moving her head slightly from side to side.

"Don't be ridiculous," he said.

"Do you want to take a walk? Let's go get Coper upstairs," she said.

A few minutes later, both were wandering around Lost-Town. Coper peed in literally every corner of the area.

"The system is twisted upside down," Francis said. "My father behaves like the BMA will last forever, but it may not. The countries of Northern Africa are soliciting more resources for the Shields, and they don't have oil anymore; they have nothing to bargain with. The Scandies are saying that they will be better on their own, like the UK is."

"Did you know about the Phelaries?" Somehow the human Alliafied wasn't interested in the local matters of Earth at all. She had never been that fond of it, but now she had another reason. A blue one.

"Yes and no. We all knew there was something out there. Don't tell me you thought we were the only ones?" Francis messed her blond hair.

"Didn't everyone? Mmm—I mean, I kind of suspected it; it just didn't keep me awake," Cate said. She rearranged her head and shortened the distance Coper— or his collar—could be away from her on her Whisper band.

"I didn't know about the Alliafied. That is new. There was a rumor about the first settlement in Europa, and now it makes sense," he said.

"What rumor?" she asked.

"The NAA and the Russians arrived separately, in different expeditions, a couple of weeks apart. The Russians left Earth first, but they got stuck in their space station so the NAA arrived earlier. It is a long story. Nevertheless, somehow, in the end they decided to build the station together," he continued.

"So that nonsense that they arrived holding hands is not true," Cate said.

"Cate, no—not at all. Put it in perspective: They had to be forced," Francis assured her.

"Yes, it's true," she said. They reached the corner on the main avenue and looked around, empty streets, and they turned back. Coper followed them.

"Well, rumor says that a meeting was coordinated at the NAA base between them, the Russians, and someone else. A deltoid alien ship arrived that day, carrying four peach-colored creatures. Sound familiar? And a very tall copper man with a cape that moved like liquid floating on air behind him."

"Mr. Rogers," Cate said.

"Who?" Francis looked disconcerted.

"One of them, who has been here for a long time. What happened after?" she asked.

"Really?" He squinted his eyes. "Well, that's when everything was set up: the bases, the Shield, etcetera. Your father conveniently found Zafor right after, and then he designed Panels strong enough to dissipate the Zafor mix across the globe. But this was decades ago, so the rumor turned into a joke, and then into nothing," Francis explained. "Are you an Alliafied like them?"

"Yes. I knew already. I just didn't know what it was," Cate said.

How could I explain to someone who is not like me?

"I thought something had happened in Europa, that was all," he said.

"I did too, until now," she said. "I thought I was the only one. Victoria is too, but she is not like me. Everything is so confusing. My head is about to explode." She grabbed her forehead.

He gave her a tender hug, pulling her to his chest. They went to a deli and got some groceries and flowers, which would be delivered to her place in the next hour. He left her and her dog at the building door.

"I cannot tell you all the horrible things we did to this thing at the moon station," he said, "every time you turned your head away."

Cate couldn't visualize Francis doing anything bad.

"Oh no!" Cate took Coper and hugged him closely. The furry beige dog licked her cheek. "Thanks, Francis." Cate waved her hand and went into the building.

"Any time!" he said.

Seeing Victoria was relieving. Moreover, the outsider creatures, besides their colors and tempers, seemed strangely civilized. What if she had more in common with them than with anyone else? She couldn't get Barrett's face out of her mind. He was in shock when Kanio had said *one of us* during the lunch, even if he'd meant Nnox. It was gratifying.

"Core: living room screen on. Search: Angel of Hell video." It was the first time she had ever done this. *I have to see it. I can't pretend it didn't happen; not anymore.*

A crystal paper-like screen came down, and the 3D spectacle began. A silver version of her pushed the Hercules several feet away. It was hard to tell if it was plasma or not. Surprisingly, it was not painful to face her fears.

She stepped onto her balcony and into the cool fall weather.

How dare my father, hidden in a forest, never explained anything in all these years? How could he isolate himself, leaving Paula with only the single answer: If anything happens, find Mr. Rogers. She is so basic. No surprise she never did something relevant on Europa; she didn't even take part in the decision to go back to Earth. Cate had always felt how Paula seemed anxious around her.

Facing her living room, she alliafied. She closed and opened the palm of her right hand a few times. She concentrated and guided all of her energy to it. Suddenly she had a shapeless hand, extrapolated in thousands of dimensions in different tones of dark silver. The space between her fingers disappeared; it was filled by silver fire. She barely tapped the glass with a fingertip and it crisped sideways in a one-foot radius. It vanished beyond dust.

"Are you there? What is this?" Cate said out loud.

Her Ereo showed up by her side.

"You are a Lario, and you can reach the fourth state. You won't ever have to look for excuses again about what you are and what you are capable of. No Alliafied does," he said.

CHAPTER 14

....

THE AMBASSADOR

A few days passed, and Kanio was in the third and highest floor inside the purple ship. The ceiling, the same oval shape as the walls—transparent from the inside—allowed him to view above, to the sky and the surroundings. *And this is what they call sunrise hour.* It looked like a storm had just passed. He was told the day before that the sky would be getting clearer in the next few days. It was not like he cared, but humans did like to discuss the composition of the sky...all the time. However, whomever had told him so wasn't counting on the Phelaries readjusting—just a bit—the Reflector Panels and the S-Z formula. Nnox said that given the empirical evidence that there was probably a human mistake somewhere, so he'd wanted to evaluate the entire Shield; plus, they wanted to solve the nitrogen issue.

In the end, Barrett Mountdragon said yes to Nnox's invitation to come with him to Death Valley. Kanio wondered why.

Today was important. He had realized that if he wanted humans to get used to have him around them, he had to show himself first; so while talking about weather, Kanio also mentioned to these humans that he would like to leave Atlantic Island, and had asked for someone who could take him around Manhattan— he specifically asked for a person who knew the city very well, dominant in human culture, who wouldn't feel threatened by the metal situation. Also, an excellent Thunderbolt rider, as that would be the vehicle of transportation.

He reached the purple bridge and a short chubby man dressed in a paneled rubber charcoal-colored suit was standing outside with two cycles by his side. Kanio came down and went to him.

"Good morning. I am Lucca Selv, the Italian Ambassador," the man said when he saw Kanio coming closer. "I got these two. I had the impression you may want to ride a blue one; this one matches your tone," he continued.

Why would I? All of my things are already blue, Kanio thought. "I'll take the black one," he said.

"Yes. Si. Are you familiar with it? I sent you a short VR manual."

Kanio nodded. "The way the cylinders release energy is similar to our Helo-Ryders. The driving seems standard. However, it touches the ground. That is quite superb," the blue Alliafied confessed.

"Well, it is too expensive to levitate. Maybe in a few years." Lucca's arm went up, with his palm twisting sideways; his left eye started wandering in a less than comforting way.

"Why do I think you do have something that hovers?" Kanio looked for a way to be more communicative.

"I'll show it to you next time."

Lucca's eye looked more stable. His hands were on his hips, his legs apart—forming an inverted V. "Let's cross the bridge to Park Avenue in Manhattan and we can talk more about what we will do. Do you need a helmet? Of course you don't," Lucca said. His hands moved all around.

Kanio smiled back at him.

They left Atlantic Island on the black and blue cycles and crossed into Manhattan. They stopped after crossing the bridge. Two Letaneos tracked their way on two small Helo-Ryders—gray-silver standing capsules with black bellies and two long turbines on the side. Once they crossed the bridge, the Helos fell on their bellies, still hovering, and the back ends became taller, bending forward.

"I saw their Helo qualcosa changed; well, these ones do too. I have asked for Park and Fifth Avenue to be closed for us and traffic diverted to the tunnels beneath them. Let's go south through Park Avenue; it's a two-way avenue—choose any side you want. On 14th Street we will stop in Union Square and you will see a monument that Americans love; it's between a casa and a pantheon. But we will skip it. Then we will turn left to take FDR Drive all the way south, then north again. Your cycle has the entire trajectory already; just wanted to give you some details...most importantly, once you begin riding and reach 50 mph, raise the right pedal with your foot and then press all the way back. Capisce?"

"Si," Kanio said.

"You go first," Lucca said.

Kanio moved the right grip of his cycle and the engines turned on. He gently pressed his palm on it, and the Thunderbolt jumped forward. Heading south, he picked the right side of the Avenue, split by Indian Hawthorn trees. As Lucca explained, when he reached 50 mph, after raising it, he pressed the right pedal down further—and with that, the windshield expanded upward, like a jelly-rounded screen. The lower fairing started expanding, like panels overlapping one another; each overlay made a hard sound when it cut the air. The new side panels expanded like wings backward; the seat rose. He accelerated. He was at 100 mph. It was not only about the speed; it felt like sometimes it touched the ground and sometimes like it didn't. Kanio could see in the rearview mirrors a lime-green aura in their wake, mixed with a few cherry petals.

Kanio stopped; he looked up and saw the SkyShot being inserted into the sky. First it was like a dark purple stain, and then it got the brushed-away look— probably by the effect of the Panels.

"You will get used to it." Lucca arrived seconds after.

"I've seen worse. You will survive," the Phelarie said.

People were starting their regular Saturday: a few runners in the streets; walkers greeted one another. Cafés opened their doors. In their path, everyone stared at them when they glided by.

Once on the tip of the island, they took a quick break. Kanio pressed his thumb and index finger in front of his right eye and created a one-inch magnifier screen while expanding them. There was very large grayish statue a little more than a mile away. "Why a half-woman?" he asked.

"It sank. It used to be a whole body, and the hand was holding a torch. Liberty," the Italian responded with a bold accent on his laugh.

"Liberty is relative," Kanio said.

"Agreed. The day is nice; let's go to the beach. Andiamo." Lucca turned his cycle on and continued. Kanio followed. They got into a tunnel and left Manhattan. He told the Letaneos to go back to Atlantic Island. In the panel, he could see a new route. The next hours they drove among enormous green trees and, later, by a marble sidewalk hedging the ocean. He passed Lucca, who never drove over 100 mph, Lucca was not unscratchable like he was. They returned to Manhattan. An hour later, he was taking 5th Avenue and soon after they arrived at the Metropolitan Museum. They spent a couple of hours on paintings and armor, and then they moved on to the top floor outdoors.

"Central Park. Almost as green as the Union's meadow. Most of the buildings you see on the other side are around 300 years old," Lucca explained.

The skyline was a mixture of Gothic concrete buildings and glass towers.

"That pond used to be full, but with the heat and then with the Shield, it became a source of diseases. It has enough water to serve as decoration now. I wouldn't be surprised if it's a hologram, indeed. The *Americani*." Lucca stared at the pond; actually, it did look dubious.

"We have only seen Italian paintings inside. What about the others?" Kanio asked.

"No need," Lucca assured him.

"I appreciate your time. I have to ask, aren't you too young to be an ambassador?" Kanio felt Lucca was cynical enough to not get offended by such a question.

"Aren't you, for being an Aekiou?" Lucca said back with a huge grin in his face.

"I learned quickly. Just happened." Kanio copied his grin.

"Likewise. Just happened. It's a story for another time," the little Onerian said.

"I am going to put you in contact with Nnox Levantone; you two may connect," Kanio said.

"Is he the other one?" Lucca asked.

"Yes. Let's walk to the other side of this terrace."

"Like Cate Weelah?" Lucca asked with a loose tone.

"Do you know her?"

"Yes, from even before."

"Before?" Kanio was intrigued.

"Before she became like you." Lucca indicated Kanio's metal body.

Kanio had a file on Cate, as Steban Weelah's daughter. It mentioned her annoying sister, the boyfriend Mountdragon, Dr. Park's daughter, the French son of the BMAs number two, a couple of students from Fox-Stone, and a Miss Walker in Manhattan. There was nothing on an Italian Selv.

"What do you think of her?" Kanio interrogated the human.

"She is nice. I saw her twice at Apollo, a few years ago; haven't seen her since then." Lucca pointed at the sky, to the moon.

So they all have been in Apollo. Kanio wondered if Lucca might be his way in.

"Why there?" Kanio asked.

"She was working for Dr. Park, but nothing major. I just went for lunches; they won't let me pass the reception hall." Lucca laughed.

There it goes. Kanio looked back to the park.

"She could be introverted sometimes." Lucca stayed quiet and then he said, "I'm glad you showed up; it kind of justified her. I know it hasn't been that fun for her."

"Fun?" the blue one asked.

"Fair," Lucca added, and then reiterated: "And fun."

"It is not always about fun, my human guide." Kanio liked Lucca, besides his frivolity. Years of living with Nnox had stretched his patience. "There is not much I can do about 'fun,' but I can do something when it comes to 'fair.' What do you think I should do to get closer to her?" He would like to hear the Italian's insights; the closest he had gotten to Cate was her golden sister, and that did not work well.

"Go to her. Don't wait," Lucca said right away.

"Next week, after..."

"No, sooner. She may go to Mars tomorrow. I know she is somewhere in downtown Manhattan. Ask CDD to give you her address," Lucca interrupted him.

Kanio took few steps back, pressed his band on his left wrist. "I need Catherine Weelah's address in New York City."

"Who are you talking to?" Lucca stared at him. "I didn't mean as soon as now."

"Try Victoria Weelah...no, it is in Manhattan, in downtown," Kanio said, and then turned to Lucca. "I have a device like your Whisper, but behind my ear."

"Alice Park?" Kanio asked again.

"No headaches?" Lucca still looked amazed.

"No. It works when I turn it on. Wait—nothing." Kanio moved away from him when Lucca was about to touch his ear; he continued talking to Central at the Union.

"Oh, *aspettare*," Lucca said loudly. "She uses a fake name sometimes. Francesco teases her about it. Walker?"

"Catherine Walker?" Kanio asked. Ten seconds passed. "Okay, Lucca, we'll be in touch. I'm taking the black Thunderbolt with me."

maria beta

CHAPTER 15

....

AN ELEMENTAL IMPASSE

S end the directions to this Onerian Thunderbolt," Kanio asked Central at the Union Building, and a 3-D map came up on the screen in front of him beneath the windshield. A pink path highlighted his optimal way along the moss-green topographic map. The time of arrival changed intermittently. Traffic evidently was different now than it had been earlier, when the main avenues were closed for him. In some places, cars advanced attached to one another in a string, making them hard to shortcut through. These might be the CDD-controlled transit paths. The two-level streets moved relatively faster, but the problem seemed to be on the roads that were filled with public passenger vehicles. It seemed the 2-Fl buses, the ones that take passengers above and CDD-controlled cars below, were not moving at all.

"A disaster," he complained. No chance to use the pedal trick.

"It's 4 p.m.; they call it rush hour," a Phelarie from Central said.

"What about that FDR from the morning? Can you do something?"

"Maybe a few traffic lights..."

"Do it," Kanio said.

He knew it was not correct that he misused his perks, but he was a goal-oriented character, and soon after, he was at a park in Downtown Manhattan. Two old men were sitting on a bench. Their clothes were old, pastel, and ugly. They didn't seem to care about getting a glimpse of him. He left the Thunderbolt in a parking space for another type of vehicle designed for Onerian children. The sign said *Bicycles Only*. The Thunderbolt took up six spots of these kids' toy spaces.

"Is this the right block?" Central at the Union responded Yes into his ear. He paced inside onto the dark streets.

He reached a wave-like silver building.

"Open this." Central opened the simple door for him. To his left, in front of two silver elevator doors, was a long vertical panel with four screens to the side.

Kanio checked the buttons on the panel. He decided to figure out how to get into the elevator. He struggled with an indigo fiber-optic sensor coming from one of the screens.

"This is mature behavior from you, the Aekiou of Phelio," his Ereo said unemotionally from behind. It flowed by Kanio's right side. "Why don't you press the large button and say the number of her apartment, or say Walker? Announce yourself first." Kanio's Ereo had been talking to the Aekiou since his second cycle, right after his mother disappeared and his father began avoiding him. A cycle in Phelarie life was close to four Onerian years.

"When it comes to all the features I have been regarded as, mature has not shown up on the list. I want to go upstairs on my own, and then knock on her door," Kanio said.

"These buildings are not connected to Central; they have an older Onerian code than the ones you have seen. You could overwrite the entire code," the Ereo proposed.

"That is too far," Kanio said, still dialing different instructions into the building system. One of the screens blocked him, but he managed to get into it again.

"Because you never go too far," the Ereo said.

Kanio turned around, but there was nothing to say back. He knew his Ereo's irony was right. "I am aware I do sometimes touch the borderline, more often than I should." He unalliafied. He was wearing a dark coal scale suit. High collar. The cape, dark coal as well, lost the motion feature from the alliafied effect and fell heavily downward.

"I wanted to use the surprise factor." He pressed the button. "Walker."

The Ereo was gone.

Nothing. He pressed the button again.

"You?" a female voice said. "You want to come up?"

"No, let's go out; show me around."

A few minutes later, Cate Weelah came out from the elevator's silver doors. She was wearing a red suit with a pale rose shirt that tied with a nice bow below her chin. The jacket collar intertwined all the way down to her waist, and her hair was pulled tightly back, like a tail.

"Who is Catherine Walker?"

"I used to introduce myself like that to not be related to Steban Weelah, and then it just happened. If people, media or anything, looked for me, they couldn't find me. What I have is under the name of Catherine Walker. It was a very good cover...until now." She seemed happy. She was smiling.

"I want to know more about humans, Onerians. Show me around," he commanded her.

"I am supposed to meet Patrick Jameson in about twenty minutes—my sister Victoria's friend, about..." Cate said.

"Don't do that. The only one who can decide when can she leave that room is me," he said. He grabbed her by her shoulders; she twisted them backward. He realized it was a little strong and lightened his touch.

"When is that going to be?" Cate asked. She blushed.

"Soon. But she must help us with something be-fore—simple. In the meantime, if she is with you, she can leave the Ryder, but not the Island; is that okay?"

"For the meantime."

"Take me around."

She moved her hand as if to say Follow me.

They left the building. There was a light gray haze that covered the top of the buildings in the area. Suddenly the building became neon in a disturbing way. He stared at it.

"Oh yes. It's during the night. It supposedly as-similates an ocean wave. I chose it because it was the cheapest block in the neighborhood, back when I got it a few years ago," she explained.

He pressed his left shoulder, pushing down the button in the center, and the cape rolled up beneath his shoulders until it was invisible.

"I like the cape," she said.

"Too much attention," he explained.

She directed him to the right and they inserted themselves into smaller and darker alleys every time. He could tell every block they crossed had signs on the buildings that were in languages other than English—mainly Asian and Middle Eastern.

"Do you like New York?" he asked. He recognized some neon lights: signs for *hardware* and *savings bank* in Mandarin.

"Well, I managed to live a life. A couple of blocks away there is a cafeteria I like," she proposed.

They kept walking. She remained quiet for most of the way.

I thought she wasn't afraid of me anymore, he thought.

"Here," she said. She pushed an old steel door and a large bright orange countertop guided their way inside. Long rectangular lamps hung all around. Four empty tables sat to their right. They took one.

"Your sister is fine, trust me," Kanio affirmed to her.

"Put yourself in my position; imagine it was your purple Nnox," she said.

She was right, but not entirely.

"Put yourself in mine. Your sister threatened the entire world with an illusion of what she can or must do, based on what everyone knows you are capable of. Humans don't know she is not like you. I would be upset at her if I was you."

A neon-pink-haired woman served them cups with a crystalline brown liquid inside. The woman's eye makeup was silver and black, and took almost half of her face.

"You cannot tell me how to think or feel when it comes to my sister," she said.

"I am giving her options, but she is not taking them. I am counting on that, with time, it will turn around. Perhaps you can help," Kanio said. This might be the way to bring her closer to him. Cate was unique in hydrogen and probably from the fourth state; he needed her close to him. *Who cares about her golden, second Leeve sister?*

"Do you like coffee?" she asked him.

"No." He had tried it already, and found it worse than Olpenia milk. Nnox did like it; he liked that horrid milk as well. When they were growing up, during training, and the instructors became distracted, Kanio always managed to give his pair the glass of that grayish condensed liquid.

"Try it," she insisted. She stared at him.

"I am just doing this so next time I ask you to try something, you do." He sipped some from the cup. He took his time to swallow it. *Same disgusting taste...*

"I want the regular cheeseburger," Cate told the waiter, who had just come to take their order, "with some extra secret sauce, please."

Her presence was enjoyable, even when she was not metal.

"How did you end up here on Earth?" Cate asked.

"Answering a solicitation for help." He stretched his back. He was definitely exaggerating this last remark. He hadn't even wanted to cross beyond Io, Jupiter's third moon, in the first place; and then he and Nnox had found out about an out-of-control golden Alli-afied, which seemed a good reason to go all the way to Onerio-13 or Earth.

"Thanks for the books and holos about this metal thing."

"You should have received them before, way before," he said. "Is your Ereo helping you?"

"I like him. Thanks. We do talk a lot."

"Good," he said.

"I've been having questions since..." she paused. "I don't remember. The day after the car crash. And no one had answers. Victoria can transform, but she is not like me. She can control it."

"That's because of your character. You are a little bit erratic," Kanio said and pushed his cup away.

"Ugh." She stared at him with deep green wide-open eyes, as if this was the first time someone had brought up her behavior.

The truth was that since he had known her, she had come and gone with no compass or target on her actions. She jumped from a window, then showed up early the next day. She complained about her sister's imprisonment and the purple ship, yet she wandered around in it for an hour after she said goodbye to Victoria. He didn't complain, but she was far from predictable. Cate looked muddled. If he wanted her to get close to him, he was the one who must bring her back to her feet. It was understandable that she was nervous. He had been taught to deal with this quality since he'd had memory.

"And because you are so much more complex and mighty than her. You are like me."

"Like you? Really?" She looked awestruck.

"Probably." He didn't want to tell her what she was capable of. Not yet.

"What is being an Alliafied? What does it mean?"

"It's about elemental energy and how it flows through us. And how we control it. It's beyond this skin characteristic; it allows us to engage with who we truly are. Don't be afraid of it."

"Do you know who you are?"

"I know. I'm the Aekiou. Do you?"

"No. Catherine Walker?" She laughed.

"It's fine; take your time," he said.

"How many can do what we do?"

If she only knew, he thought.

"Like Victoria? Probably hundreds. Like you and me? Hmm." He thought carefully. "Maybe thirty? Also, some decide to remain hidden."

"Why is that?" Cate interrupted. The waitress came back and brought water. Cate grabbed a glass and drank it entirely.

"Because not everybody wants to leave their home and endure a tough way of living. It is training. Lessons. Lectures. Isolation. It's not easy to be one of the brightest and most gifted. Learn to maximize what you are. Learn not to subjugate a lower state or Leeve just because they are."

"Like Victoria did." Cate pressed her lips. The hamburger arrived.

He alliafied his right hand and grabbed her left. Human skin was soft. "Alliafy it," he said. Cate turned it into dark silver liquid metal, still chewing her food. Her hand was now warm. Kanio pressed it with his blue right hand; some silver and some blue dust waves were released every time he pressed, pushing her liquid silver skin down. He unalliafied his hand and released hers.

"I am a Lario," Cate said proudly.

"Only Larios can iterize, and only a few. You have some Phima in you too." Kanio was half Thendor, half Phima, though his Alliafied consistency was Thendor as was his father's.

216

"You are not just any Onerian. How do you feel about standard humans?" he continued.

"They hate me; I hate them back," she said and took another bite.

"Again. Don't be erratic. I mean, how do you really feel about them?"

"Okay, it's not hate; I don't know the correct word for it. From the crazy shrink to my silly classmate, they make it hard to even just walk around. Not only for me; you don't know how it was for Victoria as well." She sounded angry.

She finished her meal and asked for the check. "I'll get this; I don't think you can pay."

"I can." He grabbed the tablet that the pink-haired woman had just brought and pressed his right index fingertip on the reader. "It will get better, I promise."

"I've heard that before." She had an entire third glass of water and they headed outside.

*****

It's hopeless. It's helpless. Part I.

He didn't know where they were going, but she seemed to know her way around—she managed to avoid the soggy alleys with the most disgusting smell; Phelaries had a sense of smell better developed than humans—so she must have already known that something rotten was in that way.

"Do you like Earth? New York?" Cate asked.

"I thought it would be drier."

"Well, you have only been in a nice place," she said.

"I have the evaluations of previous expeditions. We have been monitoring the planet's environment more constantly since the ozone layer ran out," he said. They don't deserve their independence, Kanio thought. "I am going to visit some places in the next days. Very damaged. So irresponsible. Selfish."

"What about the people?" she asked. She chortled.

"That is not relevant," he said.

"Ah? Why is only the planet important for you? Why bother?" Cate stared at him.

"This is not the only planet of its kind. But humans enjoy so much getting divided, which makes it easier to coordinate them as a whole." Kanio knew that Onerio was key in U4, as was Brogio—the green planet where Colt Behar resided—two of the few that had life by themselves. They created balance. And he also knew that Cate, as Victoria and all its inhabitants, were clueless and totally unaware of it. Earth was frail but it did self-sustain, and how these people gamed their own planet seethed him. "Was it divide and conquer?" He raised his eyebrows.

Cate shook her head. She opened her jacket, pulled his arm, and guided him to the right, into an alley filled with pink and red light bulbs hanging above.

"Indian," she said.

"I thought it was an Italian," he said.

"I mean this alley—the restaurants."

"Italians. The ambassador probably agreed with me," Kanio said.

"I saw you on TV. I was wondering when were you going to bring it up."

"Was he also a boyfriend of yours?"

"Stop it." She poked his arm.

"Where are we going?" he finally asked. Fog began to fall like a thick drape on a wall.

"Don't know. You said you wanted to walk around," she responded. "You also said you will help my sister."

"And I will, soon, when it is right," he said.

It was dark enough that Kanio didn't realize what he had stepped on until it moved. He looked down. It was a weak and old man—he raised his head; he could barely open his eyes between his deep wrinkles.

"Go to a shelter. A storm is coming," Cate told the old man. The grizzly man pulled himself into his jacket.

"Goooo eway!" he yelled at her.

Kanio drove her away by her arm.

"We do not have them in Phelio. That man is the sign that you have failed as a society."

"You don't know why he is there." Cate was a compassionate person, after all.

"He should not be there. Why is not the question."

"Sometimes it's hard to choose; decisions are not simple," she added.

"That is why you failed, you should have guided him better. On Phelio nobody is forced to participate in the system. But either you are in or you are out. What we aim for is not an ideal system or idealist leader, because many times there is none—so we look for better citizens." He wondered how this could not be clear to her.

"No options in the middle?" she asked, twisting her mouth.

"We help the ones who get stuck in the middle; no transparent oversight, like here. On Phelio, he would have been asked to decide. If he wanted to live an ordered life, we would have taken care of him. If he wanted to choose something else, he could—but away."

"Away?" She looked surprised.

"Away. Esserkon." He looked the other way.

"Esserkon? What are you saying? Like killing them? You can't mean that," she said.

"No. Nothing."

"What is Esserkon, then? Will you take Victoria there if she doesn't help?"

"No, Cate. Esserkon is the gray planet. No one will take Victoria there. Don't ever think that. And you should never go there." He shouldn't have brought up the issue. It's hopeless. It's helpless.

"Is everything okay?" She grabbed his arm.

"I like to talk to you. Discussions with arguments help build your thoughts," he said to her. He heard a few drops touching the sidewalk. "Let's go back."

"I know this place, Earth—Onerio, as you call it— isn't perfect, but it's what we have." She let go of his arm and advanced farther.

"You will be able to make a comparison when you get to know a civilized world."

He could distinguish the delicate reflection of the streetlight on her wheat-gold hair.

"This is civilized," Cate grumbled.

"Now you like this..."

"Don't move; give me your finger, your index finyer." A rough male voice interrupted Kanio and pushed the Phelarie from behind.

Kanio was already metal blue; his shine illuminated the dark night. It was the same old man they'd seen a block back, standing strong, with the same deep lines on his forehead. Closer, his face was gray; the whites of his eyes were yellow-green, with dilated pupils. Kanio seized the man's wrist, and he loosened his grip so that the sharp tube with golden dots fell out from his hand. *Crack.* He broke the old man's wrist. Kanio released it and the man fell to the ground.

Dark-silver Cate stood beside him. They looked at each other. The man's mouth was fully open, a mouth with not many filthy teeth.

She bent down to get the tube from the floor and broke it. "Let's go."

Kanio nodded.

"Are you okay?" he asked.

"Yes."

"Was he really intending to chop it off?" He showed her his index finger; he knew that was not possible, but he'd wanted to make a point.

"No, no, he probably just wanted your fingerprint." She pushed his finger away, and touched his chest with hers.

"All this mess...for coffee?" He softly pulled her platinum hair. It moved differently than any other Alliafied's hair. He could identify different strings in it instead of a single chunk of metal like the others'.

Drops fell randomly. They slumped back beneath the full covered dark night, until they were in front of the turquoise-colored changing building again, beneath the glass canopy at the entrance.

"Do you still think it is civilized?" he asked.

She smiled at him; she looked ecstatic. Slightly, she raised her head, leaning it to her left.

"I have to go. We will do this again," he said.

A couple of blocks away, a Letaneo was waiting for him by a blue Helo-Ryder.

maria beta

CHAPTER 16

....

TITCHER PARK

The next morning Cate woke up with her head mostly covered by her pillow. She'd forgotten to fully darken her windows, and after four hours of hail, the most unusual thing happened: sunshine. She'd fallen asleep with the idea that she had been on the best date of her life, one of not many. But was it really a date? For him it was probably a political meeting.

She checked her Whisper: Only two texts from Alice and one from Paula. Coper was lying at the end of the bed. He came closer and stretched his front paws on her chest. She scratched his head and pulled out a red jelly treat from her night table.

"Do you want to meet the blue giant?"

The puppy took the red tub with his mouth, jumped to the floor, and left the room.

"Air-man!" A long phony howl. "Where are you?" She covered her head with the pillow again.

"Good morning, Cate. You can call me Ereo by now." He looked fatherly at her.

In red sweatpants and a gray FoxStone pullover, Cate went to the balcony with a mug of coffee in one hand and a tablet in the other. The door opened sideways, still with the melted hole in the middle—*that wasn't practical*, she pondered. This was probably one of the shiniest days of her life. She looked down, where they had stood some hours before. Her Ereo flowed by her left.

"Supposedly, centuries ago, people could spend entire days on the beach. The sun shone like this almost every day, and it was harmless. I am afraid of the water, in any case."

"You are sunken into melancholy, a strange human behavior. It will pass," the Ereo said.

"Why hasn't he called?" She supported her elbows on the balcony.

He disappeared.

Three hours later, silver Cate was having lunch with her sister, still in the purple room, but outside the crystal jail. Dressed in black letiqa pants and a diagonal-necked black mallow sweater—it felt like a marshmallow.

"I'm not going to walk around this island in this gray suit! Please bring me something decent," golden Victoria said.

"What are you? Six?"

"Sometimes. I have clothes in Sunally; those will be fine."

"What do you think of this Kanio?"

"I have only seen him once, a few days ago," Victoria said.

"He told me that you will be retained here only for a while; that they just can't pretend like nothing happened. And that you have to help him in something."

"Bah, we'll see," Victoria complained.

"He was very nice and polite. We were almost mugged, but we were alliafied so it was nothing, really."

"Listen, he seemed very smart, and I'm sure he is very nice. I've heard mixed reviews about him, that's all," Victoria said. She stood and went to look for something on the table behind the crystal.

"What? From Mr. Rogers?"

"Yes, he kind of explained to me the Phelarie Organigram once, but I never thought I'd meet them, so I didn't pay much attention," Victoria said.

Victoria? Not paying attention? Hard to believe.

"What are those mixed reviews?" Cate asked.

"That he is reliable, but he is always looking for an excuse to get away from his duties or everyday tasks,"

Victoria continued. She sat again by her, but with a tablet in her hand.

"Then why is he so important?"

"Because he achieves them anyway. He ends up doing more than he is supposed to, and he doesn't brag about it, so everyone then loves him," Victoria explained.

"What is it that he wants you to help with?" Cate asked.

"He thinks someone from his side offered me support to carry on with my mini-coup or whatever, and he wants to know who."

"Did someone?" Cate interlaced her fingers.

Kanio might be right; so far he has been.

"Cate, I am—we are—human beings from planet Earth; we are an independent planet. I don't have to answer to him about anything, and he can't keep me here for much longer. Remind him of that when you see him again, please," Victoria added.

"If I do," Cate said.

"You will. Listen. Learn from him. Or ask him how can you learn more," Victoria said.

This was a comment that Cate would never have imagined coming from her sister. Cate thought Victoria would have preferred if she'd stayed as far from them as possible.

"Do you need anything else?"

"No. They have given me full access to news, TV, holos. I've watched like three movies already. I can't remember the last time I saw one. Did you hear that Saki broke up with that Danish actor? I wanted to show you the gossip I found." Victoria checked the tablet.

"I didn't like her latest song. Clothes? That is for sure," Cate asked.

"Oh, I deleted it."

"I want to meet Francis for a coffee at the Union."

"Is the cafeteria open as usual?"

"Everything is as usual; just these peachy people everywhere. You will see tomorrow."

"I see." Victoria looked disappointed.

"Maybe we can watch a movie." Cate went closer to the glass. She opened her right palm and created a small cloud of dust and slapped it against the glass; it shook it, but nothing more.

"It's well fortified," Victoria said. "Let's do that; I'll ask these muppets to get us pizza." She came closer to Cate and kissed her cheek. "You have to be in a higher Leeve, if you want to break it," she whispered.

Can I?

Cate kissed her back. "See you soon!" She waved her hand as she walked out of the room.

Cate was about to go down the purple rubber corridor to the outside when she saw Nnox watching the sky with two Letaneos.

He might be here, she thought.

"What are you doing? Come here." A deep and apathetic Nnox caught her distracted. He strode fast in her direction. He probably felt her.

"You are back?" She paced down to meet him.

"What were you doing? I know what you did in there," the purple creature insisted, his big chest blocking most of her sight.

"I still can't control myself." She shrugged her shoulders.

"How do you like seeing the sun? Have you before?"

The sunshine itself is gone, but the pastel orange color above looks quite nice. He did look like Kanio; so annoying.

"Ugh."

"No worries. It will be dark and somber again; we just reset some stuff to see how they work," he said to her.

"Stuff? You play Titcher Park with our survival tools. Nice. You think..."

"Sometimes I do not think. You see, that is the difference between Kanio and I. He thinks too much," Nnox interrumpted her. He extended his cape backward, and walked away, into his ship.

Did he say that because he knows about last night, or because he doesn't? Her thoughts tortured her. She didn't care about the formula and the Panels. Cate jumped into the droid car and was driven back to the Building, where she'd left her Triton at arrival a few hours before.

*****

After Cate left, Victoria spent much of the afternoon watching The Unburiable, one of the most successful holo-series of all times. She saw the 3D-character drama developing in the dark holo-cube inside her room.

She had the idea the Phelaries were filtering the news for her. However, she had approval for some shows from her district: Texan talk shows and Mexican soap operas. "My favorite actors' dreams and lives; I live through them every day," she'd said once. It was very hard for her to contain her laugh. She knew that Patrick would put everyone back together, and she knew it wasn't a coincidence that Arthur Harlow, Alex's father, had walked the red carpet at Ariana Jimenez' birthday bash in Austin the night before. That was a sign. She wouldn't know if Ariana acted or sang—maybe neither, as Mr. Harlow was probably unaware as well. Yet he was there in Texas, attending an event with Patrick and Maurice Sellenton from Florida in the New Sun—one of the main backers of her failed campaign. She was not alone.

A peachy creature entered the room. "A person from the Senate wants to pay you a visit. We said yes. Is it okay with you?" he asked.

"Sure." She paused the holo and went outside the room. She tried to look relaxed and not show her anxiety. *Why did Patrick take so long? What if it is Maurice?* The plan was that no one knew he was behind too.

"You have 20 minutes; please do go inside," the Phelarie greeted someone outside.

"Thanks." A familiar male voice crossed the door.

She froze when she recognized him: *Unbelievable. What does he pretend? He is not related to me; he is nothing to me.* She rearranged her hair.

"Hi," Alex said.

After they broke up, they only saw each other alone once. She explained what she pretended to do with the old, saggy previous government, and how they will put McCully against the wall, and he'd agreed to not do anything to stop her. Patrick and Maurice coordinated the rest of the backstage work.

"Are you okay?" Alex walked perfectly straight in a spotless blue suit with a green tie and a few related NAA pins on his chest. Surprisingly, he looked almost dead.

"Why are you here?"

"I am going to get you out," he said.

"I can get out."

"Off the Island, I mean."

"Alex, don't do this to yourself. Or to me. Don't interfere in my life ever again. Go. Say hi to your father." She headed back to the room and picked up the holo-control from the bed.

"It was me. Not the polls. I'm sorry," he said.

"What are you talking about?" she asked him.

Is he finally admitting to how much of a coward he is?

"Us," Alex said. He came closer to the glass, he unbuttoned his collar, and loosened his tie.

His acts were so familiar that they made her feel even angrier.

"Alex, it's been forever. It's too late. It's done," she said. She turned on the holo.

"It was too much. If you can ever forgive me..." he continued. His sight was drowned in misery.

"I won't. I can't. This is a joke." She closed her eyes out of fury and covered them with her hands. She exhaled deeply and walked around. "This is actually the most outrageous scenario for this conversation with you, trapped in this glass cage and not capable of getting away from you." She touched the purplish glass and in desperation murmured, "Nnox. Purple thing. Get him out."

"You have to listen to me. I need to explain," Alex insisted.

"Are you doing this on purpose?" She looked to the other side.

"No, no, please forgive me," he begged.

"It is too late. It's been seven years, Alex. Not weeks or months."

"Please." He was not giving up. He touched the glass.

"There are few things that I have clear in my mind, and one of them is that I don't want to see you," she said. "I don't want to talk to you, ever again."

"I haven't been with anyone all this time. I never forgot you, and it's because..."

"Alex. We finally meet." Nnox approached them in a purple superliquid state. His cape flowed in a wave-shape a few feet from the floor.

"He needs to leave," Victoria said directly to Nnox. Her arms cut the air.

"Then you are gone," Nnox addressed Alex.

Alex looked to Victoria, and then to Nnox. "I'll be back with an answer," Alex said to Victoria.

"No, you won't." Victoria moved back to her bed, with that sharp agony that she thought she'd gotten rid of years before.

"If you try to come back, I won't let you get onto this Island again—even if Kanio appoints you as the Prime Minister of the entire planet." Nnox smiled at him.

"Victoria, we'll talk again." Alex walked out of the room.

Nnox got close to the glass.

"Is everything okay?"

She nodded.

He wandered around the room and then came back to the glass.

"I am glad you called."

"Why?" She couldn't focus on an idea.

"I was hoping you could help me, at least in return," he said. He supported his right shoulder on the glass.

She remained skeptical; she never thought the word help would come out of his purple mouth.

"I want to know more about humans. You are both human and Alliafied. It makes sense, finding out from you," he explained.

"No, actually I am your prisoner," she interrupted him.

"Well, it's true." He walked back. "That is what happens when you do bad things, but, you see, I like you despite your attitude," he said.

Victoria took the control and raised the holo-series' volume.

"In the meantime, you have access to almost anything you want in this VIP suite—books, food, exercise, your sister's visits, and the like. Now you can even have a morning run on the Island," Nnox added. He did sound ironic.

"Are you stronger than me?" Victoria paused the holo.

"Was not that obvious when we met?"

"And than Cate?"

He released a sarcastic laugh. "I would never have left someone I care about the way he left you," Nnox said.

"You wish you were a bit like him. He doesn't need a metal shield to be a superhero," Victoria said.

"If you like him so much, maybe I should call him back," Nnox said.

"Do you care about anyone but the Aekiou?"

"No."

"So then your choices are easy," Victoria said. For her, life was all about the decisions and choices you make.

"They are. I have no one else," he said.

A moment of silence hit them. She couldn't find the right words to say. She hated Alex, yet she'd discovered five minutes before that he still touched her feelings like no one else. She hated Nnox, yet she'd discovered five seconds before that he was not as soulless as she'd thought after all.

"What kind of tool is Titcher Park?" he asked.

"It's not a tool. It's a game for children. You can build houses, buildings, cities. And they come with little people. I loved it when I was a child. Cate would tear apart the little heads, though."

"I see." He smiled at her. "Good night, Victoria."

He left without saying any other word. It was for the best.

The next morning, Victoria was having breakfast and reading the Texan yellow press on a tablet. The same peachy Phelarie man from the day before came into the room with a two-square-foot package and left it on the floor in front of her.

"From Nnox Levantone," he said.

She opened it. It was the latest Titcher Park—the Union Building version.

maria beta

CHAPTER 17

....

THE SHIELD

It had been almost two weeks since the day the Phelaries arrived. It was mid-October, and Cate had decided she couldn't avoid a visit to her parents anymore. Paula's calls and texts had become intermittent—and most importantly, she felt she was finally ready to face her father. She was dressed in black, and he was in yellow.

"Steban, you have to explain—anything, please." This was the first thing she'd said when she sat by him in the library room.

He had stayed mute for almost an hour, his eyes closed. *Is he going to act as if I'm not here?* Cate hesitated about leaving him at least twenty times, but she was already there, so she took a magazine and read it. He looked at her and then he stared out through the shaded window.

"Latima, get me the book we discussed yesterday," he said.

The funny robot went to the back of the room and brought a beige book with some red letters on its cover to him.

"Give it to Catherine," he instructed the robot. "Have they asked you about the Panels? The SkyShots?" he asked Cate.

"No," she responded, "but they do know I'm your daughter."

"Don't tell them anything. Take the book; everything in it is wrong. I have to rest."

"Is that all?"

He closed his eyes again.

"Thanks, Dad. I'll tell Victoria you send her your best regards." Cate, disappointed, took off. In all these years, she had never managed to confront her father. She waved goodbye to Paula, who was in the garden with her magenta gloves. She could tell her stepmother was coming after her. She sped up, hoping to avoid her.

"Doors open, engine on." She quickly jumped into the car and threw the book into the backseat, almost hitting Coper. She drove by the roundabout and was out of Sunally in less than five minutes.

"CDD, take the car; destination: FoxStone," she commanded. She needed to go to the University and pass by her other house to grab some winter clothes. As soon as she released the car, she took back the book from the seat behind her. It was *The Shield Experiment,* the first book her father had written about the Panels and the Aurean Shield. It didn't mention anything about Alliafied, Phelaries, or Aekious. There were some pages marked. She tried to check some, but she got easily distracted. Steban Weelah had definitely wanted to show her something with that book. She'd have to re-read it, then. When it came to science, her father had been a mentor; when it came to communications, he had surely been something else. But what could he have said? Reminded her that she was not his daughter? No matter what, in his own special way, he had always been there, and she couldn't be ungrateful for that.

Once at FoxStone, she made a first stop by the University and went to the Dean's office; she saw the door open and went in.

"I'm sorry; it's quick. Sorry I missed the practice. I can't go to Venus next month. Priorities," she tried to explain.

"I understand; it's fine," the Dean said. "If there is anything I could do to help, let me know."

"Thanks!"

Before she was at the door, she turned her sight back to something old on his desk.

"Is that *The Shield Experiment*?" Cate asked.

"Yes, I was told it was a good time to re-read it."

"I was told that as well." Her chest tightened. "Thanks again," she said.

She took a walk around the campus; it was filled with news crews. She skipped them by taking a detour through the Chemistry building. Then she ran into a familiar face: Sabrina's.

"Cate! I haven't seen you in a year, or more!"

"Oh wow! How've you been?"

"I saw you were in that reception at the Union; why are you talking to them?" Sabrina pursed her lips; her expression wasn't one of curiosity.

"They are not that bad, really," Cate responded, a little surprised by the question.

"How are they?" Sabrina pressed the books in her arms against her chest.

"Like us—like me. You shouldn't be worried. As long as life as it is continues, it will be fine." Cate wanted to continue with a relaxed mood to antagonize her friend's.

"Anyway, nobody acts like they're worried. The University gave a few talks in the amphitheater, and that was it," Sabrina explained. "I heard yesterday that your sister may have some issues."

Cate nodded.

"Is that why you are here? To talk to him?"

"Is he here?" Cate asked.

Days had passed, but there hadn't been a concrete sign from him besides some documents and a set of powders and stones that a peachy girl brought to her apartment at Lost-Town a couple of days before. They came with a signed letter from him; though; it said: *'Knowledge is buildable.'* Besides that, nothing else.

"Yes, he is. Kanio? Kenio? In the Conference Center. Only a few were invited."

Cate pulled a holo-screen from her Whisper band and checked her emails.

"I was. Let's go."

"I don't know," Sabrina said.

"He is okay; trust me. Come on!"

They paced quickly through the campus till they reach their destination. Cate could see a couple of Letaneos at the door, and some guards in purple and some in green.

"What are those things?" Sabrina asked.

"Letaneos."

Sabrina squinted her eyes.

"His SWAT team," Cate replied.

Two New East guards stopped them. "Do you have an invitation?"

"I have the email," she said.

"Did you confirm?" the man dressed in green said.

"Ask him! Ask the spider-man!" She raised her voice and swayed, looking for the polished-rock creature's attention.

The dark character nodded.

"Thanks!" She pulled Sabrina in.

"Hey no!" the guard complained, but the Letaneo nodded again.

"I'm one of them. I'm silver!"

They squeezed in between some students; the room was full, no empty seats, so they stood at the back.

"Are you here for the water?" a man from the crowd asked.

"No," Kanio said. His voice resounded in the whole space. He was standing entirely in blue on the main stage. He shook his head.

"Any other resource?" another person asked.

"No. Another question. A different type of question," Kanio demanded.

"What are you looking for? Why are you here? We know you are visiting the tubes and the stations. I don't take this transition to a new government?" A woman stood up. It was the Portuguese Eugenia and her crazy hair.

Kanio took one step forward. "As I said. We will analyze different matters, including the Shield, and we will see where can we find improvement, and how to achieve it. Also, from now on, you will see across the NAA our Phelaries, people from Phelio, these nice people here who helped to organize this event." He indicated the Phelaries at the doors and around the area. "We are harmless. You know Catherine Weelah already." He looked at her. "We are just like her."

Everyone turned around and set their eyes on her; there was a buzz in the air.

Oh, damn it. Cate wanted to iterize and disappear through the walls.

"Until you have a proper government, a working government, we will make the final decision in these matters, either myself or whomever comes afterward. So if you don't like having us around, you will have to go and vote. Vote correctly. If not, I'll be back."

Some of the people laughed.

"I don't think he meant it as a joke," she whispered to Sabrina.

"Thanks for coming." He left.

Some people clapped, while others stood up quickly and left as well.

"Cate, he does know you," Sabrina said.

"I told you!"

"But I didn't think that well." Sabrina looked surprised.

"I don't know if well, really; we are just alike," Cate explained.

Sabrina smiled dryly. "I don't like them. Sorry. And they are not like you. They are from that place. Phelio? And you are from the NAA."

"Cate Weelah! You are a celebrity now. When are you coming on my show?" Marisa Gomez, her eccentric frames, and her special O. "I have to go; see you soon!" She pinched Cate's arm and left with her holocamera man behind.

Sabrina and Cate laughed. They followed the crowd out.

"Do you want to have supper?" Sabrina asked.

"I can't. I'm going back to the city. I want to leave before it gets dark. Take care," Cate said.

"Thanks! You too!"

They hugged each other.

Cate walked to her car. A little in the clouds.

He knows me. Do I know him? Why am I like him?

A beam on her Whisper band. A text from Alice. "My mother saw you at the Conference; he said that you should be careful." She checked her newsfeed and Marisa Gomez mentioned: "Kanio already has a special connection with a human."

Oh no! What if people react like Sabrina did?

Head down, reading her texts, she finally got to her car.

"What is it?" someone asked.

246

She raised her head. An unalliafied Kanio was standing in front of her.

"So?" he asked again.

"How did your speech go?" She tried to look relaxed.

"It's not relevant. It was for them, not for me."

"Ah?" Cate said. *Did I hear right?*

"I've been trying to reach you. Central doesn't have access to your Whisper," he complained.

"Oh, might be because I have the non-tapped one." She air quoted. "I need to go back to the one that spies on me."

"I'll send you one. Or I can arrange a Zoun for you." He touched behind her ear.

"Inside? No, I'm fine with the plastic attached to my neck."

He smiled. "It has other benefits besides the communications property."

She shook her head.

"I'm glad you came, but you arrived late. I have to go now. Dinner with the Harlows; just wanted to know how to reach you."

"No. Alex! You don't even eat."

Cate pursed her lips.

"I do, sometimes. Also, the Dean of Physics missed my speech, and he is already gone. Can you introduce me to him? Maybe coming from you is better. He is close to your father, I've heard."

"They used to be. Sure. I can try."

"I'll see you tomorrow." He walked away, became blue, and the cape hovered behind him.

She heard a flash. She looked around; a bunch of students were staring, lifting their necks and taking holos. And not too far away, a jumbo lens, the professional type.

She received another text from Alice, "You are with him! Again!"

*****

The next morning, Cate and Victoria were rambling across the green lawn. Actually Victoria ran side to side and Cate strolled placidly. "No collar this time!" she told Coper.

"So the book says the most important thing is the Panels," Cate said to Victoria when she trotted close by. "So, that is not true?"

"What does the book mention as the Shield?" Victoria left at a slow speed.

"The Stations, the tubes, the satellites and its Panels, and the SZ SkyShots or fake-ozone powder," Cate said when Victoria came back. "Would you please stop. This is important," Cate added.

Thank God I don't run, Cate thought.

"What about the formula?" Victoria asked.

"What formula?" Cate asked.

"The formula for the SkyShot. That shit above us. Only a few know the exact composition. And Dad is one of the few."

"Are you sure? I thought you could find it on the Internet."

Victoria twisted her lips. "Cate, I'm sorry to tell you, but I found out about it when you broke up with that idiot, Barrett."

"What do you mean?"

Victoria completely stopped. She exhaled a couple of times.

"When Barrett broke up with you, I think it was because he had no reason to go home anymore. When Dad retired, Barrett asked him for the formula and Dad said no. He said he was his brightest assistant, whatever, plus a Mountdragon. Dad said no to giving him access to the SZ formula and that he wouldn't propose him to be added to a list. I overheard the conversation. I'm sorry. After that, we never saw Barrett again. I asked Steban once about that list, he said I misheard."

That idiot, Mountdragon. Cate was furious.

maria beta

CHAPTER 18

....

SZ

Cate had spent all day in Soho with Alice, doing something she hadn't done in ages: shopping.

"What do you know about the Shield?" Cate asked.

"The same that you do," Alice said, distracted, while checking out some scarves.

I don't want to tell her about Barrett; it's embarrassing, Cate thought.

"What is it that your mother does, exactly?" Cate asked Alice.

"Something with Zafor; how to purify it so it doesn't poison us."

"And does she know Steban?"

"Oh yes, I saw your father at my place a few times. Just didn't know he was your father back then. And it's not like he ever went to school to pick you up. I think I recognized him at your fifteenth birthday."

"Oh God, that zoo." Cate pressed her temples.

"Can I ask you something? I've never asked this before; I'm sorry if it's inappropriate."

"Alice, of course, what?"

"Do you know who your biological father is?" Her humungous cheeks seemed to drop.

"No. We don't have any interest. There were important instances when he should have shown up. Either he doesn't care, or he is dead." Cate took a black scarf and tried it on.

"I'm sorry. But tell me about Kanio. Why do you think he is nice?" Alice put on a hat that looked like a pumpkin.

"Don't you think it's too much?" She poked the hat.

"Oh, it's not." Alice smirked sideways. "So what is it about him, and don't say it's because he sent you the Whisper Z. Those work with a private satellite. I'm a little jealous," Alice added.

"He took me on a turbo-boat ride the other day; we went to see the 'sunken lady,' he called it," Cate said.

"You? Water? There has to be something else."

"He acknowledges me," Cate admitted.

Alice smiled. "When was the last time you got a facial?"

"I've never..."

"Let's go!" Alice hugged her.

Cate entered her apartment carrying more bags than she should. A few fell from her arms just as she crossed the door. Her band was beaming, *'Incoming Holo Turnfelf.'*

"Accept," she said.

A shadow of blue sprinkles was in the middle of the room.

Should I be mad? Kate wondered. *This is a little too invasive.*

"How is Miss Park?" he asked.

"Kanio?"

A few seconds passed and the hologram of his entire figure became clear.

"The image breaks a lot." Cate paced into her living room.

"The building's blueprint was outdated; the system couldn't find all of the coordinates," he said. "Do you need more books? Information?" His right arm pushed air to one side. His left hand's fingers kept screwing something.

"No, please. I've had enough for a while. I like the ones about Larios. How the cells enhance with air. "

"If you need help with any interpretation, you can always ask us, or your Ereo."

"How do I reach you?" she asked.

"You have to call Central first, or you need the Zoun," he said.

"So you can speak in my head when you wish? No thanks," she said.

He laughed.

"What are you doing?" she asked.

"I'm reviewing some saline levels," he said.

She opened the bags and started checking her purchases. She actually got something in a color. Blush.

"I spoke with your Dean. He left for Venus; he said that because of your absence, he had to go. He was polite. He asked me if I wanted to join the next time."

"Good," she said.

He pushed the air to his right with both of his palms. His image became clear.

"Tell me about Alex Harlow." He took a step closer to her.

She stood up. "I don't like him; I still can't believe what he did." She clenched her fists. *I hate Alex, but okay, less erratic,* she thought. "Alex. He was very close to us, to all of us, I mean; he was the closest to a brother I've ever had..."

"No. No. Is it true that he kind of saved the Alliance?"

Kate moved her head in denial. *Why do I bother?*

"What was it with that scandal with Agrippa, and the father of your boyfriend, Mountdragon?"

"Don't mention ever again that he is my boyfriend," Cate said.

"Never again. So?"

"Well, this is Victoria's version. Which is very close to reality."

"Go on," he said.

"Years ago, Alex and some other members of his party discovered that other senators—from all parties— together with executives from Agrippa Corp., the company that manages the Quartz tubes and the Reflector Panels for the Shield..."

"Mountdragon?"

"Yes." She nodded.

"Essentially, they agreed to build the case for more tubes than was really necessary. In certain zones of the NAA. The poorest zones. The scandal was nicknamed Agrippagate. Alex was in his early thirties and it was his first term as senator, but under the circumstances he ended up heading up the Committee on Banking and Housing."

"Interesting. Why him?

"I guess he had a familiar face; his father Arthur has been working in the NAA all of his life. There are pictures of Alex as a child, standing right behind Arthur when he gave his acceptance speech as New Governor for the New East. And you know how important the New East is."

"And then Alex became known worldwide."

"So, while in Banking and Housing, he was the one who gave the major push for all of the housing reconstruction in California in the New Sierra. Among other reconstructions. This was a game changer. The East and West were so far apart back then that no news channel was tracking how long the Kansas sandstorms were lasting in the New Sands; there was no interest in crossing the country anymore. The image of Alex giving away new homes to people far away, on the other coast, symbolized the reason why the Alliance was created in the first place," Cate explained. "But this is public info; what do you want to know."

"If things would have ended differently with your sister, would you still trust him?"

"I don't know. You have to ask someone else," she said. She leaned on the window, looking outside.

"I don't know anyone else here; you are one of us— you are the closest I have," he said.

We are close?

Cate sat down.

"I'm always coming to you. You can visit too," Kanio said.

"You are always busy solving the world's problems; you saw me yesterday and just waved."

"I was busy."

"What is going on with Victoria?" she asked. "Why is everyone out and not her? I feel bad, having a normal life." She pushed the bags away.

"In the Universal Law, what she did is inadmissible. And I'm giving her a way out, if she comes out with who backed her and her adventure."

"Alex probably backed her, Patrick, who knows who else."

"No. She contacted someone from where I am from."

"How do you know?"

"I just know." He wrinkled his nose.

"Trust me, and I'll trust you,"

He sighed.

"There is something that we just found out. And that will delay your sister's release."

"What?"

"There is a person—and Alliafied—who recently escaped being transferred from one prison to another. We inspected his cells, all of his tracks, accomplices, and in the documents we could recover, he was aware about a golden Alliafied taking control of Earth in his name. Golden? Alliafied? Do you know of another one?"

Cate didn't know what to say. Hard to find an argument.

"It has to be a coincidence," Cate said. *How can I defend this?*

"I know. But when your sister's event was announced at the Centarkof, a few didn't act surprised, and said that the Rule wasn't working. This is bigger than your sister and McCully. Yet she insists she knows nothing. Do you believe that?" Kanio pushed some air to the left.

Nothing? Victoria? She remained quiet. "I don't know, really," she said.

"Then I don't know really when she is going to leave the Island. I have to go." He disappeared.

Cate snorted. *Damn it, Victoria!*

She heard some noise. "Oh no!" She had left Coper inside the room. "Oh! Come out! Come out!" The puppy came out, all moody, and went into the kitchen.

She went back to the couch and crossed her arms. *Victoria, Alex, the Panels; what is really going on?*

She grabbed a tablet, "Search Steban Weelah, Joanna Park, Zafor."

"There is nothing with the combination of those three words," Core said.

"You won't tell him the things I'm searching for, right?" she asked.

"No," the Ereo said to her left.

"Larios, Phima, whatever. Core: Find SZ SkyShot composition."

"Unavailable," Core said. A series of links appeared with suggestions and guesses about the secret formula.

"Read number 2."

"Zafor is not believed to be lethal, but it is believed that large amounts would create a series of allergic reactions and side effects."

"Number of deaths?" Cate asked.

"Zero."

"Number of people affected with side effects?" Cate asked again.

"Unavailable."

"Side effects?"

"Unavailable."

"What is the alternative?"

"Unavailable."

*****

Two light-green metal Phelaries were playing on the green lawn; a square purple ring was displayed right below the large ivory staircase. A big crowd of Phelaries and humans were cheering on their champion. It was nice to see different color guards feeling relaxed.

"Is this a fight or a game?" Cate asked.

"They are Leeve 2, like me," Victoria explained to Cate. They were watching from a balcony to the right arm of the stairs. Both were alliafied, surrounded by Phelaries. The human guards were mostly on the other side. Victoria had on a black bracelet that tracked her steps and didn't let her go above the building's third floor.

"Where is he?" Cate asked.

"Whom?"

"Kanio."

"I don't know," Victoria said. "I can't care less."

On the ring, one of the Phelaries swung his leg, tackled the other one, and pushed him into the ground. They stood up. The crowd applauded. In between the guards, the purple man went down the stairs. The Phelaries began clapping and whistling.

"He is supposed to control gravity; he doesn't control light or particles like Kanio, so let's see what he can do," Victoria said.

Like me, Cate thought. "How did he capture you?"

"He seized my wrist and then pulled me into a helo, and then he took me to that ship. So humiliating." Victoria twisted his lips sideways.

The two Phelaries stood side by side and walked toward Nnox. Their hands were covered by green flowing dust. When they were at a certain distance,

Nnox crossed his arms on the air and both men flew back. The crowd cheered.

"Let's go inside," Victoria said. "I'm allowed in the Cafeteria; it must be empty now."

"Why don't you help them? There is a document that mentions you, from where he is from."

"What document?"

"Kanio said that someone from where he is from talked about a golden Alliafied taking control of Earth, supposedly before you did this."

"That is awkward." Victoria rubbed her chin.

"I want to ask you something. Do you know who our father is?" Cate asked Victoria. They went up to the second floor. Humans stared at them. They unalliafied.

"Rogers put me in contact with him. His name is Tykan Grage. You always said you never wanted to hear about him. I just followed. I'm sorry."

They went to the coffee machines. "Take this." Victoria grabbed a silicone mug, filled it with coffee, and gave it to Cate.

"Is he like us?" Cate took a sip and burnt her lip. "Ouch!"

"Yes. Do you want to know more?"

"No, it will be another disappointment," Cate said.

All these years, all of my struggles, he doesn't care.

"I'm sorry, Cate. There is not much to tell, really."

"I have to go. There is another storm tonight. I'm meeting Francis before that. I want to know what the deal is with the formula in the BAM." Cate pressed her cheek against her sister's.

"He won't help you. No one knows who knows."

"Do you think Alice's mom may know something?"

"What do you want to know?" Victoria asked.

"Why is it important?"

"Who cares about the formula and the Panels. I need to get out," Victoria complained.

"Do you want me to help you escape? Maybe Rogers can help."

"No, and I think those two would bring me back in again. Go, Cate; say hi to Francis."

CHAPTER 19

....

THE PAIRS

Cate drove back home later in the afternoon. She went straight to the parking complex; earlier was better, given the anticipated demand due to the upcoming storm. She received a message from the building that someone was waiting for her; a blurry image on her wristband. *Oh, Francis! Always early, and me...always late.*

"Text Francis G: Be there soon." She walked faster. There were guards every two corners, sending people to their homes. She alliafied, with the sole purpose of avoiding them; it worked, and she kept going without stopping. One of the few privileges of being immensely different. It was a weird combination of blue fog and gray wind. And then, at a certain distance, she saw her building entry, a blue vehicle, and a man standing by it.

"Where have you been? No one has seen you in like a week," Cate asked impatiently.

"I just landed. I had to go to my Ryder up there," Kanio said, he lifted his chin. Unalliafied and no cape. That was probably why the image looked confusing.

"What else did you find out about Alex?" she asked.

"It's not relevant. This time, I want to know about you, only you," Kanio said.

Cate looked at him and tried to find the right answer. He pulled her arm. "Come on. We'll take my Helo-Ryder."

"A real storm is coming," she said.

He alliafied. His palms opened up. "That is not a problem, to us."

Cate and Kanio jumped into the capsule vehicle. Cate sat behind. Ice began to fall on them, but it dissolved when it touched the veil surrounding the vehicle. He drove to Manhattan Bridge—one of the bridges that connected the Island to Brooklyn—and stopped almost in the center of its bikeway. The view was surreally perfect. Hazy. Tall buildings disguised as lighthouses. Spotlights diverging around them. They both shined and supported their elbows on the metallic structure. The river had waves of its own. Sometimes the water reached high enough that it splashed over the bridge barrier. It was hard to visualize, but the roaring sound of the waves colliding into one another meant that the Island protection blockades had been lifted up.

"I found out I like fish. And apples, strangely, green apples." He seemed thoughtful, regarding this revelation. He looked down at her. "So, you?"

"I like them red."

"Interesting. And I thought your life was mainly centered around the brown worm." he smiled wickedly.

"And you can make jokes." She smirked back. "Well, so, um, I was born on Europa, Jupiter's most famous moon. Came to Earth for the very first time at eight. Became an Alliafied at seventeen. Spent the year after on Earth's only moon. Then I locked myself in college during the week, and in these streets during the weekends." She indicated Manhattan with her head.

The bridge was tumbling. The wind turned stronger.

"We should jump, and then climb up," he said. He grabbed the barrier and looked down.

"Not happening." Cate walked backward.

He laughed.

"How is it growing up as the famous Steban Weelah's daughter?"

"You do know my biological father is not him?" she responded.

He nodded.

But yes, I'm Steban Weelah's daughter.

"In any case, not that fun." She shook her head. "You have this stupid idea that he has done so much for everyone's regular life. The entire world idolizes him so you feel you do too. But honestly, I am not sure what he has done for me besides creating that Shield. As a father, Steban can be cold and sometimes apathetic."

She shrugged her right shoulder. Kanio stared at her quietly and then shrugged his right shoulder too.

"And then there is Paula. She was not bad. She was just not enough. I wanted more. I know Victoria did her best, but she also needed her." She walked closer to the barrier.

"Her?"

"My mother," Cate said. "She died; I never met her. You know," she grabbed the barrier strongly and looked up to the sky, "I was told that she was up there, in heaven. And I foolishly thought Paula meant *space*. Paula kept pointing out there, somewhere." She pointed up to the sky. He stared motionless. She continued, "When we were traveling here, in the beginning, I was so excited. The few moments I was awake, I watched everywhere; I was glued to the window. Never found her. I thought I might have seen her floating like a fairy. Don't know. In any case, we got to Earth, and then Paula revealed to me that heaven was not what I knew as space. It took me a while to understand."

"Seems that hurt you. Is this Paula a good person?"

"She is; she is, indeed—and Steban is as well. I shouldn't have said what I said before," Cate She rethought her words, but again, she still kind of thought the same. Her father's latest actions were another instance of the usual attitudes she had experienced so far.

"Catherine Weelah, if it helps you, you are describing an average Phelarie father," he said.

"I'm not an average person, Kanio from Turnfeld," she said back.

"No, you are not." He grabbed her wrist and pulled her closer.

Is he flirting with me? This is so confusing, she thought.

"Do you know who your father is?" he asked.

"No, do you?"

"There is a Lario Leeve 4 who visited Titan several times..."

"I don't want to know. I'm fine with whom I have right now." She sighed. "Do you have people with you? Like relatives—friends."

"It's not relevant, but..."

Not again... He says relevant again and I'll throw myself into the river.

"What is it?" He looked surprised.

"Nothing; you were saying," she said.

"Well, hmm—there is my father, who is known as the Khun." He moved away from the bridge barrier.

"Of course; how convenient."

He immediately turned back to her, lowered his eyebrows, and came back to her side.

"My Ereo," he added. He swung his head side to side.

"Friends?" she specified. *Is he around, all alone? The purple clown and the air-man?*

"It is strange. I cannot find a correct translation for friendship," Kanio said. "What is friendship to you?"

"A sentiment, a bond?" Cate said.

"It is your Onerian word; what does true friendship mean to you?"

Cate laughed to herself.

"Yes, it's tricky. I guess it is an emotional bond. And my real friends are those whom I feel safe with. I also think I don't have many friends," she explained.

Two, three, and the air-man...maybe, who else?

"Me neither. But add me to your list: I think you are safe with me," he said. He supported his back on the barrier. His blue shine irradiated more, almost two inches of blue mist around him.

She wanted to believe it, yet she still couldn't completely. There were many reasons why she should be distrustful of him right now. *The come and go. Victoria retained in that purple island, or ship; everything looks purple these days.*

"My friends would be Nnox, whom you know; a few others—and I have a laiko," the Aekiou continued.

"A laiko?"

"His name is Raushed. It is like a pet, but a very special kind of pet," he said proudly.

"Coper is very special! You just haven't seen him in action." She tried to build the irony.

"The yellow doormat, in action?"

"Oh! That is so mean!"

"Maybe one day you will prove me wrong," he added.

"Kanio, do you still like having me around?" Cate asked.

"Yes, of course," he said.

Then where have you been? She wished she could say that out loud.

"Do you feel the same way?" he asked her.

"Probably, yes," she said. *I have felt more alive in the recent weeks than...ever,* she thought.

Cate had surrendered to the fact that her life would remain in an insipid phase for the rest of her days. Although she understood that it was the wrong part of her human essence—the one that was dragging her down—she didn't fight back. It might have been because of unapologetic indifference, laziness, or frustration against failure; she never knew.

She chose obliviousness and self-inflicted ignorance; yet she underestimated hypocrisy, and didn't consider the weight of indifference's counterplay when she was cast away. Perhaps she was too selfish—and she deserved being segregated, anyway.

"Do you think I'm selfish?" Cate asked.

"I think you are cute." He stood in front of her.

"Cute? *Coper* is cute," she said.

"Sweet, then? Might be translation," he clarified. "You are funny sometimes."

But why is he doing this? And he wants to jump from the bridge...

The sound of the river's waves calmed down.

"We will release your sister. I'm convincing the Centarkof that she was just a pawn in the human show, and about that file," he paused, "that she probably was a pawn too."

"Thanks," she said. This time he was the one who brought up the subject of Victoria, which might have been a good sign.

"And I would like you to come to a station with me, next week; I want you to be more involved in what we are doing here, there, everywhere," Kanio said.

"I can't. I have stuff to do, which includes visiting my sister and making sure she is okay until you release her. Plus I need to work in FoxStone for the next expedition," she added. "I can't believe they haven't fired me."

"Because you are an Alliafied. They are privileged to have you around. Come with me. We have to change the current tubes. There is too much damage on Earth's crust. I want you to see how we do it. And I want to go to Antarctica after," Kanio said.

"There is mostly nothing left. Most of what you see is artificial," Cate assured him.

"Maybe Nnox can take care of your expedition," Kanio said.

"I don't think he would be the most appropriate. It involves dealing with other people."

"We will have to find someone else," Kanio said.

They both discussed her college life for a while longer, and he compared it with his life on Phelio, growing up with Nnox and the others.

"I think Victoria dislikes him." Cate laughed.

"I don't think he would care; she isn't the only one, for sure," he simply explained.

"How come he gave you your first punch?"

"I was still deciphering how this thing works, so I just let him. His strength is different than ours; it relies more on his pair than ours—but do not underestimate it; it is quite deceiving indeed." He decreased the tone of his voice.

"Pair?" she asked.

Kanio remained quiet for a while and circled the path. A blue haze followed his route. "Cate, there is something you need to know." His sight was intense. "Listen. The pairs." He took a step back and looked up to the sky. He swung his right palm and a string of light was shot up to the sky, half blue, half silver, kind of electric, kind of fiery.

"Give me your hand," he asked.

She gave it to him, and repeated the swing. This time it was not a string, but a thick thunder of the same substance that went up into the sky. Half blue; some orange. Sparkles fell. She felt her blood warmer and her pulse speeded up. He released her hand.

"We Alliafied work better in pairs; our energy enhances, and we can pick sensors and molecules from the other. Always have a pair; be close, mentally and physically."

"Like Victoria?" she said.

"No, it would be more appropriate to have someone from a higher Leeve. Like yours. This is not a blood-related bond or true friendship—you have to match; you have to trust. The right pair will have an impact on the gravitational attraction between the elements that you manage. It is important," Kanio insisted. He looked to the other side. "If you are alone...it's not good to be alone."

"I see. You sound worried," Cate said. *I've never seen him like this before.*

"Because it's not good to be alone."

"But you are not. I'm here; Nnox is close by," she added.

"But someone is. Colt. He is one of my closest Alliafied. We were all trained together. His pair got old and distracted. We think he was poisoned. The Khun is aiming for Colt's pair to recover, but he will be alone in the meantime, and that is not good; there are beings out there that do not like us," Kanio confessed.

"Send Nnox to him," Cate said.

"Nnox is mine; I am his. Plus, it is the Khun's decision, and we do not interfere with that," Kanio said. "No one can."

"Why is the Khun so important?"

"He is Protector of the Law, and responsible for our purpose being achieved."

"What purpose?"

"Our purpose is to regulate, protect. We do rule, but our decisions are supported by consensus. And we guarantee that these decisions take place. We can, because we are Alliafied. Unbeatable and incorruptible," Kanio continued.

"But you must do something."

He grabbed both of her wrists.

"We must do something, you and I, but we must wait for now. Will you come with me to Pirthee, in Phelio? When the time comes," Kanio asked.

"What? No, I can't!" Cate exclaimed. A few moments before, he was mentioning a visit to Antarctica; and now he wanted her to go all the way out of the Milky Way.

"Why? What ties do you have here? A hypocrite society that rejected you until I forbade it? Cate, there is nothing here for you."

What is he talking about? Cate couldn't believe what she was listening to. She pushed him away.

"You have no family. You have no friends. We will be better for you," Kanio kept going.

That is mean. I'm not really alone. Not that alone.

She took a step back.

"Kanio, you never say 'please,' or 'sorry.'"

"We don't have them in our vocabulary. Same goes for 'thanks.' And it is not relevant."

"It is. They are. They give special meaning to what we say, to what we mean."

"Cate, I mean what I say; I do not need to put flowers in my sentences. I want you by..."

"Kanio, my place is here, with my low-level sister and my useless dog—that is we for me right now," she said, "and probably your place is with Nnox and with that friend of yours that you are leaving behind."

She waved her hand and took off. *It's true; I feel more alive than ever, but not safe enough.*

maria beta

.

CHAPTER 20

···

AN ANGEL FROM HEAVEN

The mellow black curtain turned into a solid rock after Kanio crossed into the Kof. The panoramic glass showed the green lawn covered by three inches of opaque blue snow from the previous night's storm. Still, some light-blue flakes managed to fall from the gray sky.

Nnox, always alliafied, lifted his head from his concentration state. He had been putting some plastic pieces together.

"How much longer do we need to be here?" Kanio asked. He sat at the table, staring at the dark-grayish scenery.

"I've sorted out winters. I need time for summers. You don't want them to evaporate in the transition; I want to be here by the beginning of summer in the north," Nnox explained.

"Seu. You have to make sure the adjustments we made in the south are not too drastic for the north," Kanio said.

"That is called biased evolution," Nnox added, leaving whatever he had been doing.

Kanio shook his head and walked along the long table.

"How are the negotiations going?" Nnox continued. He picked up a plastic piece from the table.

"Alex understands and agrees, and I committed to back him in anything to get it achieved. We will do an entire American Alliance, and people will migrate to the south or the north; the center will be gone," Kanio responded. "The point will be an adequate transition that doesn't translate into populations migrating only to the north. Are you still wasting your time with this park thing?" Kanio engaged in the game with his friend. *Toys? For adults?*

"You see, this is an Onerian hospital. Victoria recommended it." Nnox gave him a plastic piece that looked like a little man with a red cross on his white hat.

"And it is you whom I've entrusted with my life, oh, so many times..." Kanio gave him the toy back. "Does that mean you got closer to her?" Kanio asked.

"No." Nnox left the pieces by the game. He walked away. "I have met with her a few times. She has become more communicative. She says that she has no big name behind her, that anything she would say wouldn't be of major help—also, that we cannot hold her there forever. She said that she managed to send a message to the Khun Kof and the U4 Centarkof."

"She has sent nothing, but someone did. The Khun said that I have to let her go."

"But we have the records: chaos in Brogio, and a golden Alliafied in Onerio. They are dated before this happened," Nnox added.

"But it is not enough," Kanio said. "He did not say when, but he did say soon," he added.

"Soon is relative." Nnox laughed. "Listen, leave this nitrogen dump when you think it's time; I'll stay here longer. I have Rogers if it is necessary. Also, the Khun needs you close to him." Nnox got closer to him and continued, "The golden Alliafied out of control. Colt and Angot divided in Brogio. Angot is hopelessly bedridden; we don't know if he will make it. This could be only the beginning. We need to gather ourselves, Alliafied, and be aligned," Nnox said.

"Time has passed since the last rebellion; my father is not sure how many of us he can really rely on," Kanio said.

"When I say gather and align, that also includes Cate," Nnox added.

"I know. But her mood switches when anything sensitive arises. Her tolerance is low; when in conflict, she shields away. It is not easy to reach an agreement with her." He was overwhelmed. "And I do like her," Kanio confessed.

"I know you do. When she is around, or you talk about her, you have a good mood. You didn't even have a mood before." Nnox went back to the game.

"I connected with her yesterday," Kanio said.

"I saw it; everyone in the New East did," Nnox joked. "I mean, several news channels covered it."

News? What? he wondered. "We should have brought her in sooner." He took a chair and sat, not interested in what everyone else thought.

"We were told to stay away; even the Mirabele offered to adopt her, but the Khun rejected the idea," Nnox added. The Mirabele were a powerful Lario family; their two daughters were very special. Cala, one of Kanio's closest Alliafied, smart and trustful, but stubborn and territorial; and Iria, easygoing and cheerful, but unreliable and crazy.

"She spoke about her mother. I knew she was dead. She does embrace the grief; humans evidently have a different attitude toward the long-gone ones," Kanio continued.

"She probably was waiting for you to ask. But I am sure that, as always, you were successful in avoiding the conversation about feelings—and, of course, about parents," Nnox said.

What else could I have said?

Avoidance had been the attitude he had seen regarding both of his (for different reasons) well-known parents. He'd put in his mind the target of making it up to her, somehow, someday; but this was one of the things that Phelaries, especially Thendors, found hard to understand about life. The moment. For them, stars could be aligned from time to time—someday, somehow, all the time.

"It is curious that besides Cate there is another being extremely heavy in hydrogen," Nnox said.

"Eh?"

"Your mother."

"What is curious about that?" Kanio reacted instantly.

"Humans call it Edipo's Syndrome."

"We don't talk about her." Kanio stood up and walked to the panoramic window.

"Well then, it also reminds me of Olto and Zela-ya. Just that Olto couldn't manage oxygen as you do." Nnox referred to the father and mother of the Phelarie culture. Both lived like plasma. He was white; she was black. Olto was almost pure metallic hydrogen, and Zelaya almost pure carbon.

"I'll never be like Olto." Kanio sat at the table. "People will remember me for getting lost with you for two quortos in the sands of Yaguora." Kanio, once again, successfully switched from the subject of his parents.

"No, people will remember you for connecting yourself with others and for not putting a shield of metal between you and them—like your father the Khun does," Nnox said. He grabbed a few pieces of Titcher Park and melted them in his hand.

"We will see," Kanio said.

"So, when are we releasing Victoria? It's true. I don't think she will end up saying anything relevant to us."

"She stays with you for a little longer," Kanio said.

"And Cate?"

"It's too late; she doesn't want to join me or learn more. She'd better stay here with her Leeve 2 sister and that golden worm. Avoid her," Kanio said.

*****

"I saw you! A gossip column posted a picture of you in the middle of the storm on a bridge. Was it the Brooklyn Bridge?" Alice said when Cate called her.

"Manhattan."

Cate lay on her bed, in black fluffy pants and her FoxStone pullover.

"Literally it was a blue and silver dot, nothing more, with the headline: An angel from hell and an angel from heaven," Alice said.

"Why am I still the bad character in all this?" She kicked her bed with her heels.

"Well, my mother said that in general people like him. But I got the impression she doesn't like him. They had a few meetings together."

"Your mother doesn't like anyone, Alice; what did she say the others say?"

"That Kanio doesn't pretend to be anyone's close friend; he maintains a distance but he does make an approach—an effort," Alice said. "That is what the column also said. I still can't believe he went to your house and picked you up!"

"It's not the first time. I am like him; it kind of makes sense he reaches out to me, despite how everyone else sees him as a god, and I'm still the girl that was that night out of control. Why is that?"

"I don't know. I guess because he arrived on Earth in a purple spacecraft, and you drive around in a standard green Triton." Alice laughed.

"Makes sense. Do you think I can see your mother this week?" Cate asked.

"Oh, I know she is very busy and she is not receiving anyone. But I'll ask," Alice said.

"Great. Gotta go; I'm meeting Francis. I stood him up last night."

"Oh, Cate, well, dinner next week. Bye!"

Cate pressed the Whisper on her ear and took it off.

An hour later, she met Francis for breakfast a few blocks from her house.

"Yes, it is almost a fact; Alex will become the next Prime Minister," he said. He offered her a croissant from his basket. It smelled like butter.

She took it and put some chocolate cream on it. The cream was frozen and didn't slide well.

"It is so annoying that after all my sister is going through, Alex is the official winner in this situation," Cate complained.

"Cate, he already said openly that despite the polls, as soon as he has the power he will get her out and give her an absolute pardon. He is not a bad person."

"What polls?" she asked.

"The government conducted a poll," Francis said.

Oh, that poll...

Besides New South, New East, and two other New Houses, the results were undecided about the future of the golden Alliafied. Before the coup no one knew her in New Cascades, New Forest or in the New West.

"He left my sister over nothing. You stayed with me, close, always, no matter what," she exclaimed.

"But I wasn't on my way to be the next Prime Minister. It is hard to judge."

Cate avoided his sight. The coffee was bad. "In any case, can you give me a lift to the Union? I want to go see my sister, and I want to talk to Kanio specifically about her release. Last night we couldn't define anything about it. I assume you also know about the Manhattan Bridge."

He sipped his espresso and pressed his band on the check-reader tab on the table.

"My father appreciates him. He says he gets straight to the point. He hasn't asked for anything related to the Treasury Department yet, so there has been no reason for me to meet him." Francis stood up as well and took a final sip.

"Yes, he has a way with words; it takes a little to swallow them correctly." Cate smiled.

Francis didn't say much more, but took her to Atlantic Island.

Once at the Union, Cate went directly to the purple vessel, and on her way to Victoria's room, she crossed words with the purple ship's owner.

"Good morning, Angel of Hell," Nnox greeted her.

"Don't tell me you read local gossip as well." Cate sounded mad but she was not.

"Why not?" he said.

"You are not funny," she said.

"If it helps you, Kanio doesn't read it," Nnox continued, walking.

"Why is he from heaven and I am from hell?" Cate raised her voice.

"Bye, Cate. Do not pay attention to it," Nnox said.

"Where is he?"

"At the Kof," he said from afar and soon he was gone.

Cate visited Victoria. The Phelaries had recreated a mini movie theater and set up a big white couch. They had watched a movie and had pizza for lunch. By the end of the film, Cate's side of the couch was completely marked by tomato sauce stains. Of course, her older sister had also read the gossip column and thought it was funny.

"So, he told you to go to Phelio? That's surprising. Was it his idea, or the Khun's?" Victoria asked Cate.

"Well, he gave me arguments for not staying here, but none to go there with him. I can't imagine going beyond Europa."

"Yet you always wanted to go far."

"Just not that far." Cate stood up. "Why do I have to choose? It's not like he is leaving now."

I'm finally on my feet; I don't want to go away.

"Don't think about it. Go home and rest; I do know you went home late last night," Victoria said.

"As everybody else does." Cate shook her head.

Cate made her way out and discerned a peachy Phelarie walking up to the ship. "Is the Aekiou still in the Kof?"

"No, he left," he responded.

"Is he here?" Cate smiled at him, trying to come across as friendly.

"No, he is not. You should leave now."

"Thanks for the pizza."

"Too salty." He kept walking and left her talking to herself.

Where could Kanio be? she wondered.

Despite the confusion and the gossip column, she couldn't wait to see Kanio again. She went back to the ivory building in one of those small approaching cars, and while going up into the building, she saw Kanio coming downstairs on the other side. She raised her Leeve and waved at him. He kept going down.

"I thought you knew him," Francis said.

This is very annoying. She swallowed her saliva.

"Come on; let me take you home," the French blonde said.

Something was wrong; maybe it was just nonsense paranoia. She used the Whisper band to connect to Central and asked to talk to him; the answer was 'UN-AVAILABLE.' As soon as she entered her apartment—as soon as the door closed behind her—she called out to her Ereo: "Ereo! Hi!" The Ereo appeared in front of her, and in front of the repaired window; he had no reflection, even though every other piece of her living room did on this dark night.

"Please ask Kanio where he is. Did he see me? I want to see him tomorrow, or before he leaves for the Stations," Cate begged him.

"Cate, I am not a communication device."

"You must, please," she insisted.

Why? Why? Why? she tortured her mind. Maybe I should go with him to the Stations.

"Wait." The Ereo disappeared for a minute. "Cate, he is busy; I am sorry," he said.

"I just want a when."

"There is something else," he said, looking straight out of the window, as if she wasn't there.

"What?"

"I will not be able to come visit you anymore."

The Ereo was gone.

"I don't understand. Is it your decision? Is it his?" Cate said out loud in the empty apartment. "You said I'll never be alone again. Ereo? Ereo?" She waited for a few minutes for an answer. She looked outside without being able to fix her sight. She sat on the living room couch; her nose was warm and dry. She grabbed Coper and scratched his stomach, trying to hide some tears from him and from herself. She kept waiting.

How could he?

maria beta

CHAPTER 21.1

....

ANGOT FIRAKEM

The room was dark. The walls were made of blocks of gray stone. An old man rested on a white bed—he looked pale, demolished. Blue tubes had been inserted into his arms, and two round screens hovered behind the bed. Angot had lived more than two centuries, but until the last Phelarie cycle, his health had been spotless. He had always beaten Colt, his pair, when it came to sport duties. The thought of those hunting days in Brogio's dark forest, beneath the thick blue ocean of the planet, was giving him strength, and the thought of his daughter Ahlora back in Phelio was keeping him alive.

He was asked by the Khun to remain on the planet Brogio after he helped to build the atmosphere sanitation process, and he had stayed here for almost twenty cycles. Colt was his third pair; the previous one didn't deal well with too much nature. Colt arrived on Brogio by mistake, as Nnox would say, only just two cycles before; and he didn't become his disciple, but his partner. Angot knew he was the one who was supposed to leave first, but never this soon. Right after he began having the poison symptoms, he was told he would recover quickly; yet his condition had worsened during the last two rotations of Gyo, Brogio's shiniest moon.

Two Phelarie guards were standing in the back of the room. An explosion was heard from outside. They turned around. Another explosion erupted, closer, almost inside. The dark brown doors were blown into a hundred pieces, toward the room. Through the brownish smoke, a giant crystal sphere entered the room and someone jumped out of it. Pale white, thin skin, dark veins, still in unfastened white robes; greasy long black hair stuck to the side of his face—he had the appearance of one who hadn't seen light in tens of cycles, because he hadn't.

One of the two guards jumped backward, to where a silver suit was opening, ready to absorb him. The helmet moved from the back forward, to cover his face. He flew over Angot. The second guard moved back and opened her right hand, where a clear rectangle expanded. She spoke to her palm and then turned it around.

The greasy man moved his hand from left to right, pushing the particles in the air to the first fighter close to him. The silver fighter evaporated. The second female guard pressed the clear rectangle on her left wrist and moved backward, looking for her suit. She looked at Angot, but he shook his head. He was too weak. He couldn't alliafy. He heard the terrifying laughter approaching.

*****

"I have been trying to meet with you for days. I don't have patience like Kanio," purple Nnox addressed copper Juveo Rogers.

Nnox was sitting at an oval table in one of the rooms of his Ryder's top floor. He'd invited Juveo to sit with him when he arrived on Earth, but Juveo somehow never acknowledged the request until now.

"Probably because of that, you are not the Aekiou," Juveo replied back. He took his hat off his head. He walked slowly into the purple room, his sight hooked on the gray display above. Juveo had this special manner that seemed like he was never really there.

"What is it with the Onerian suit and hat?"

"I got used to it. I'm a Balio; I adapt well." He blinked. "Not only physically."

"You were supposed to be in control of the planet, and the Weelahs. Who is Victoria talking to?" Nnox stood up and joined him.

"No one that I'm aware of; I have always been her contact for Phelio." He remained looking above, probably at nothing.

"Did she tell you that she was going to expose herself the way she did?" Nnox inquired. He faced Rogers.

"No," Juveo said.

"Who is her father?" Nnox kept asking.

Rogers lowered his head and looked straight at Nnox. "You have no authorization to ask that, or to make me answer to you. Nnox, you are smarter than this," Juveo continued.

"You see, this is not me, Rogers—it is Kanio. He shall be back tomorrow, and you will have to respond to him. He *does* have the authorization," Nnox said. He kept his distance. "In the meantime, you can't leave Onerio. You are not requested to join Colt at Brogio. We and the Khun are confidant Angot will recover soon. And you will be here, stuck with me."

"Poisoned, right? How do you get poisoned these days?" Juveo went back to look at the cloudy day outside.

"I am sure I have been poisoned a couple of times. I have to go; you know your way out." Nnox left the room. It was pointless. Nnox had always felt that Juveo and his generation behaved like they were above the young Aekiou and his half-Asfeolio pair—they always went straight to the Khun and Karakel, as if the sapphire-blue Alliafied didn't exist. Kanio kept telling him to let it go; they were all Leeve 3, and that it was not relevant. His father had wanted to incorporate them as well in the ruling coalition, and it had worked. More systems had joined. The rule had expanded. A clear line now divided who wanted to live by it and who didn't. And Phelio was the epicenter of its mandate.

maria beta

CHAPTER 21.2

....

COLT BEHAR

Colt Behar hated to alliafy. But lately, given Angot's sudden sickness, it had been suggested that he should do it more often—practically always—and that was the advice he had been following closely. But not today. Today, they were celebrating his arrival on Brogio two cycles before. He'd accompanied Kanio, the Aekiou, to help in the relief efforts after a series of tsunamis had intermittently hit Starz Island.

The room was crowded. Some were seated; some were mingling around. There was a buzz from the mix of everyone's conversation. The large room was built from blocks of beige stones and, in front of him, Colt saw the second sunset of the day. The millennial fortress resided on the top of an angular cliff. He was sitting at the head of the table, together with representatives of all of the ruling tribes of the planet. The seat in front of him was empty. Angot should be there—or should he be with Angot? *Will I stay on Brogio if Angot dies?* he thought.

He wanted to postpone the celebration, but the Dellhus had said that the planets and the moons were changing faster than normal in this season, the tides had become thicker already, and soon they wouldn't be able to leave from their hidden lands in the deepness of the ocean. Colt, as Angot, appreciated the Dellhus so much that he couldn't say no to them. The short and muscular green creatures didn't get invited to many events.

His wristlet became warm and tightened; a rectangle popped up, and it was Angot's guard's face.

"Colt! Run!" she said. The image switched; it was Angot in his bed, and behind him, a man he knew but he couldn't remember well. "They are here." She ended the message.

It's been so long. What is he doing here?

He looked sideways; there was no one to trust. He felt his blood flow coming up to his chest, his heart pounding.

"How many cycles more do you think you'll stay?" A pale yellow-skinned man to his right asked.

He stood up and alliafied. Metal green, as emerald was his major component. Silence; everyone looked paralyzed. He looked right, and beyond the windows were three Dunners on the way. Colt jumped on the table, ran, jumped through the large window at the end of the room, and fell onto a terrace that converged into an esplanade. Fast. He kept running until the end. He slid down from the stone wall, pushing his legs inward, until he was some five feet below the balcony. He held tight to the stones. He punched the wall once and it cracked. He punched it again, and a hole large enough to fit him opened up. The Dunners were turning vertical, as they were ready to stop and disembark on the terrace. He went into a basement, where his silver Z-Zella jet was. There was no time to spare, he had no pair, and he knew that even at Leeve 4 he would not be strong enough. He didn't have time to analyze the situation any more. He climbed quickly into the cockpit. He shot the stone wall in front of him, not even realizing if it had shattered or not, and between the ashes he flew away. From a small screen to his right he could see the entire terrace falling apart behind him. "Kanio, I hope you get this..."

"Communication network has been corrupted," the Zella system interrupted him.

He accelerated toward the horizon.

maria beta

CHAPTER 22

....

DC

Cate arrived at the Eagle Station in Washington DC at around 9 a.m. Marcus was waiting for her. "Long time, ha!" she said.

"Good morning," he said.

He walked her to a Black Oceanic and opened the door for her.

"Good morning, Cate," Patrick greeted her. "Come in. Always happy to see you."

"This is a surprise." She kissed his cheeks.

"I can only take you close to the building. I have to be a certain distance away from all governmental buildings." He tapped his Whisper band. "But I got you a meeting with Rogers. And clearance for two hours."

"Clearance?"

"Walk around, go to the Cafeteria, to the rooftop, let people see you, let people remember that Victoria exists and that you two are Dr. Weelah's daughters. Text Marcus when you are ready and I'll meet you later for lunch," he said.

"I don't like it here. But, well, okay."

"I wish I could leave this place. It's so dreadful here; everyone is in a panic." He looked outside. They were crossing through the Mall.

And I thought things were bad in New York. There is the National Gallery. Maybe I can make a quick stop. I used to come so often, and I've never come back...

"I like your handkerchief; it's so much better than those NAA pins." She smiled at him.

Patrick looked like a normal citizen.

"Would you believe I miss them? I wear them at home," he admitted.

Apex Tower – Exit 200

"Hey, but this is the way to the Tower," she exclaimed.

"Yes, Rogers' office is there now," Patrick said.

"I don't want to." She felt shivers all over her body.

"Cate, it's time to grow up." He looked like he wanted to choke her. "We have all made sacrifices after your acquintances arrived," he said.

I haven't seen them in like a week.

The vehicle stopped.

"I can only take you to here; just walk through that path. Good luck," Patrick said.

She got out of the car and walked through, while the shadow of the silver skyscraper began to swallow her. She lifted her chin and went up the big stairs that years ago she'd run on her way down. The floor was like glass, as if time hadn't passed. The Hercules recognized her. Two followed her with their gaze.

I want to turn silver. I want them all to see how can I come in and out, just like that. But not today.

She passed through a reader and pressed her thumb, cleared. Floor 65, Elevator Delta; she went up and entered into the Space Affairs Department.

"Hi, good morning. Can I see Mr. Juveo Rogers, please?" she asked.

"He is busy," a dark-haired woman said.

"Are you talking to me or to someone else?" Cate asked, as the woman's sight remained on the screen in front of her. "Sometimes I think there are still hidden robots among us," Cate added.

The woman looked up at her.

"Catherine! Come over." The snowy woman from years before appeared behind her. Her hair was completely platinum and her glasses frame was blue.

"Hi! It's you." Cate approached her. "I need to see Mr. Rogers."

"I know. She is always supposed to say no." She giggled. "Let's go see him," snowy woman added.

She took Cate into a hall.

"I still remember when you woke me up and told me it was time to go home," Cate said.

The woman smiled warmly.

"Are you one of them?" Cate asked.

"Yes, but not like you," she answered.

I'm one of them as well...of course. Cate felt like slapping her face again.

"I'm a Lario," Cate said.

"I'm a Phima. Leeve 2," she said. "You know that we Phima cannot be alliafied all the time."

"No, why?"

"Cuckoo cuckoo," she twisted her finger by her ear.

"Why are you different? Not like those two. You are...you talk..." *Those two are just so unbearable sometimes, Cate thought.*

"Well, Mr. Rogers is a Balio; he adjusts better to new environments, he has been here for so long. And I'm not under the metal shield all the time."

"Does the shield make you colder?" Cate asked. *That would make a little sense.*

"Catherine, eventually you will see yourself as apart, and you are Leeve 4 like them. Untouchable. Unattached. There is so much to learn. Go inside; the door at the end."

"Thanks," Cate said.

Cate crossed a silver door; the only metal door on the floor.

"Why is this the only metal door on the floor?"

"In case I need to electrify it and turn it into a weapon." Mr. Rogers met her by the door. "You should do the same at your place. Please. Come inside; sit down. Why are you here?"

The room was yellow. A big stone of Quartz sat on a corner.

She alliafied completely. And so did he. She sat in front of him.

"My sister. I thought you cared about her."

"I'm doing my best. I have already been interrogated twice. There was a document; I can't tell you much."

"I know about that chaos on Earth," she said.

"Chaos in Brogio, a golden Alliafied on Earth. They are freeking out. But there are no links, so she will be fine. Kanio could have sent her to Phelio right away, yet he kept her here."

Cate pursed her lips. She sighed. "So, what is next?"

"Lets just wait. How close are you to him?"

"I don't know."

"Go back to New York; I'll keep you posted if anything changes."

This visit is not much worth it, she thought.

"How is Phelio?" Cate asked out of curiosity.

"It's like Earth is supposed to be. You should visit someday." He began checking documents on his desk.

"I think I've never thanked you for taking me out of here that time."

He raised his head. "You are one of us, and we won't leave you behind." He went back to his papers.

She left the floor and waved good-bye to the silver-haired woman. The woman stood up and walked her to the elevator. She pressed 'Lobby' and indicated 'Beta.'

"Can I be one of you, and also one of mine?" Cate unalliafied.

"Of course you can; don't let anyone have you believe otherwise."

"Thanks!" Cate jumped in the elevator.

Everyone can take a side. Why can't I? I wish it's because I loved them both so much, that I just can't make up my mind... The doors opened; the man to her right came out. *Inertia. What is wrong with wanting to keep my insipid human life? And also discovering what an Alliafied is,* she kept wandering. The doors moved. She looked outside to the wall in front: 'Reflector Department.' She alliafied her hands and put them in between the doors right before they closed. She stepped out the elevator.

To her left, it said 'Satellites,' to her right 'Reflector Panels'; she kept on that way. She moved along using her fingerprints, until she reached a door that woudn't open. She didn't think about it much; she alliafied, itirized, and crossed the door.

The people in the room on the other side inmediately stood up, panic showing on their faces. Quickly they began to leave the room, quietly, avoiding her sight.

There was a woman sitting in a corner, silent, biting her nails.

"Come help me. Log in to your computer," Cate said.

The woman did, and stood up.

"Don't leave, go back, sit there," Cate instructed her.

The poor frightened woman had goosebumps on her skin and started weeping.

Cate typed in the browser: SZ Composition.

The answer was: "*Unavailable.*"

"Pure Zafor Side effects?" she typed.

The answer was: "*In the first experiment, 2% of the sample developed a purple rash in their arms and face. 1% developed lung nodules, and 0.01% became blind.*"

"What is the alternative?"

"*PAWEL File.* Denied access."

Two Hercules came in the room.

"I'm out. I got lost." She raised her hands. They showed her a plastic handcuff. She pretended she didn't see them and kept walking; they escorted her until the elevator area, and soon she was on her way to the lobby. She was silver, just like that day seven years before, but this time she made sure everyone saw her. She stopped in the middle of the glossy floor that she'd once crossed—embarrassed, head down between her shoulders. Not anymore. She looked around, and there, that small character that had threatened her nightmares nights before.

That small raven of hell, she thought.

Cate paced fast and steady.

"Dr. Sanders. I wouldn't recommend you try locking those two. They have less patience than I do."

The woman's eyes opened and her nose turned into a small red button. "You are one of them; you don't belong here," the woman mumbled.

"I'll be wherever I feel like," Cate said back. She left the building, stepping down the gross white steps; she stopped in the middle and looked back: all along, Apex was just a tower made of glass. In front of her, it was insignificant. *I don't care if you people stare at me or not,* she thought. She felt a grin stamped on her face.

At the end of the steps, Marcus was waiting for her.

"Oh good, you are here; I forgot to text you," Cate said.

"I heard about disturbunces, some metal disturbances." He sounded annoyed. The self-driven Oceanic was waiting for them. He opened the door for her, and soon they left. "I'm taking you straight to the station."

"Can we pass by the National Gallery beforehand?" she asked.

"Better not; this is not New York."

"Very well. Eagle Station, then."

She unalliafied, her chin on her fist, and looked outside. *People here all look all the same...politicians.*

maria beta

CHAPTER 23

....

ELEVATION

It had been almost two months since the Phelaries had arrived; it was the end of November, and fall was a tough season due to the changing SkyShot composition. The formula was lighter, but more shots were released and the Reflector Panels moved slightly faster.

Cate and Alice had been kicking around dinner plans week after week for the past month, given Cate's constantly changing schedule. Finally, they were about to get together on a Friday night. Cate checked the news while getting ready.

"Our most special visitor, Kanio Turnfeld, the Aeki-ou, is leaving us, and we are all very sad; the date will be announced soon," the news anchor said.

Sad? It's not like they know him. "News off," she yelled to the screen. She sat down and remained silent. *I know him; what happened?*

She grabbed her black letiqa jacket and took off.

"When was this?" Alice asked about Kanio and Cate's last meeting on the bridge. She was wearing some fuchsia-framed glasses; the lenses were kind of pink and kind of orange. The place was covered in bamboo: floors, tables, and chairs, even the menu tablets. They ordered the full rice cubes tasting. This was one of Alice's favorite restaurants, especially because it was hidden below Penn Station.

"Two weeks ago," Cate told her friend. She looked up, waving her arms back along with her sight.

"And nothing after?" Alice sounded like a crime investigator. Not precisely what Cate needed then.

She moved her head in a big no. Cate bit her tongue. She was not hungry really. She omitted the Ereo story. The word "cruel" came to her mind, but Kanio for a moment became the light at the end of that smoky tunnel that had become her life. It was hard to match these two sides of his character. Did he really vanish just because she'd left him on the bridge? He should be the one to give her an apology. Perhaps Victoria was right and she should have been more careful—they didn't know them.

"Garlic is quite strong, don't you think?" Cate had mentioned it a few times.

"Not at all." Alice chewed her food.

A thick piece passed through Cate's throat.

"I'll be exuding garlic through my pores for days, even through the metal shield," Cate joked.

"Have you tried to contact him?" Alice asked.

"I've asked Core, his Central; nothing. I've been on the purple ship almost every day. He is not there. I can't—I don't feel him," Cate said. She remembered that night when her Ereo left. It was frustrating.

"Do you feel them?"

"The first time, it was something like high pressure; hard to describe—my chest hurt as if it was hard to breathe...and I wanted to faint, to throw up." *Like I want to do now,* she thought. "The last time, on the bridge, it was just like a mere change of temperature. I guess it is getting better with time." She broke a few cubes with a chopstick. They were stickier than usual, but it didn't really bother her. She grabbed another rice cube, and again swallowed another piece of garlic. She sighed. "In any case, I can tell when he is close by; and they are all different, so I can distinguish him from Nnox. Nnox is like a scratch on my skin. I can't feel Victoria much, really; Kanio calls her Leeve 2," Cate explained.

"Nnox Levantine? My mother told me to stay away from him, " Alice said in a serious tone.

"Did you ask your mother if I could see her?" Cate asked.

"Oh, yes; she said she is very busy right now."

"Tell her it's about my father." Cate stretched the truth.

"Do you know who also used to come to my house, with your father, those years ago?"

"No. Who? Paula?" Cate was curious.

"Your Dean."

"Of Physics? Ashcroft?"

"Yes, and a few others that I don't know who they were. I recognized him in that speech about rocks that you gave last year. His hair, and the mole in his forehead."

"His hair style, it's quite unique. Listen, I need to talk to her. Did you tell her it was me?"

The girl looked down.

"Alice?"

"Oh, it's nothing, Cate! Right now people are confused and some see you maybe too close to them; it will be fine." Alice kept eating.

Dr. Park had known Cate since she was ten years old. Even her?

"Cate, look!" Alice pointed to the holo-screen be-hind Cate. Cate turned to look at it while Alice pressed the side of the table, and a thin silverish plaque lev-itated up from it. And there it was: Kanio was get-ting out of a black Hawkline, the two-person sports car—one wheel in front, one in back; probably the ultimate, most elegant car in the world—at least that was what their slogan said. He was metallic blue, no cape; he waited by the co-pilot door, under flashes that bounced back on his blue shield. It was the entrance to the most popular restaurant in the city: Elevation.

A person came out, but was not purple, a human, and she was wearing a sleek orange dress. He extend-ed his hand to help her out. Cate could tell how her jaw dropped slowly, heavily. She turned to Alice and to the small screen on the table.

"Oh, God. Saki!" Cate looked at Alice, who was frozen and pale. Saki was Cate and Victoria's favorite singer.

Alice tapped her Whisper band on the check-reader tab by the table.

"Okay, we are leaving." Alice pulled Cate's arm.

"Where?" Cate exclaimed.

"I don't think I can get in there. My rating is not that high. Call Francis; I am sure he can get us in," Al-ice said, while they waited for the elevator to go up to the ground floor of the station. She took a yellow hat from her bag. It seemed it had bees embroidered on it.

"You want to see him, right?" Alice asked.

Cate was still in shock.

"It is ridiculous that Elevation only accepts reservations from the Tier 1 customer division—and this place, on the contrary, will never let you in if you call ahead," Alice said.

"And this is so much better," Cate said. She had been at Elevation a few times.

The doors opened and Alice pushed Cate into the elevator.

"In any case, what is Tier 1 these days?" Cate was getting anxious.

The elevator doors opened and they showed up in the bathroom of the fast-food chain King Solomon's Pizza, where they only sold half-pizzas. They walked fast toward the exit.

Catherine pressed her Whisper band on the side and said: "Triton, out. Penn, Exit 7 below 8th Avenue. Confirmed." Walking out through the passageway that led to the subway station on 8th Avenue, they turned right where a yellow parking sign showed up. She stopped in front of a window screen; it was a Halloween advertisement from Party Anywhere, and they were showing metallic costumes, blue and purple for men, and silver and gold for women. Even metal-colored capes and wigs.

"Move on, Cate," Alice called to her, though she was a few feet ahead already.

"And now I am a Halloween costume," Cate said.

They reached the exit. Hundreds of cars were parked there and the green Triton was waiting for them, its two doors opened sideways. They got in. "CDD, take control. Direction: Elevation, Tribeca, Downtown," Cate said. She was too nervous to drive.

Three minutes later, they were on 7th Avenue, moving south.

"Alice, I can't do this." Cate covered her face with her palms, leaning on the car's steering wheel.

"Yes, you can. Cate, this is nothing! I've seen you do so much more. Really. And I'm not talking about your alien superpowers," Alice said sweetly. "I'm talking about how you survived them. You need to ask him why is he avoiding you; at least you deserve that. What if he leaves, as they say?" Alice continued. "Don't you wish you'd had that conversation with Barrett?"

"Not really," Cate said. *Besides, I already know...*

"Let's just try to get inside. Then you'll see."

"I can get in there," Cate said.

"Wow. How? I mean, great!"

"Victoria Weelah." The younger sister released a long and peaceful breath, and she joined in on her friend's laughter.

From afar, they distinguished the fluorescent green cube floating in the sky, in between the illuminated purple clouds. It was always lighted to contrast with the unexpected environment. The glamorous restaurant hovered on the Hudson River, in what was equivalent to an 80th floor.

"I hate Saki," Cate whispered between her lips, crossed her arms, and pushed herself back in the seat.

*****

"Miss Walker, we are out of tables. The bar is full. We are sorry."

A blue-haired hostess dismissed them. She didn't even check if Cate was actually on the list or not. The woman was wearing a long-curvy silver long-sleeved mermaid-scale dress. The back edge ran even longer and drifted slightly, without touching the floor. It seemed impossible to pass through her and reach the massive glass staircase a few feet behind, which led to the tube that connected to the cube up in the air. Dance music could be heard from the staircase area. It was Saki's latest hit, "Aliennation."

"What did Francis say?" Alice asked.

"Same. It is a private event. At least he got invited, but he never RSVPd. I think he is popular."

"Of course he is, Cate, and you are blind." Alice looked away.

"Ugh." Cate tried to sound surprised, but she knew what Alice meant. *I can't think about it right now,* she decided. Her mind was only set up to find Kanio and tell him...she had no clue what she would say to him.

"Ladies, we are very sorry about this—there is a private event going on, and we need the area to be clear for the people who exit," a security guard in a navy uniform said as he approached them. It sure was very private; there was a large number of guards outside, from the NAA and from all the New Houses, even from the New West, distinguished by their icy-blue colored uniforms. They never left their New House.

"We are about to get a table; we will wait here," Alice said. But Cate could see how the electric-blue-haired hostess made a no-no gesture to the man with her index finger.

"Miss Walker, we promise you any other day we would have looked for a spot for you, but today it is impossible," a second security guard told them.

Cate sank in irritation. She looked back slightly and caught a glimpse of a female Phelarie coming a few steps down the staircase. A guard dressed in purple came to the Phelarie; they exchanged a few words, and then he left. He had to be there. Kanio. There was another way to call his attention without them facing each other.

"Miss, please, let me escort..."

Cate extended her palms, which were coated entirely in dark silver fire. Everyone opened a circle around her; people's mouths fell to the ground. The audience switched from civilians to security guards. She pressed her fists strongly close to her chest. She felt dizzy, but her mind was clear. She switched the energy to her expanded arms, her head up to the sky; she extended her arms in the air. It was like those tiny tongues of fire that covered her on the day of the crash, but more intense. Her body was breathing. The deeper she inhaled, the farther it exhaled.

Nothing. I feel nothing.

She came back down to liquid. She looked around. Four Hercules were pointing at her with their twisted arms. Alice was being held back, but Cate could see her smiling.

"Let's go." Cate walked through two Hercules and reached her, yet the Hercules surrounded her again.

"Stop. Stop. Cate, are you okay?" A familiar voice crossed the Hercules. Alex Harlow. He was in a black suit, with all the puppets usual insignias, jade-green tie, jade-green handkerchief on one side, and the triple star on the other. "They are with me," he said to the security guard in the navy uniform, who indicated to the Hercules to move away.

"Alex, we need to go up; help us," Alice said.

"I'll see what can I do. Stay here," he said. Alex proceeded to speak with the hostess, and this one called them with the same index finger she seemed to like to use so much.

"Come on." Alice pushed Cate toward them. Cate hated Alex; she didn't want to rely on him. *How did I get into this situation?* she wondered. The Hercules kept her in their sight.

"Let me make a call upstairs," the hostess said.

"They are guests at my table. It will be fine," Alex reiterated. He gave her his signature grin.

"Well, your guest just made quite an spectacle a few minutes ago," the blue-haired woman said. "She has to turn that thing off." Her voice was stressed, not as bold as a few minutes before.

"Kanio and Nnox are gone; it's fine with my approval," Alex insisted.

"Guests won't be comfortable; I can't make that call."

"He is gone." Cate unalliafied. She began shaking her head and sobbing through her nose.

"Who? The Aekiou?" Alex said.

Cate looked up at him and nodded.

"He was about to leave when I came down here; he was being picked up there." Alex looked at her with concern. "But come; you can meet Saki. I have spoken to her all night."

"Oh no!" Cate lowered her eyes and walked away. She left the place abruptly, walked right into the dark, and ended at a small pier close by, among the light purple haze. The river was calm. Alice and Alex followed.

"Cate, stop!" Alex moved closer. "What is going on? Listen, we don't know them yet, and I am hopeful for the future; but be careful," he said.

"Why did you do it? Why did you leave her for nothing?" Cate saw him and remembered how much she'd looked up to him—and how disappointing it was when he left her sister for being like her.

"Do you think I don't think about it? I understood later it was part of being human; it was part of being vulnerable. Look how people still reacted to you, just five minutes ago."

"I know," Cate moaned.

"I thought I was right. I was stupid." He paused. "I thought I had only two choices." Standing tall with his hands in his pockets, he stared down at the ground. "Hide myself in a cave with her, or go ahead with everything we had planned. I thought she would do the same thing if it was her. I thought she loved her career more than me." He shook his head. "I thought I did." He moved closer to her. "I hope you never have to be in my situation, and if you do, I hope you make the right choice."

"Life in a cave?" A few seconds passed. "I'm sorry," she said.

"No. The one you don't regret in the long run."
Alex twisted his mouth.

"Do you regret it?" she asked.

"Always. Every day."

Alex moved closer to the water.

"Is he really leaving? What will happen to Victoria?" Cate asked.

"He is. I asked him again to release her, but he didn't say anything. I was firm on the fact that he cannot take her with him. And he said that he won't."

"Can he do that? Why can they do all this?" she asked in shock.

"Have you seen the ship on the water? They have a bigger one behind the moon. We didn't give them access to Apollo. That station is locked. But for Earth, the best option now is diplomacy."

"When is he leaving?"

"I can't tell you," he said.

"Alex! It's Victoria."

He shook his head. "Two days. Maybe less. He just told me he wants to leave now..."

"No. No. Alex." Cate didn't let him finish talking.
Her lungs had no air; she could barely breathe.

"What?" he said.

"I need you to take me to the Union," Cate said.

"Someone will pick you up early tomorrow."

"No, now."

"It's 11 p.m.," Alex said, surprised. "I can't take you at this time."

"You can take me at this time. Damn it, you are Alex Harlow. Please," Cate begged him.

He remained quiet for a while. He looked at her, looked at Alice.

"Only you. I'll try." He pressed his Whisper band. "Hi, I'm ready. Please meet me at the entrance in two minutes." Alex moved his hand, indicating for Cate to follow him. She did.

"Alice, I'll talk to you tomorrow!" Cate said.

Around twenty minutes afterward, Cate and Alex were inside his silver Oceanic 5000, sitting in the second row. This time, they rode in silence. When they got to the tunnel that connected Manhattan to Atlantic Island, Cate moved from the second to the third row and lay down.

"What are you doing?" Alex asked.

"Something that I won't regret tomorrow. Keep going to the Building and leave whenever you want. And don't look back here," Cate said.

The tunnel gates opened automatically for his car. Soon, Alex's car entered the Union's parking lot. When he arrived at his spot, a Phelarie was waiting for him.

"Good evening, Senator Harlow. Do you mind if we give your vehicle a quick check?" the Phelarie said.

"Not at all." Alex came out.

"All doors, open," the Phelari commanded.
All doors opened. All rows empty.
"Sorry about that. Good night." The Phelarie left.

*****

When Alex's car got close to the Island, Cate moved to the third row of the car, went down to the floor, and alliafied. She thought that by being covered in metal, the tunnel scanners would confuse her with pieces of the Oceanic, and thus the Phelaries wouldn't realize her entry. It went fine. As soon as Cate stopped seeing the yellow neon lights from inside the tunnel, she iterized for one second or maybe two, and found herself deposited on the road. Barely at Leeve 1, to avoid shining, she moved to the row of trees. She walked, not thinking about it, crossing through the bushes. Behind her, the purple ship floated on the river. The vessel's shape was barely discernible amid the violet haze. Forward. The Union seemed to be covered in dust; light from the columns produced a dramatic effect. A garbage bag of mixed feelings. Alex didn't hesitate for a second. It was hard to think. What if she hadn't ever accidentally transformed that night, and therefore Victoria hadn't either? *Would they still be together?*

"We will take you to the building," a voice said from behind.

Two Letaneos were standing behind her, camou-flaged in the dark night.

"Holy...you scared me!" she said.

A Helo was coming their way.

"Tell him that he is right. I have nothing here. I need to talk to him now."

CHAPTER 24

....

THE ALLIAFIED

Kanio went to the party at Elevation—*a popular place,* he was told—to finally get to meet all of the members of the New Houses. He finished dinner and proceeded to the Zey that was waiting for him at one of the restaurant's private exits. The blue triangular Zey moved from vertical to horizontal, the square red base trailing behind, and it flew away.

Behind the moon, once in his Ryder, it landed right by ten others; he pressed a palm reader when he got out, and the triangle turned dark gray as the others. Straight to the Kof. Nnox was there already, sitting near the end of a long floating blue plaque. Behind the plaque, a transparent veil showed the inside of the intelligent blue machine. The room was like a balcony to an enormous space—the heart of the ship. A diagonal building surrounded by a park at the bottom, operational and engine rooms at the end, a set of elevators on both sides; Phelarie life in exhibition.

"Angot is dead." Nnox came to his feet.

"Colt?" Kanio asked. He pressed his right shoulder and his cape compressed upward. He paced around the desk and reached the balcony.

"He escaped; he flew beneath the thick ocean. He is probably with the Dellhus."

"What did the Khun say?" Crossed arms on his chest, Kanio continued without changing the tone of his voice.

"To send a Phelarie envoy," Nnox said.

"He wants to negotiate." Kanio turned to Nnox and strode toward his pair, grabbed his left shoulder, and said: "Negotiations take too long. What are we going to do?"

"Nothing much really. Onerio and Brogio are not remotely close, and the Khun specifically said that we must remain here, at least myself, until the first station is fully operational." Nnox took Kanio's hand and removed it from his shoulder. "Also, why do we have Seemo handling T4?"

Nnox meant that place in the universe where Phelaries are no one's favorite.

"It is not relevant. They did not come from there." Kanio looked down to the Okera, or recreational area, and the Phelaries' interactions.

When did this become such a mess?

"They escaped while being transferred to Esserkon. You see, no one escapes from Esserkon—they had to be reached before he would arrive there. They had to have someone who knew the timing and routes," Nnox added. "He is not even that powerful." Nnox raised his hands and made a despicable facial gesture. "Why do people follow him and his irrational demagogic ideas? It makes no sense to me," the purple Phelarie continued.

"Talum is charismatic—what you and I are not. And he is powerful. Nnox, listen." Kanio stopped to think about what he was going to say; how could he explain what Talum and his followers were capable of? "Colt will not last long there. Someone must go and take him out, soon," Kanio said.

"Seemo is too far. Cala?" Nnox turned to the Phelarie world and sat on the blue table.

"She would not move from Phelio, not even for you and I together, and she is not returning my messages." Kanio grabbed a seat-tower but remained standing.

"She probably heard about your late night out with the human Weelah." Nnox sounded ironically happy.

"That is hers to deal with," Kanio said. He did mind hurting Cala's pride. Before Cate, she was the only female close to him, but now there were bigger things in the picture. "I am sure Cala found out about Cate while you were talking to Seemo behind me." Seemo Fendple was more than close to Iria Mirabele, Cala's younger sicato. They were Larios; only Larios could have *sicato*—siblings, in human terms.

"Maybe I said something." Nnox lowered his tone and pushed a chair farther away.

"I went out, for hardly a couple of hours, to an insipid dinner with an annoying girl," Kanio paused, "and we lost Colt, and..."

I didn't see Cate, he thought.

"Don't blame me for this; this circus has been building for a while, way before these last two hours." He recovered his apathetic tone of voice. "And do not blame yourself," Nnox said.

"The thing is..." Kanio said within his choking anger.

"What?"

"What are we? You? Seemo? Colt?" The blue one walked toward the purple one.

"We are Alliafied," Nnox said firmly.

"There must be a reason why I picked you before the others." Kanio poked his index finger on Nnox's chest.

"You picked me because with me, you are solid and indestructible." Nnox crossed his arms.

"No, there was something else; I could have been enhanced by anyone else as well. Everyone wanted me to pick Seemo, a Phima, and make our Genyis closer. But I picked you, another Thendor."

"I don't know why you picked me, and I don't care. I just know you did," Nnox said.

"I knew you would say yes, but I never did ask. What if you'd had other plans? What if you'd wanted to go back to your system?" Kanio padded his pair's back.

"You never asked, and it has never crossed my mind that you should have. This is not who we are; we do not establish relationships by exchange," Nnox said back.

"Precisely, and that is why I have to do something. In human terms, you, Colt, Seemo, Cala—you are my closest friends. And for this, I cannot command you, but I can ask: Do you want to help me to go and get Colt out of there?" Kanio looked straight into his friend's eyes and then looked down to the Phelaries again. Their nice lives—they just enjoyed the voyage. They had never engaged in combat.

"I can't. We weren't even supposed to be here in the first place. After the Weelah Union incident, you decided to come, and I followed. Luckly, the Khun instructed us to engage, and take control of Onerio-13—install those tubes, change the mixture, finish a mission...And then that document, it was good that we were here at the end. I cannot do more. I have to follow his orders, not yours yet," Nnox said unapologetically, but then his voice became nicer. "I know that because I am your pair, you can't go without me. But Seemo wouldn't go either. No one would."

Kanio snorted and shook his head. He stepped back. *No one, it's true, no one.*

"If I ask, from today on, would you be my pair?" Kanio said without even looking at Nnox. He was disappointed not with Nnox but with himself. When it came to the Khun's decision, there was nothing he could do about that.

"I am not only your pair; you are mine, and believe me, I like having you at my back. I wouldn't pick anyone else." Nnox gave a witty look.

"We need to realign," Kanio said.

"Go. You need to be close to the Khun now. I have Rogers; worst case, I release the gold Weelah." Nnox headed toward the door.

"Release her now; she has nothing, and if she does, it's meaningless. I will leave tomorrow then, before sunset."

Kanio stood by the veil-wall. This was probably the longest conversation he'd ever had with Nnox that didn't involve Cross-Ryders or war. His father's best ever decision was to bring Nnox to him.

"And Kanio, I don't want you as my pair only because you are a Thendor Leeve 4, Aekiou of the Universe, blah blah." Nnox came back to the table. "You see, when I arrived on Pirthee, I didn't speak much to anyone—not because I didn't know the language, but because I didn't want to talk about losing my parents, or about how I lost them."

Kanio knew very well what had happened: one had died in an accident, and the other killed himself right after.

Nnox continued. "A few days passed, and I ran into you at the Medallion; you came and spoke to me in my native Asfeolio. You were still shorter than me." Nnox set his hand on his hip. "Maybe less," he said, lowering his hand farther. "It was the first time we were ever alone, and you said something like, 'We don't need to talk about them, ever, nor live beneath their shadow, ever. We will make an adventure of our own,' And you left. Now that I know you better, I am sure that you learned that U3 tribal language just to address me when the opportunity arose, to take advantage of my weak emotional situation, make me feel secure, and unconditionally trust you. It worked. But it did because beneath your casual manipulative mantra, you are kind and honest." He turned around and walked back to the exit.

"You have never been emotionally weak. You have never been weak in any way. And that is why I chose you as my pair," Kanio said. Strangely, at that moment, he finally found the true reason why he had chosen the purple Alliafied as his longtime partner: It was because he trusted Nnox unconditionally...the most solid creature that he had ever known.

Nnox left the room.

Kanio sat, fully depositing his blue back in the chair. He remembered that day. He wasn't that short. He remembered how Phelaries were staring at Nnox, just as they were staring at him when his mother had taken off.

"Probably everyone was wandering if we would turn out like them," Kanio said, referring to their elders.

"Well, you both proved them wrong," his Ereo said from behind the chair.

"And I will prove it to them again. Don't know exactly how yet."

"Will you tell him?"

"No," Aenio said.

"And Cate? Will you say something to her before you go?"

"It's with or without us; no middle ground. Leave."

The Ereo disappeared.

He meant every word he'd said. He did like to be around her. But a few *sodios* would not mark his existence. Plus, this was not the first time that he had been torn apart at the thought of someone leaving his life. Thoughts; it is important to disconnect from them. After an experience, what remains in our minds are only memories; the retrospective of them it is what manipulates the rationality of our decisions—that is why it is important to get rid of them, more important than getting rid of her. *It will be fine,* he thought.

*****

Soon the same room was crowded; the balcony window had become a screen, showing a light beige desert under a pink sky. The participants were going to debate which regions of the planet could have their amount of Zafor increased first, in moderation. Kanio and Nnox were sitting in the middle, in front of the screen. Kanio checked his armband and then lowered his head to Nnox on his right side, and said: "I'll be right back."

Nnox nodded. The blue Alliafied exited the room to speak to his Letaneos. Despite the fact that this was his original plan, he'd never really thought that it might indeed materialize. *Cate needs to pick a side; it is the best for her.* Yet now it didn't matter anymore. He went back to the room, swiped his right index to the left in the air, and the lights turned on.

"Barrett, the only reason while you will still be in control is because you will let no one but Nnox around those tubes. Hope you have that clear," Kanio said.

Skinny, bulgy eyes, Barrett stood up and went to him. "Only my team will have access."

"If anyone else comes close to those tubes' control, your Mountdragon empire will be in charge of only the sewer system of Manhattan and nothing more," Kanio said. "You can't be seen together. People are asking. People soon will be asking more."

Barrett and Nnox, who'd just joined them, assented.

"How do we get the final formula? Who else has it?" Nnox asked Barrett.

"Weelah, that is for sure; I told you," Barrett answered.

"Weelah, Ashcroft, and Park. We know," Nnox said.

"But Weelah pretends to be mute, the Dean is in Venus, and Dr. Park told Nnox, what?" Kanio explained.

"To go to hell; her exact words," Nnox responded.

"What if you exchange it for Victoria?" Barrett asked.

"We don't do that," Nnox said.

"There has to be someone else whom we can find, or talk to," Kanio said.

"Your father?" Nnox said, "isn't he important?"

"No," Barrett said with a deep disdainful expression. "I think there is a politician in the group; they needed someone to sign the final formula and to lock the code," Barrett said. "You may have better luck with him. They are easier to negotiate with."

"McCully?" Nnox asked.

"No, they stopped sending him vital information years ago. He was truly just a dummy of my father and his friends," Barrett added.

"Harlow," Kanio said.

"Alex?" Nnox asked.

"No," Barrett said, "the Senators don't have access to the Shield."

"Arthur, his father." Kanio said. "He was New Governor for the New East when the first Panel was installed in Manhattan."

The Phelaries nodded.

"I need to deal with something. I have to go." Kanio left.

"Kanio, wait. Barrett, go back to your seat," Nnox said. The skinny rat went back to the table. "You are going to see Cate."

Kanio nodded.

"I don't like another Alliafied wandering around," Nnox complained.

"What are you worried about? She is just a girl, a girl from a moon." Kanio shook his head.

"No," Nnox said firmly. "She is a hydrogen-based Lario Leeve 4."

"Take Victoria home. I'll meet you later." Kanio left. They both headed in different directions.

Kanio knew what Nnox meant, but things were already complicated, better to leave Cate out of the equation. He kept walking straight into the hangar to take a Zey and go down to Earth, until his Zoun notified him of a message to his private log from an unknown sender. He stopped. He listened but it was impossible to understand something beyond the interference. He proceeded to the departing platform where two Letaneos where waiting for him.

"Go into my log, there is a recent message that you will have access to, clean it until it's clear, it is from Colt Behar."

*****

The Zey made its way in the Union and landed by the ivory steps. The wind pulled his cape almost perfectly horizontally behind him as he took the bold stairs to the third floor, where he encountered Cate at the hall. Dark silver, completely solid with a touch of silver dust on her. The vault was semi-lit, the columns looked yellow and dusty, and the shadows were deep.

"You can go," he told a group of Letaneos around her. The six arthropods went downstairs.

"You were right; there is nothing for me here. I only have a few friends and a dog. And I'll leave with you, but you have to let my sister go," she asked.

"Your sister is already gone; she's being taken to your human parents. And you can't come with me anymore. The invitation expired the moment you said no. You'd better go now." He paced toward the large colored glass. The night was dark. The purple ship was barely discernible on the other side. He crossed his arms behind him.

"Why are you so unbearable sometimes? Are you mad?" she said unsteadily.

What does she mean?

"No, I'm disappointed." He turned to her and she was motionless. "You asked me to release her; I did. What else do you want?"

He moved closer to her. It was like magnetism.

"I thought you wanted me to learn, to train, something," she said.

"Not anymore," he said.

"No. No." She shook her head. "When are you leaving?"

"Tomorrow."

"Why haven't you said anything? I thou...I thought," she stuttered. An inch of gas evaporated through her metal shield and immediately disappeared as she went back to superliquid.

"Well, you have a life of your own. It's better not to interrupt. I asked you before and you said no."

"You only asked once."

"Why would I ask twice?"

"You disappeared. You even took my Ereo away! How could you?" Cate moved closer to him. She shoved his right arm and then pushed a wave of silver dust to the large window. It scattered away a piece of the glass; a current of wind blew inside.

"I should have left a long time ago," he said—firm and dry. As the final touch, he unalliafied. His best weapon. *She needs to learn never to say no to me again...*

She stared at him. She unalliafied as well. Fragile—almost like when they'd met that day at the Kof.

"Sometimes. Sometimes, I think you just want to use me." The wind moved her hair slightly to her face.

"Maybe I did. Maybe I do." He pulled her hair softly back. "And you should use me too, but not in the selfish way that humans and Phelaries do. We are Alliafied," he said. "But either you are with me or not. And if not, with you out of the equation, there is nothing left for me here. I don't care about this Alliance, your sister, or Mountdragon and his tubes. Time will bring up what Victoria is hiding or what happened, and we will deal with it; we always do. If it wasn't for you, I would probably have left the day after I landed." He released her hair.

"What about Nnox? You can't leave him here alone."

"He has to finish what we began; he has Rogers, and someone else will come to fill my place. I'm needed on Phelio now," Kanio said.

Her eyes were bright and wide open.

"When you asked, I thought I couldn't go through another change again. I thought this was bad, but the bad that I know; but now I don't know anything anymore—bad is you not here anymore," Cate said.

He took her hands. "You are far from the character that apathetically wanders the world, as you describe yourself. You went through a lot, but you got over it. And that—that was the past. I was... I am the present. And we are the future. You cannot deny who you are, or what you can be. You are an Alliafied, like me, for good or for bad. Make it worth it," Kanio said. "I'll arrange something for you. I promise. In the meantime, you have Nnox and Rogers. Stay close to them."

"You can't leave me." Air rushed out with Cate's low voice. "I'll go with you now."

"You can't come now." He looked away and went to the window, against the wind.

"Why?" Her head turned slightly. "You said you wanted me in Phelio? Rogers said it was fine. What has changed?" She went by his side. "I've seen you with that look before. What is it?"

He alliafied and released a string of light to his right. It helped him with stress.

"I need to meet the Khun first," he said.

"No." She alliafied. She grabbed his arm; a strange smile marked her face. "You are going to get your friend!"

Why is she doing this? Interfering with my will...

"You have to; it's the right thing to do. And you can't be alone until you find him. You know, you said so," Cate said.

What is she happy about? he shook his head.

He walked away.

"How are you going to find him?" she asked.

"I know where he is," he said. "It has to be quick and unnoticed. If I interceed in the Khun dialogues to take Brogio back, it could be seen as confrontational," the Aekiou said. "But he won't last long. He needs a pair, so I need to go there now."

"You know that with me close to you, you can protect us both."

"This is not what I want. This is not how I wanted it."

"It's time. *We* are the future. The future is now," Cate said.

He remained quite for a while.

Time is relative. And the future eventually becomes the present, he thought. At least Nnox will be happy... "You have to stay close to me. You will do what I say. Nothing erratic," he said.

She nodded.

"You can't tell any one, not your sister, no one, or else you cannot come."

She nodded.

I'll protect you all.

maria beta

CHAPTER 25

CLEOPATRA

'How does it feel to be ouside? It is not like you have stars to watch in this filthy sky anyway," Nnox said to Victoria.

Nnox was unalliafied. His slick black hair fell to his left, covering half of his face. Long ears, skin tone slightly olive. He shook his head with half-open eyes; the hair moved, exposing his left eye. Dressed entirely in coal black, with a long cape falling down from his squared shoulders—long enough that it remained dancing over the floor—and a silver octagonal pin with a strange asymmetrical round figure with a rhombus in it carved on his chest to the right. His chest looked quite muscular. Square jaw, thin lips. He looked more imposing than he did while covered in purple.

Both unalliafied, no cage separating them, felt different to Victoria. A sense of equality.

She remained mute.

"There is a branch on Phelio that would support your pledge," Rogers said, and Rogers always stuck to his word. If she had told Cate everything, Cate would have allowed her to carry on anyway, as the final outcome had zero effect on her life—though, considering how close she had become to the Aekiou, it was better that Victoria had left her sister in the dark.

Of all the Alliafied out there, it had to be Kanio Turnfeld himself who came, she thought. Although she knew of his elevated alliafied status, she didn't have the slightest sense that she had zero chance in front of him—or against the other purple Alliafied.

"My Helo, you've been here before. Up," Nnox said.

The capsule vehicle's roof moved up.

She got inside and sat in the back. "Why are you not purple?

"Protocol; now I can," he explained.

"Where are we going?"

"To Sunally, then you can leave the NAA and never come back if you wish. Though I have the impression you will be knocking at the Kof tomorrow morning."

"I don't know if it will be to talk to you precisely," she added.

They took the tunnel to cross Manhattan.

"You know I would have never put you there unless you hadn't plotted against your government and against our Etheean Phelarie," Nnox said.

"You mean the Khun? Your empire?"

"There is no translation. Don't stress about it. You see, he makes sure that the rest of the show can carry on. He shares some features of what you can call a leader, but he is not a dictator. When the American revolution took place..."

"I don't want a history lesson right now."

"You see, in my history chapter you would be more like Cleopatra."

"Don't tell me, and you are Marcus Aurelius." She chortled out of her lungs. "Oh god, I forgot what laughing was." She managed to composed herself. "I'm far from an Egyptian queen, especially in this bodysuit. The gold, perhaps," she sighed, looking down at the horrendous gray suit.

"The gold, and also because she was so proud and ended up so lonely." He raised his eyebrows through the mirror to his right.

"In different circumstances, perhaps we could have been friends," she said.

"We make the circumstances." His eyes turned sharper in an invasive way. "Why is it still so hard to understand that we are on the same side. We have an Alliafied in trouble—his pair was murdered, and there is someone mean out there chasing him. We—including you—have to be closer now, more so than ever."

"Stop it, Nnox. We have never been close at all. We only played chess once."

"And I won." He laughed.

Nnox turned pearly purple—the cape, the suit, and his hair, which instantly went back behind his left ear. "Alliafy," he said.

So she did. He accelerated. The highway was empty. And the Helo was faster than any car she had ever been before.

"Why did you people never ask for Cate? Why did you never come for her?"

"We did. After what happened on Jupiter's moon, I think Rogers convinced your father that it was too late, and that is not true. I was almost in the same cycle that she was when I joined Kanio and the others. Then, after the car accident, we asked again. He said, again, that your human father said no. For some reason, Steban never wanted to talk directly to us after Cate was born," he said.

"He is special. And you guys are kind of far away." She justified her father.

"There is an emotional aspect about you humans that I cannot understand," he added. "You are more Phelarie than you think you are."

Victoria raised her head and looked at him from behind; she wondered, *How much does he know? He talks about the past and about Steban so casually.*

"Strangely, your sister is the contrary," Nnox continued. "I understand why Rogers never went to her; he wouldn't have been able to control her or to reach an agreement."

An awkward moment passed. He pushed some buttons and music came out. When they arrived at Sunally, the Helo parked at the roundabout, in front of the white house. Nnox came out of the Helo and helped Victoria jump out.

"Nnox?" she asked.

"What?"

"Why is Cate so important?"

He looked up to the sky. He truly had thin and long ears. He then bent his head slightly down toward her. "When you are close to her...can you tell how you become thicker and lighter at the same time? We are all special, even you. But I just caught a glimpse of her once, and it was different; she never wants to connect to me. I wonder why." He pursed his lips.

"Yes, I wonder too." She followed the lip grimace.

"I think you wish you were human," Victoria joked.

"Sometimes I do; you have a different concept of freedom than we do."

His head moved to the right, he took two steps back, he grabbed his chin and then moved his head to the other side.

"Cate is leaving tomorrow with Kanio. By tomorrow, we will decide your new role on Onerio and in the NAA. As a Lario, perhaps you are capable of showing more loyalty to this side, to your kind." Nnox shrugged his shoulders.

"What? Is it because of me?" she said out loud. "Is that why you let me go?"

Did I put my sister in a Phelarie silver trail?

"No, at all. And don't blame yourself. She likes Kanio. This will be good for her."

"You are an idiot."

She went inside the house.

*****

Cate arrived at her apartment and went straight to her storage closet. It was the next day but still night-time.

"Core: Call Victoria sister."

"Unavailable."

"Leave a message: Meet me in Sunally."

She grabbed a bag and put in all of the jumpsuits she could find.

"Four messages from Alice Park," Core said.

"Tell her I'm fine and to come over right now. No, tell her to go to Sunally."

Do I need toothpaste? she thought.

Then she saw a ball of hair coming out from the room.

"Coper!" She hugged her furry pet.

"Am I not the worst puppy owner ever?" She picked him up and carried him in her arms to the kitchen; she rubbed his head, and then fed him some puppy treats that were on the counter. She put him back on the floor, and became aware that he had definitely peed more than once in the apartment. "These are probably expired, but they are good, right?"

She looked for something in her fridge and found nothing much, really. She still had the flavor of garlic in her mouth from the night before.

"Core: Order Winky Eggs from the Mexican downstairs; grapefruit juice, too."

"Memo received the order. Ten minutes," the system confirmed.

I will leave with him. That moment when she saw Kanio arriving with Saki at Elevation felt like weeks ago, but it had probably been just twelve hours that had passed since then.

She made some coffee and proceeded to the balcony. She put some of the pieces of the night before together—Kanio, the ship, the river, Alex at Elevation, Saki. Then a short warm breeze blew behind her. The much-missed flowing figure was there. Her jaw dropped down with the emotion.

"He said this time I am assigned to you forever. He said to specify to you the time length."

"Oh! Will he keep his word? This is awesome. Really!" She put her palms on her heart.

"He always does."

"And so do I!" she added.

His eyes opened wide.

"I'm aware I'm reckless. I may not be the most stable person out there. But I will try to do this right," she said.

"Kanio will need you. You can't blink," he calmly said. "You can't leave him alone. He will rely on you, as no one has relied on you before."

"I won't."

"I know you mean it, but you have to work on your willpower."

I will, she thought. "I think last night was the most exciting and exhausting night of my life. It's hard for me to read him sometimes," she said. *I wonder if that is what keeps me captivated; I wonder if he cares about me as I do for him,* she thought.

"He does. Cate, this is serious." The Ereo shook his head; it looked as if it was disconnected from his body.

"It's serious. What will happen when I'm there? The food? Will I be able to breathe? Will I have to be alliafied all the time?"

"Physically, you have a few variations from them. No long ears. Different digestive system, but you can eat their food. Their lungs are almost flat. In that sense, well, your lungs are flatter than an average human being's. The main similarity with them is that as a half-Phelarie, your skin can go through the alliafied process. In Brogio, you will be fine; its atmosphere is as pure as Earth's was a thousand years ago."

The Ereo disappeared.

Ding ding! a sweet sound came from the speaker by the door.

"Come in," Cate said, and a wheeled-trail robot entered the room. Cate pressed her band at a reader on the side of its square menu head, opened the door at the robot's chest—a heating box—and took out her Winky Eggs.

"Incoming call from Victoria sister," Core said.

"Accept."

"Hey, I just connected to a Whisper again. Are you okay? Tomorrow? Why?"

"This is what's right. And it's today," Cate said.

"I'm heading to your place," Victoria said.

"No. No. Where are you? I'll be in Sunally in an hour."

"I'm already here. Okay. Let me know if you need anything."

In one of the drawers was the blush scarf that she'd bought with Alice some weeks back; she grabbed it and put it in the bag. Cate ate half her food while getting ready; she picked a black silicate-linen skirt and a gray turtleneck sweater. Once ready, she pressed her Whisper band on the side and said: "Triton, downstairs."

*****

In Sunally, inside Steban and Paula's house, carrying Coper in her arms, she stopped in the entry hallway, in front of that old picture of her mother with her blond braid and Victoria as a toddler. Victoria, grown-up, did look like her; same narrow eyes and honey light-blond hair.

"I don't remember anything about her, if you've ever wondered." Victoria showed up from behind, in a navy blue jumpsuit, crossed by golden stripes.

Cate immediately released the dog and jumped into Victoria's arms.

"Why are you leaving with him?" Victoria said. Both walked inside the house. Coper followed, waving his short legs behind them.

It smelled like carrot cake. Cate closed one of the windows so Coper didn't go outside.

"You know why I am; you all did your best, but I need to try, after all this time. I want to know what this is," Cate said. "I want to learn. I want to know who I am."

I don't even feel sad, she pondered.

"Another chance, or another perspective?" Victoria asked.

"Another chance. Yes. And I think you have to talk to Alex." Cate couldn't't find the right argument to justify it, but the fall of their relationship was the metal trick as well.

"Really? Coming from you?" Victoria supported herself behind the camel sofa, looking toward the big window. It was gloomy outside. Nothing to see.

"I saw him. He is just a normal person, and he doesn't have the robotic mind that these two others have," Cate explained.

"Cate, it is different for me. You weren't going to marry him and spend the rest of your life with him."

"I know. But just think about it. See it as a chance, or a perspective." Cate sat by Victoria and rubbed her back. Coper jumped onto the sofa behind them.

"Actually, I *don't* want to think about it." Victoria made a flippant gesture with her mouth, as she looked the other way.

"You know your father doesn't like him!" Paula entered the scene, raising and waving her palms, dressed in beige but with an orange belt that reached her chest. Coper saw her and immediately jumped down to the carpet and hid beneath the square wooden coffee table.

"Well, I am very sorry but I need to ask you to keep it here for a few days. Until we figure out what to do. Someone will pick him up; don't know exactly when," Cate said seriously. She was tired of the inquisition against her tiny dog.

Paula turned pale, almost green, and remained mute.

"I'll take the puppy; please breathe, Paula," Victoria said.

Paula remained mute.

"Can you take him with you?" Victoria asked Cate.

"I don't know," Cate said. She couldn't contemplate leaving him behind, though she knew she always did. Yet he was always unconditionally waiting for her to come back.

"How long will it be?" Victoria asked.

"My Ereo on the way here said that a year..."

"A year..."

"Are you leaving, Cate? To the moon again?" Paula asked.

Cate nodded. *Why waste my time explaining to her?*

"And you can come back right? Do you trust him?" Victoria asked.

"Any time; yes, I do," Cate assured her.

After picking up his friend... I can't tell her; she won't let me go if she knows.

"Your father is awake if you want to see him now," Paula said. She elegantly avoided the dog conversation.

Cate walked straight to her father's library. She knocked twice and opened the door.

Steban was standing by the window. The first Sky-Shot had recently happened. Lativa stood by him.

"Let's move to the purple sofa." He moved slowly. Lativa followed him.

"It's burgundy, Dad." Cate felt a blade inside. He was not her father, yet he was her dad after all. She approached and helped him to sit down. "I'm sorry. It's *almost* purple," she said.

"We had to adjust the windows one level up," Steban said.

"Darker?" Cate asked. She hesitated to bring up whether he had visited the oculist lately, but decided to mention it to Paula instead before leaving—though it was true that the days had become a bit brighter lately.

They discussed a bit about the weather, and then out of nowhere he said: "*Phelio*. It's far." He settled on the sofa; his back was more curved than the last time, and he supported his right hand on Lativa.

"I'm sure a part of you wishes you were coming too," she said.

"I was invited when I met them, when we created the Shield and Panels; but a trip for me could have been years. Too long. Life is not that long," he said.

"I can travel faster while being alliafied," she said.

He smiled at her.

She also knew that as half-Phelarie she would probably live two times as long as a human.

"Why didn't you ever tell me about it? About them?" She went straight to the core.

"I don't like them. They are different," he answered in a bold tone.

"They are like me. You don't like me?" She smirked at him.

"No, Cate. You are my daughter. The only thing you have in common with them is the elemental process. Far from them. That is the only thing I wanted for you. I only told Paula about Rogers because I'm not blind; they can do what we cannot." His hands trembled. "Kanio seems different, people from the university said. But they all work as a community, all around this Khun, like a queen bee. And the Khun runs an agenda of his own," he continued.

This was one of the longest speeches Steban had ever given to her regarding her personal life. Cate couldn't infer if this was good, bad, or very bad.

"I feel sometimes like I have no place here. Maybe I do have a place there," she said.

"I understand. It is good for you to have choices. Paula was always afraid of you; she didn't recognize it. She said that when she took you out of the pool, you seemed so strong and proud; while trying to get out, you pulled one of the bars from the brass stairs with no effort, and your eyes were bright as magnetic light bulbs," he said calmly.

"And you? Were you ever afraid?" Cate asked.

"I was afraid they would come and take you away; at least now you are taking off on your own will."

"I am."

"Do communicate," he said.

"I will. Thanks, Steban. I see now that it was not easy." She kissed the old man's forehead. She felt like asking about her mother, but it might be too cruel asking about the woman who was so close to one of them—the ones he wanted her to stay far away from. She continued on her way to the living room.

"Cate," Steban spoke again.

She stopped before opening the door.

"Be careful about chemistry. It makes you interpret things in a different way than you should."

"Is that what you had with Sarah?" she asked. Sarah, her mother. It just came out.

A moment passed. A second moment passed. He never answered.

"Advice taken." She left.

Was it the chemistry he felt for my mother? Or does he mean the chemistry Sarah felt for the Phelarie father? In any case, they all ended up broken-hearted.

CHAPTER 26

....

PURPLE RAIN

The sky was a deep purple hue that matched Nnox's ship. High clouds. Cate and Victoria were under a tent at the end of the green lawn, some feet away from the floating purple vessel. Far left was the blue square-bottomed triangular figure called Zey or Zentinel.

Earlier, Cate had asked her Ereo, "What if I am more like them than like humans? If I am like them, can I still be like Victoria? Like Alice?"

"Deep inside, you consider yourself human, but you do not consider yourself to be part of humanity," he said.

"Victoria has never questioned her humanity, even though Kanio and Nnox keep pointing how much like a Phelarie she is," Cate said.

"While, on the other hand, you have questioned yourself ever since the day when you woke up in that room. Just give it a try with this new phase. You don't have to decide now; you don't have to decide ever," he said. "It will not be easy for you to find an explanation for what the conjunction of their coexistence may be about—human and Alliafied, Cate." He left.

Cate was with Victoria, and it was better not to analyze or discuss the matter further. It would be heartless, saying something that might imply that they were different.

"Well, now I'm nervous," Cate said to Victoria.

They looked at each other, both beneath the tent.

"Just don't see your life, or this visit, as a science task; it's just a trip," Victoria said. "Go see what is out there, and then come back." Victoria even then managed to sound serious and confident. She grabbed Cate's arm. "What about the pairs? Am I supposed to take care of the purple egomaniac? For how long?"

"He cares about you, I heard," Cate says.

Kanio told Cate once that Nnox respected Victoria, and even if he didn't agree with her procedures, he supported her willingness to change. As Kanio put it, "I think he admires her stubbornness." But Cate skipped that part and opted instead to tell Victoria about the end of her conversation with the Aekiou.

"And most important is that he rarely cares about someone else. Kanio told me that Nnox said that the only respectable human is you, and that then he said, 'Oh wait, you see—she is a Phelarie too,'" Cate said, chuckling.

They both laughed, and then got trapped by frustrating melancholic silence.

"For what it's worth, I've seen more of you in the last three months than in...can't remember. But we may not see each other at all in the *next* three years, more?" Victoria said.

"What if I never come back?" Cate asked. It wasn't really a question—it was a distinct possibility.

"But you can come back, right? You said so."

"Yes, I can, and I will." It was not the moment to mention the possibility.

"And listen." She grabbed Cate's temples. "If anything happens, do something. Send a hidden note—send the puppy back," Victoria continued.

"Oh, come on, Victoria."

"Send Coper back, and I'll know you need something."

"That won't happen, but okay," Cate said, thinking, *Here is paranoid Victoria Weelah.*

"Also, you need to listen to this, even if you don't want to: You will meet Tykan Grage. Our father."

"No, I don't think he cares about us, really," Cate said. She looked around. "Maybe it's time to leave now." She started looking for Kanio. She saw a bunch of people close to the river, and some close to the Zey. She could recognize his blue in between the people close to the triangular-shaped spaceship.

"No, listen. I always thought our father was dead. There was this Dr. Stevens, who died a few years after we moved to Earth. I swear I look like him. His daughter looks like my twin. I thought it was him, and after he died I thought that we wouldn't ever find out." The older sister sounded rational again.

"We have to go; it's ten minutes to the fourth Sky-Shot release." A peachy Phelarie approached the sisters.

"Two minutes...one," Victoria said.

"He is a Phelarie, very close to the Khun, and he will probably try to reach you," Victoria continued.

"Why did he never contact us before?" Cate hated this conversation.

"They are different, so don't expect the father-daughter relationship that you didn't have with Steban. But if anything happens with Kanio, he is there," her sister said.

"Why would he want to be in my life now?"

"Victoria, Catherine." The female Phelarie was back.

Victoria pulled Cate toward her. "Don't forget what you are, and don't let Kanio forget it," she said. The two of them started walking toward the triangle.

"I don't know," Cate said. From afar she could distinguish Lucca talking to Nnox. The Italian was almost on his toes, making dramatic gestures with his hands. The purple Phelarie was standing perfectly straight with crossed purple arms, staring down at him, not even nodding.

Closer to the vessel, to the right, Barrett Mountdragon was standing with another group of people.

"Barrett is the best example of how insipid my life was before," Cate said. The years since their breakup had been a mere parenthesis. What was coming was what mattered.

To the left, close to the Zey, Alex, in a navy blue suit, and Kanio in his characteristic pearly blue were shaking hands. Kanio looked at her. It was time. Her chest burnt and it was not that fired-up reaction she'd felt when she was alliafied and close to him. This was how life blushed from within. The blue Zey's front wall opened to the left.

"I need to ask you something." Cate took Victoria's arm.

"Yes, what?"

"Did you know if Dean Ashcroft ever work with Dr. Parker?" Cate had forgotten about it with the day's rush. *It has to mean something.*

"Alice's mother? No, no idea."

"Go to them. Ask them about the formula; just ask."

"She will kill me for wasting her time," Victoria complained. "I'll ask him."

"Ask him if it's important!"

"Everything related to him it's important." Victoria said.

"And what or who is Pawel?"

"I guess Park, Ashcroft."

"And Weelah..." Cate finished the sentence.

Victoria took a deep breath. "I'll take it from here."

"I want to thank you," Cate said.

"No! For what?"

"When this happened, I thought there was no way out. I lost hope, and you found it for the two of us." Cate hugged Victoria.

"I don't know if it was hope what I was looking for. I was so angry," Victoria said.

They gave each other a final warm hug.

"Cate," Kanio called to her.

"I love you." Cate felt a few tears running down her cheeks.

"I love you too," Victoria said back without a single drop.

It is probably the medication she takes, Cate thought.

They met Kanio, Alex, and Nnox, who had just joined the group.

"Ready?" Kanio said.

"Alex," Cate greeted him. He gave her back his signature grin.

"I'll see you two before the semi-cycle ends," Nnox added.

"Be on time, Seu Kalema," Kanio said to him.

"Seu Kalema," Nnox said.

Kanio and Nnox patted each other with a discernible trace of sentiment.

"We will talk soon," Kanio said to Victoria and Alex.

A few purple drops touched Cate's hand, and a purple drizzle started falling on them.

He offered his arm to walk her to the Zey.

"Bye," Cate said.

Victoria waved her hand.

"This rain will clean the atmosphere; we will see some blue while we are up there. You will like that," Kanio said as they were about to enter the Zey, which emanated bright sky-blue light from inside.

"Wait." Cate looked back one last time before stepping inside. It seemed like Victoria and everyone else believed she was joining a cosmic quest to find out who she was, or if there was something out there for her. It was true, but the true motive behind why she was really letting go so easily of this human life of hers...was blue, and standing right in front of her.

*****

As the small vehicle took off, Victoria stared at it as it moved straight upward.

"There she is. You won't be separated; communications work perfectly these days," Nnox said.

Victoria saw a flash of platinum through one of the Panels of the Zey.

Victoria alliafied, and tried to shine as golden bright as her Leeve 2 status allowed.

"You can't forget the dog," she said as she unalliafied.

"What dog?" Alex asked.

"You haven't met Coper?" Nnox looked at Alex.

"You haven't either," Victoria said to him.

"Do you still want me to take it?" Nnox turned around, dramatically holding his cape, and walked back to his ship.

"Do you have a dog?" Alex asked sweetly.

"I have to go." She headed back to the tent to pick up her bag and coat. She was not ready yet to talk to him about the dog, or anything else.

The grass was muddy thanks to the rain. Her boot's heels plodded through the grass. Once in the tent, she grabbed her navy coat. Patrick approached in an impeccable gray suit and a yellow tie, carrying a gray umbrella.

"What just happened? I should have left with her, but that is not an option now." She shook her head.

"This friendship between Cate and Kanio changed all plans."

"Cate is unpredictable; that is how she always has been. People say my mother was like that," Victoria said while getting her small blue bag from a chair.

"And you?" Patrick asked.

"I'm like my father," she said, sharp and clear. "My real father."

It's true they only spoke a couple of times. He came with instructions and assertions, and he was the one who'd guaranteed her that as soon as she took full control of the NAA, he would be the one to watch her back. Yet, she failed. Also, as Steban had stated as well, he mentioned not to trust the Khun and his intentions toward Earth. She'd withheld this information from Kanio before because, evidently, negative opinions about the Khun wouldn't seem adequate to deliver to the Aekiou—in this case, also the son of the same Khun.

"She will be okay." He sounded reassuring.

"After years and years of watching her struggling, it's fair to let her try," Victoria said.

"So, he left you in charge after all; brilliant," he said.

"Not me, really; it's Alex. Let's walk back. And I have to handle Nnox," she added.

"This fellow will be around for a while. He is managing the conclusions of the Stations. I heard they are having problems with disturbances in the southern hemisphere. But we will leave that to them to deal with," he said. They both laughed.

"My dear Victoria." Mr. Rogers suddenly showed up; he took off his hat and kissed both of her cheeks.

"Rogers, where have you been? Thank you; why did I never see you in my purple prison."

Patrick snorted.

"It got complicated. They found a file in Phelio that put you in a complicated situation."

"Chaos in Brogio. A golden Alliafied in Onerio. Yes, I know," she said.

"But you missed the most important part: And soon the days of the Thendor will be over." Rogers raised his eyebrows. "Why do you think he left running like a chicken behind his Thendor father."

"What does that mean?" She asked.

"Let me go talk to Harlow, now that he is important." Rogers put his hat on and left.

"These people..." Victoria shook her head.

"What should we do in the meantime?" Patrick asked.

"Rebuild everything as we originally wanted it," she said as she turned her palm to the rain. The drops were thick and dark purple. "And find out what they really are up to. All of them."

maria beta

CHAPTER 27

....

BEYOND DUST
BEYOND MATTER

Before crossing the atmosphere, Kanio suggested to alliafy, as it was safer for Cate given the pressure and the speed they would eventually reach. Cate looked through the window for a final glimpse of what people made her pretend was home.

"A new government, led by Alex Harlow, will officially begin on Monday."

"Alex?" Surprisingly, she smiled.

"For two years, until elections or whatever time we are sure people will vote, and we have provided viable candidates to vote for. It will be announced on Monday.

Your sister will be a link between Alex and Nnox," Kanio explained. "We will also tell her on Monday."

"A link? I don't think she talks to any of them. At least, not to Alex for sure."

"It is not relevant; that will make her closer to Nnox, and Nnox needs a pair while I am away," he said. "Despite she is only a Leeve 2."

Level Two. He always manages to bring it up.

They crossed the stratosphere and she gave more attention to the bright, light blue interior. It simulated a small media room, with a short ladder connecting to the upper deck, where two Phelaries were maneuvering the Zey.

"When was the last time you went to Europa?" Kanio asked.

"About two years ago. I travelled with the Russians. They have New Alaska, but they are still not fully convinced, and are still betting on Titan to become the next new world. I think they just don't like sharing with the NAA," she explained.

"And they are right. There is not enough space on Earth, and I wouldn't like sharing with the NAA either," he said.

"In any case, it was funny. I felt like I was invited as an exchange for bodyguard services; people are still afraid of crossing the asteroid belt, and I needed a ride to New Greenland, so it worked for both of us." She kept recalling that expedition. "And they explained to the crew that I can cross through fire and electrifying frostiness, and so on."

"In the end, it's all dust and matter," he said. He pointed to the window behind her again. On one side there was the moon, and to the other Earth and its splotches of mauve and blue.

"I've never seen the blue of the oceans like this. Your purple trick worked," she said. "I lived there for a year," she said, "the moon."

"Developing weapons?" he asked. "I didn't see you as that."

"What do you mean?" she asked back.

"Apollo is the largest NAA war station," he said.

"No way."

"You didn't know? Look, that is my Ryder." Kanio showed her a blue rectangle that began to emerge from behind the moon to the left. It was almost twice the size of Nnox's. "It is connected to me and my toys." He sounded proud.

"How?"

"It is made of a material that absorbs our KIO—um, DNA—and, remember we have your Whisper already in the head. Which reminds me..."

"No. You are not putting anything inside my head," she said firmly.

"Do you want to come?"

She rubbed her head behind her right ear.

"And I have a suit for you waiting in your chambers; three, actually."

"Like yours?"

He nodded.

My toys, she thought. Despite her excitement, she looked back out at the blue vessel. The rectangle was composed of multiple vertical rectangles, or so it seemed. As they approached, it looked more mosaic-like, with two dented lines crossing it side to side.

"What does Nnox say about not having the bigger ship? I've never seen something like this."

"His is faster. I used it once for twenty sodios, and when I connected myself to it, it turned blue," Kanio said. "My father got mad, though. He doesn't like when I transcend the rules of the establishment."

"Is a palladium creature part of the establishment?" she asked.

"You are hydrogen."

He went up to the deck; she could hear him saying something in his strange tongue, with a lot of *O*s in the words. He came back and stared at his Ryder from the window, as if she were invisible.

"I was trying to make a joke," she said.

What have I done?

"I know. But you were part of the establishment, from a long time ago." He remained staring outside.

"Once we leave the Milky Way, we will split into a smaller crew, and we will head directly to Brogio, the green planet; we have time to prepare. You will like Colt. Did you tell Victoria?"

"No. Did you tell Nnox?"

He moved his head in a *no.*

"How will we find him?" she asked.

"I received this half a *sodio* ago. Listen."

He pressed the middle of the back of his left wrist and a message began: "Kanio, I hope you get this," a distressed male voice said; the audio was crackling. "You know where I'll be."

"This is the last thing he said before losing communication. The first time we went to Brogio, he and I, we discovered this place by mistake. I think he is hiding there. I know where to go."

He still remained calm when he spoke, but she knew this might not be an easy task. "He addressed the message to you because he knew you were going to go after him," she said.

"And I will. You were right. And we will be fine," Kanio said and went back to the deck.

We will be fine, she thought.

She stared down at Earth and could tell the mauve cloud had turned into thick gray mud. He came back.

"Do you want one?" He extended his arm and a shiny and perfectly round red apple was in his palm. He kept the green one.

"Thanks," Cate said.

"You're welcome," he winked at her.

the girl from the moon

maria beta

the girl from the moon

Made in the USA
Middletown, DE
27 September 2020